Forever Home

A Windsor Peak Novel

Book 4

Denise Latham

Dedication

To all our first responders, who put others before themselves every day. Thank you for making the world a safer place for everyone. And to all the parents, wives and children who support them, and give them a safe place to return home to at the end of the day.

Chapter 1

"Good morning," JJ Monahan grinned at the woman working the airline counter as Zoe groaned inwardly. He was using his sugar-sweet voice, and she knew something was about to happen that she wouldn't like.

"JJ," she whispered, tugging on his arm. He reached for her hand, squeezing it lightly to indicate she should be quiet, continuing to smile at the woman he was charming across the counter. When she started to speak again, he pulled her into his chest, wrapping his arm around her and dropping a kiss on her head.

"She just can't get enough of me," he said to the worker. "We just got married, and now we're headed off for our honeymoon. I'm a law enforcement officer, we rarely are able to get away like this, so it's almost too much excitement for her to handle."

"Oh, how thrilling," the woman gushed. "Let me see if I can do anything about your seats." She typed away at the computer, furtively smiling up at his handsome face, as Zoe struggled to disentangle herself from his seemingly endless arms..

"I'm going to hurt you," she nearly growled, yelping when he leaned down and took a nip from her neck.

"Promises, promises," he whispered, winking at her as he released her. "Let me do my thing, please."

She collected her bags, fully intending to stalk off and leave him behind, when the attendant handed tickets across to him. "Not much I can do from here to New York," she said. "But I was able to upgrade you for the flight to California. I hope you have an amazing trip."

"Thank you so much," JJ said. "You're an angel."

Picking up his carry on as well as hers with one hand, he clamped the other onto hers and hauled her away from the ticket counter towards security. "See, you never trust in me," he said. "This is the number one thing we need to work on in our relationship."

"We don't have a relationship," she reminded him. "And we are most certainly not married."

"Not yet," he said. "A little fib won't ruin her day, and it scored us first class to Los Angeles. You can't possibly complain about that."

"Patrick offered to buy us first class tickets," she pointed out. They were flying to spend a few days with her sister, Emma, and her boyfriend Patrick before they all drove to Las Vegas. Patrick Burrows was a huge movie star, and the cost of two plane tickets would be nothing to him. But even Zoe secretly would have felt bad accepting them from him, despite needing to poke JJ about it.

"I'm not accepting a handout from my friend to celebrate my nuptials," he responded. As they approached the TSA checkpoint, he handed her the purse he was carrying before pulling out his own wallet and badge before greeting the agent. "Morning."

"Good morning, officer. Do you have a weapon in your possession today?" The agent glanced at the open wallet on the counter in front of him, which showed JJ's badge across from the spot where he had pulled his license out.

"No, sir. This is a pleasure trip only."

Zoe tried to resist laughing at him before putting her license into the scan machine. No matter how ridiculous he was, she was always amused by him. That would likely explain why she still spent the majority of her time with him, despite his constant desire to be in a relationship with her. Yes, he was handsome, with his chiseled jawline constantly covered in a five o'clock shadow, his baby blue eyes and sandy colored hair. He towered over her at just over six feet tall to her five-foot four, and his shoulders reminded everyone that he had been a linebacker in college. And unfortunately, he was the nicest person she knew.

They had met almost two years prior to this trip, when she moved to the small town of Windsor Peak. The move had been unplanned and unexpected, moving from France to Vermont. But when she found herself answering an advertisement for a chef at a locally owned restaurant, and then connecting with the owner, she felt like it was the perfect place for her. The small town had looked like the perfect place for her introvert self to live a solitary life, but when the Sheriff decided he liked her food and started showing up every day, her life turned upside down. Now she couldn't shake him if she tried, although she had to admit she didn't try very hard.

She followed him to the small departure gate where they would board the flight to New York, where they would connect on a larger plane to California. He glanced around, then pointed at the small newsstand and coffee counter. "Do you want me to grab you a coffee?"

"No, I'll be okay. Thank you," she said. "Let's just sit."

"We have almost two hours," he pointed out. "I told you we didn't need to be this early for our flight."

"What if we had hit traffic?"

"From Windsor Peak to Burlington?" He cocked an eyebrow at her, laughter in his eyes. "Unless a moose decided to hang out on the highway, that's not likely."

"We can get something to eat if you want," she said, gesturing towards the restaurant. "Or I brought a deck of cards, we can play a game."

"Deal," he said. "I just ate, since you were nice enough to bring us breakfast sandwiches. I want to save some room for the treats we'll get in first class."

She led him to two chairs separated by a small table that faced the window, pulling the cards out of her bag once she sat. "Gin Rummy?"

"Sure," he said. "What are we playing for?"

"We never play for anything," she said, feeling confused.

"Always a first time," he answered. "Winner gets to ask the other person a question and they have to answer honestly."

"That's it?" She stared at him, even more confused. "I thought we were always honest with each other."

"We are, but this could be different," he said. "Something deep, maybe."

"Are you trying to make it dirty?"

"I mean, that's never off the table," he laughed. "But I'm game for that anytime, you know that."

"You're ridiculous," she groaned.

"We have fun together," he argued. "And no matter how many times I've been humiliated, I've never backed down. I think it shows my commitment to you, I'd do anything you asked."

"I still feel badly that I made you eat that hot chip."

"That crazy thing nearly killed me."

"That was hysterical," she laughed. "I felt bad though, I didn't think about it getting into your eyes."

"How could it not? It was all over my body, I think."

"No, it was on your fingers, and you touched your eye. I think the package specifically said not to do that."

"Impossible to think rationally when your entire body is on fire," he said. "But I did it anyway, because I never back down from a dare."

"Neither do I," she pointed out. "I sang that Celine Dion song at Karaoke for you and wore the other half of the electrical plug outfit on Halloween. Although maybe I'll find something you'll say no to."

"You couldn't," he said confidently. "I'd do anything you asked."

"Let's just focus on the game," she said. "I might win on the first hand."

"Not going to happen," he said as he picked up his hand. "And if you try to cheat, I'll catch you."

"I have never once cheated in all the games we have played," Zoe said, watching as JJ shuffled the cards.

He dealt the cards, then placed the deck down on the table. "You go first."

She chose a card and discarded, studying the man in front of her more than her cards. "Maybe I do know what I'll ask you when I win."

"What's that?" He quickly discarded before meeting her eyes.

"I want to know your biggest secret."

"I don't have secrets from you."

"Really?" She laughed as she picked up another card. "What is it that JJ stands for again?"

"Oh, that," he said, waving a hand. "Not important. If you want to waste a question where I'm obligated to tell the truth on that, feel free."

"It has to be something truly terrible since you won't tell me," she guessed. "Is it a girl's name? Judy? Jasmine?"

"Not that I'm saying there's anything wrong with that, but no," he answered. "Maybe it's just become so fun now that it's driving you crazy, I don't want to tell you."

"I don't think that's the case," she argued. "You would have told me the first time I asked if it was. I think it's something sinister and you want to protect your good guy image."

"You think I'm a good guy?" He went out, winning easily as he grinned at her. He did the math quickly on both of their hands of cards and put notes in his phone before looking up at her again.

"What? Oh, did you want an answer?" She shuffled the cards quickly as she responded. "You know I think you are."

"Then why not date me?"

"Thought we were married?"

"That's coming," he said confidently. "But why not date me first?"

"JJ," she sighed. "We've been over this. You've become my best friend since I moved to Vermont. I'm not going to mess that up."

"I think that ship has sailed," he said.

"You think I've already messed us up?" She stared at him incredulously. "How?"

"You've been sleeping with me for months," he said in his matter-of-fact tone, as if she needed the reminder. As much as she tried to resist him, once she let herself have one small taste, he had knocked down more of her defenses than she wanted. "I've basically moved in with you."

"You have not," she laughed.

"Really? When was the last time you slept alone?"

She frowned, thinking back over the last few months. Her life had been a whirlwind, with her long-lost sister Emma reappearing in town, followed by their shared father. The same man who had never appeared in either of their lives before but decided to turn up when Emma was rumored to be dating one of Hollywood's biggest stars. The drama and emotion that their father had stirred up had upset Zoe more than she cared to admit, and having JJ's strong, warm body next to her at night had been comforting.

"I guess I will be tonight," she sniffed in response.

"Not happening," he said. "Patrick told me his house only has two bedrooms."

"That's not true at all," she said, rolling her eyes. "Emma took me on a Facetime tour, and there are at least six."

"It's unfair to the cleaning lady to dirty a whole extra set of sheets when we're leaving in a few days," he argued. "We'll discuss this later, I guess. In front of Emma."

"No," she said quickly. "I don't want Emma to know anything."

"She's going to figure it out when I'm her brother-in-law."

"You're ridiculous, you know that?" She couldn't help but laugh with him, which is how she had let down her defenses with him to begin with. He had a sparkle in his eye and a joy for life unlike anyone she had ever met, and it drew her to him. Her dark, battered heart apparently hadn't given up after all, because when he smiled at her the way he was now, she could feel it skip a beat.

"You say ridiculous, I say optimistic," he said. He stood quickly as an older couple struggled to pull their carry-on luggage through the row of seats, easily lifting both bags and placing them near the empty seats. The couple thanked him profusely before he took his seat again and picked up his cards.

"Always such a good guy," she teased him.

"No big deal," he responded. "Unless you want to reward me?"

"I did happen to pack some food, knowing you can't go more than ten minutes without a meal." She pulled a small cooler bag out of her large tote and offered it to him. "I didn't pack a ton since we'll get food on the plane, but just enough to keep you from getting hangry."

"I knew you loved me." He pulled a wrapped sandwich from the bag and groaned. "I don't even know what this is but I'm so happy already."

"I don't understand why you aren't grossly overweight," she grumbled, laughing when he took a bite and sighed. "If anyone else ate like you, they would be. Your metabolism must be through the roof."

"I'm happy to need to work it off, as long as it means I get to eat what you cook," he replied. "I'll spend hours in the gym to make up for it."

She studied her cards as he quickly ate the sandwich, secretly loving the way he enjoyed her food. As a chef, seeing the joy her food brought to someone was the best feeling in the world, and JJ reacted the same way whether it was a sandwich or a filet mignon.

"That was amazing," he said, patting his stomach. "Now let's finish this game so I can be declared the victor before we board."

An hour later, she was grumpily putting the cards away as he ran his victory lap around the seating area. She bit her lip to keep from laughing when he dropped back into the chair next to her after high fiving all the kids, and some of the adults, who had been watching his spectacle.

"I told you I was going to win," he said. "No welching on our bet."

"What's the question?" She glanced over to the flight crew as they started speaking into the microphone, announcing the boarding procedure. They were taking a small plane to New York, where they would connect to their flight to Los Angeles.

"Time to board," he declared, jumping up and grabbing their bags. "I'll ask you later, I never said it had to be instant."

She watched as he offered to help the couple next to them, then gestured for her to go down the jetway in front of him. He easily lifted their bags into the overhead before helping the other couple with theirs, then sat next to her and took her hand. "I don't think I mentioned it, but I'm scared to fly, so I'll need your constant touch."

"You are not," she laughed, but couldn't bring herself to pull her hand away. His hand dwarfed hers, and the rough edges of calluses rubbed against her softer skin, making her more aware of his touch. She turned to watch the airport fall away behind them, focusing on the excitement she felt about seeing her sister again. Not the butterflies caused by the man next to her.

Chapter 2

JJ placed his suitcase and Zoe's near the door before crossing to open the door to the balcony. The guest room had a private little deck overlooking the waves crashing on the beach, with a small sofa and table to relax on. He could see himself sipping a coffee or a final glass of wine while overlooking the breathtaking view, at least for the few days they were in California.

Hearing the door open, he turned to see Zoe enter the room before she noticed he was there. She was staring at her phone, a frown on her face, which he wanted to immediately fix. Her pixie cut blond hair was sticking up slightly in the front, making her look even more adorable. Everything about her reminded him of a fairy, from her small, upturned nose to her tiny feet, the dusting of freckles across her cheeks and the twinkle of laughter always present in her green eyes.

"Hey," he called to her, seeing her jump slightly when she realized she wasn't alone. "Come see the view."

"This house is amazing," she said, joining him to lean on the railing. "Imagine waking up to this every morning."

He smiled at her profile before tugging her closer to him. "I already wake up to the best thing I can imagine."

"You are so corny," she groaned. "And we are not doing this the whole trip. We agreed it was a casual thing, and you're acting like we're in a relationship."

"Are you seeing anyone else?"

"That's not the point, and you know it."

"I think it is. If you were involved with someone else, then I'd back off. But you're not, and neither am I. And we make each other happy. That's what a relationship is," he said. "Or what it should be, at least. Just have fun with me this week, that's all I'm asking. Don't spend the whole time fighting your feelings."

"JJ," she rolled her eyes. "You have to stop assuming I'm in love with you."

"You are," he said confidently. "You're just too scared to admit it. But we'll get there."

She turned to leave, and he grabbed her hand, pulling her back so she was at the railing with him behind her, his arms holding her close. "Take a minute and enjoy this with me."

She sighed but then leaned her head back onto his shoulder, closing her eyes briefly. "It's hard for me to relax."

"I know that," he said, moving his hands to gently rub her shoulders. "That's why I'm here. Want to tell me what was bothering you on the phone?" He massaged her until she turned and buried her face into his chest, gripping tightly around his waist.

"It's nothing, just my mother being her usual self. Thank you for making me relax," she whispered. Tipping her chin up, she kissed him softly before stepping back. "I'm going to unpack quickly and take a shower, okay?"

"Is that an invitation?" He winked at her and laughed when she scowled.

"You really know how to ruin a moment," she called over her shoulder as she went through the door.

He headed down the stairs, where Patrick and Emma were nestled together on the couch until he appeared. "Hey," Patrick said, jumping to his feet. "Want a beer?"

"Sure, that sounds great."

"We were just thinking about all the things we wanted to do while you're here," Emma said. "We thought you might be tired from the travel, so we planned a dinner here for tonight. I have a chef coming in, so Zoe can relax with us. Then tomorrow maybe we can enjoy the beach and then do some Hollywood sightseeing."

"That should be interesting, considering we're bringing Hollywood with us," he said, gesturing to Patrick.

"I'll wear a hat," Patrick replied. "No one will recognize me."

JJ and Emma shared a look and burst out laughing. "Sure thing, bud. We'll see how that goes. But all Zoe cares about is the food, and all I care about is making sure she has fun."

"That's so sweet," Emma said.

"And maybe a round of golf," he amended with a smile.

"That we can definitely do," Patrick grinned. "I'll see if Zane and Liam want to join us, that will make for an interesting afternoon. Then maybe Nat can join us for dinner."

"She can come here and hang out with us," Emma offered. "Or if she's busy, I'll take Zoe on a little tour, show her some of the sights."

"Perfect," JJ nodded. "Are we all set for the concert in Vegas?"

"We are," Patrick said as he handed him a beer. "Front row, just like you asked. And I sent the message along as well, although I have no idea what is happening."

"Thanks, I appreciate that. You'll see when it happens."

"When what happens?" Emma asked. "What message?"

"That's between me and Patrick," JJ said quickly. "I'm sorry, I don't want to force him to keep secrets from you, but just this once, for me."

"It's not anything bad, is it?"

"No, it's going to be good," he smiled at her. "Very, very good."

"Now I'm suspicious," Patrick laughed as he sat back next to Emma and pulled her close. "You sure it won't make things hard if I'm there with you?"

"You said they'll have security, right? And looking at the layout, if things get tight for you, you can duck out. But I'd like you both to be with us," he said.

"I'm sure it will be fine," Patrick said. "I can't wait to see what this is all about. I never knew you to be a Luke Combs fan before."

"Zoe likes him," he explained. "And one of his songs is perfect. Well, a lot of his songs are great, but one just fits the occasion perfectly."

"I'm so curious about this," Emma said. "Maybe you can give us a little hint?"

"No hints," he said, shaking his head. "Let's change the subject so it doesn't drive you crazy. How have things been out here?"

"Great," Patrick responded, grinning at Emma. "We've been having a great time but can't wait to get home."

"Although I have become quite accustomed to the life of leisure, so I'm not entirely sure how I'll go back to my four a.m. wakeups to be to work on time," Emma said with a smile. "But I do miss Vermont, and seeing you guys every day. And Patrick's family. Oh, and Whiskey."

"They must sell whiskey out here," JJ said.

"She means the horse," Patrick explained. "She facetimes with the trainer at least once a day, convinced the horse can see her on the screen."

"She misses me," Emma argued. "It helps to hear my voice."

"Of course it does," Patrick dropped a kiss on her head. "We'll be home soon. And we'll talk about the work thing later."

"I'm going back to work," Emma said, her voice sounding like a warning to JJ's ears. "We already talked about it. You'll find plenty to do while I'm there, and I need to make my own money."

"But I—"

"Nope," Emma cut him off. "I'm not living off your money. End of discussion."

"Do you see how stubborn she is?" Patrick said to JJ.

"It must run in the family," JJ said as he heard footsteps on the stairs. "I feel your frustration, trust me."

"Are you talking about me?" Zoe demanded as she came into the large living room. "This place is amazing, Patrick."

"Thank you," he responded. "But I'll be selling it. We went looking at houses in other areas and fell in love with one that has a more small-town feel. I've realized I need more land around me, and this place doesn't have that."

"You have a whole beach outside," JJ pointed out.

"That's not mine, though," Patrick said. "This other house has a few acres, we could keep horses here too, and not feel like we're in a city."

"You aren't thinking about moving her permanently, are you?" Zoe asked, looking worried.

"No," Patrick and Emma responded together, then laughed. Patrick gestured for Emma to answer for them both. "He will have to be here for long stretches of time for work, so it's important he likes where he lives."

"We like where we live," Patrick corrected. "If I'm here filming, I'm dragging your sister along. You're welcome to come as well, but she will absolutely be here while I am."

"Caveman," Emma teased.

"You loved that house too," Patrick said.

"I did," she sighed. "It's stunning. And it's not a house, it's practically a hotel."

"It's not that big," he laughed.

"It is," Emma nodded to JJ and Zoe. "And there are several guest houses."

"We'll call the best one now," JJ grinned. "Just name it after us, and we'll come visit often."

"Do you have a shoot coming up?" Zoe accepted the glass of wine Emma had poured for her.

"Not for a few months," Patrick answered. "I talked to my agent and manager to keep me at one movie a year, ideally. Sometimes with the series they like to do things back-to-back, but it can be grueling. One a year would be perfect, between filming and promotion, I should be able to spend at least six months in Vermont."

"Back and forth, he means," Emma corrected. "If the shoot takes three months, he'd be able to come home until the promotion starts. I'm starting to learn all about it."

"I'm looking forward to a more balanced life," Patrick smiled.

"Are you getting used to life in Hollywood?" Zoe asked her sister, sharing a look with Emma that told JJ they had discussed it already at great length.

"Patrick's friends have been wonderful," Emma said. "I was so nervous to meet Natalie, and she was nothing like what I thought she would be. They have all been so welcoming and made me feel way more comfortable than I could have imagined. It's still a weird place, but I'm okay as long as Patrick is with me."

"Trust me, I'm not leaving her alone in Los Angeles," Patrick laughed. "Someone would try and steal her away from me."

"Oh, you're ridiculous," Emma laughed. "No one even notices me."

"Trust me, they do," Zoe said. "I see you in magazines and on social media almost more than I do Patrick. The mysterious girlfriend still gets clicks, apparently."

The doorbell rang, and Patrick glanced at his watch. "That's the chef. My assistant will let him in, but I'll just go say hello."

JJ sat back and enjoyed listening to the two sisters lean their heads together and talk quietly and quickly, Zoe reassuring herself that her little sister was indeed fine. He hadn't realized how worried she had been about Emma before this moment, assuming they had been in constant contact with each other. The weeks apart must have put a strain on Zoe, because he saw now that she was more relaxed, quicker to laugh, than she had been at home.

Patrick returned and led them all out to the deck, where they could have drinks before dinner overlooking the ocean. The outdoor setup had everything a person could want, including a comfortable looking outdoor sectional, a flat screen TV, fire pit, oven, full outdoor kitchen and bar. JJ assessed the setup and grinned at his friend. "I could get used to this life."

Chapter 3

Zoe woke to the sound of waves crashing, the soft sunlight of dawn falling across her face. She stretched, surprised to find the spot next to her empty. JJ had been curled around her most of the night, despite her best efforts to keep a tiny bit of personal space for herself. He had laughed and tossed aside the pillow she had put between them, pulling her even closer than she would have thought possible. Somehow, she had become accustomed to sleeping so close together, although she pretended nightly that she wanted him to leave her to sleep alone.

She sat up and glanced toward the open door, where she could see him standing at the railing. He was only wearing his boxers, giving her a chance to admire his physique before she surprised him by sliding her hands around his waist. Touching him had become second nature, and she soaked in his warmth in the cool morning breeze.

"Good morning, beautiful," he said, pulling her around so he could kiss her on the head.

"You're up early," she said.

"It's nine in Vermont," he reminded her. "I'm not one to sleep in. Besides, I got to see the sun come up over the Pacific, never thought I would have a chance to do that."

"I wish you had woken me."

"I will tomorrow," he promised. "You looked so peaceful, and you never get enough sleep."

"I really did crash, I guess the travel made me more tired than I would have thought. Even your snoring didn't wake me."

"First of all, it's you that's snoring," he said. "Second, I think it was more emotional than you expected to see Emma again. Almost like a part of you was afraid you had lost her again."

She considered his words, then nodded slowly. "I think you're right. I missed her for so many years, and the months with her in Windsor Peak went by so quickly. I didn't even realize what I was feeling, but when I saw her again, it was just a sense of relief. She's still here, she's real, and she still wants me in her life."

"Of course she does, you're amazing."

"You are way too good for my ego," she laughed. "I'm just so happy to have my sister back. She's all I have."

"You have me too," he said, sounding more forceful than usual. "I'm not going anywhere."

"I know," she said softly. Despite her resistance every step of the way, he had never faltered. From the first time they met to the night before, he had always been respectful of her and careful, never pushing too hard, but also never letting up in his pursuit of her. She just wished there was something that could help push her past her fears, to let him in fully. At the same time, she knew there was a big chance that if she did, he would realize she wasn't all that he thought she was.

They stood together in silence, watching the surfers and the few lone people running along the beach, before she shivered. "You're cold," he said, rubbing his hands up and down her bare arms. "Let's get you inside and get warmed up."

She laughed, then had to bite back a shriek as he suddenly picked her up and carried her inside, dumping her on the bed. "That started out so romantic and then you had to drop me," she objected.

"I'll make it up to you, I promise."

***

The sun had fully risen by the time they had showered and made their way downstairs, JJ distracting her every step of the way. The only thing that had finally worked was his unending hunger, and the promise of an omelet if they went downstairs. The smell of coffee indicated that someone had gotten downstairs before them, and she smiled when she saw Emma pulling bowls out of a cabinet.

"I'll cook breakfast," she said, giving her sister a quick hug. "It's the least I can do for you guys."

"This is supposed to be a vacation," Emma argued. "But considering Patrick and I didn't even know where the bowls were, we might be better off letting you do it."

Patrick emerged from what she assumed was a pantry, holding a loaf of bread and an armful of fresh vegetables. "Man, I'm happy to see you," he grinned at her. "We haven't had a good breakfast since we got here, and as much as I'd like to try to make something, I know we're in safer hands with you."

She took the food from him and pointed for everyone to sit. "Let me work my magic, please. You guys plan out the day while I cook."

She took the cup of coffee JJ had pushed her way, taking a big sip before starting to chop up peppers. Cooking soothed her, made her feel comfortable even in the most unstable moments. But like this, surrounded by happy voices and people she cared about, she was truly in her element. She made quick work of prepping for omelets, toast, and home fries and was sliding plates toward everyone before taking a bite of her own.

"Delicious," Patrick praised. "Thank you for doing this."

"Anytime. I feel bad that I didn't get to cook for you last night."

"I wanted you to have a night to relax, it wouldn't have been fair to have you cook after a full day of travel. And tonight, we can go out to eat, I want you to see some of the fancy spots out here," Patrick said.

"We're going to golf, if you don't mind," JJ told her. "Then meet up with you and Emma."

"That sounds perfect," she smiled at her sister. "What are we going to do?"

"A little shopping, and some sightseeing," Emma said. "Unless there's something particular you want to do?"

"Nope," she shook her head. "I just want to spend time with you. Anything is fine."

Patrick glanced at his watch when they finished eating, then stood. "I should jump in the shower if we're going to make our tee time," he said, gathering his plate and coffee mug.

"I'll clean up," Emma offered. "You go get ready."

"You should too," Zoe said to JJ. "We can take care of things here."

They cleaned the kitchen quickly and said goodbye as the men left. "Try not to miss me too much," JJ teased her as he headed through the door.

"You guys are so cute," Emma said. She settled onto the couch and gestured for Zoe to sit with her. "Let's catch up on the gossip before we head out. The traffic might be a little better if we go later."

"We can just stay here if you'd rather," Zoe offered.

"No, I want to show you around. And I haven't really had anyone to do girly stuff with, other than Natalie, and that's a scene to go out with her. You can't imagine the circus that unfolds when she goes out in public."

"It must be the same with Patrick," Zoe guessed.

"Maybe," Emma looked thoughtful. "But I feel like people are more respectful of him and his space? Maybe it's the size difference, she's so tiny and people just crowd her. Patrick, they tend to be a little more in awe of, I guess."

"Shopping with her must be fun."

"Oh, the stores just close right down," Emma laughed. "It's very Pretty Women-esque. Champagne, people bringing you clothes to look at. I tried to tell them I was just there to keep her company, and next thing I knew, I was in a dressing room. She refused to shop alone, she said. I can't even imagine how much she spent, and I somehow ended up with bags of clothes I could never have afforded."

"That's nice of her," Zoe said.

"It doesn't feel like she has many friends, which is sad," Emma said. "It's been nice to bond with her. But even better now to have you here, I'm so excited to spend the day with you."

They planned their day as they finished their coffee, then split up to go finish getting ready. Soon they were zipping down the Pacific Coast Highway in one of Patrick's SUV's, Emma appearing comfortable behind the wheel.

"You've really discovered California," Zoe commented. "I'd be scared to be driving on these highways."

"Trust me, I was at first. But Patrick insisted I get used to it so that I'm not trapped at the house when he's working," Emma explained. "Thankfully I can hook the GPS up to the car, because I would never find my way around if not for that. This is a far cry from where I grew up."

"Me too." Zoe looked at the Pacific Ocean, the bluffs around them, and the sheer number of people on the streets. The small town she had grown up in was nothing compared to this, and Canada rarely got the weather they were experiencing on this beautiful day. "Where are we headed?"

"Patrick made us appointments for manicures and pedicures, he insisted. The spa is right near Rodeo Drive, so I thought we could walk down there for a bit. He called one of his friends, who will meet us at one store. Don't try to fight whatever happens, trust me," Emma said, rolling her eyes. "I had no idea he had put this much thought into the day, but he wanted to make sure we would both be able to enjoy our time together and have no stress. After all that, I thought I could show you around a bit before we go meet the guys for dinner."

"Sounds perfect. I don't remember the last time I did anything to pamper myself, so I won't complain about the mani-pedi. Even though my nails are so short, they'll probably be horrified."

Emma laughed and held up her right hand, showing her the short nails. "Mine aren't much better, but that's okay. We both work with our hands too much to have long nails."

Zoe relaxed as they talked and sang along to the radio, making the time in traffic go by much faster than expected. She raised an eyebrow when her sister pulled into a valet stand, but kept her mouth shut as Emma looked like she knew what she was doing. They both climbed from the SUV, Emma accepting a ticket in exchange for the keys, and walked toward the entrance to the spa.

"This place looks amazing," Zoe whispered. "Way fancier than anywhere I've ever been before. And I lived in Paris!"

"I know," Emma said. "Everything out here is to the extreme. I hear stories from Patrick's friends about how they had to live on people's couches, or didn't have electricity or water, while they were auditioning. They worked in places like these valet stands and the expensive restaurants to make ends meet, but then had to take buses hours to get back to their cheap little apartments. It takes a lot of dedication to stick with it."

"Although Patrick never had those problems," Zoe laughed.

"Trust me, they give him a hard time constantly about his good luck. Hello," Emma smoothly greeted the woman behind the counter who was eyeing them. "We have appointments under Burrows."

Zoe saw the woman's forehead move the slightest bit, the most her Botox would allow, as she recognized the last name. Her eyes quickly swept up and down both of them, her lips pursing in what could only be described as disapproval at their casual skirts and tank top attire. Zoe even had flip flops on, having thought it would be best for a pedicure, but a quick scan of the room showed only high-end footwear abandoned next to spa chairs.

"Somehow I think we would be more welcome if Patrick were with us," Zoe said just loudly enough for the woman to overhear, her back stiffening as she walked. The receptionist led them to two leather chairs, separated by a curtain from the people on either side of them. A second woman came by with glasses of champagne, offering a selection of cocktails if they preferred. They both accepted the glass and said it was perfect, glancing at each other.

"Get used to it," Emma said. "This is what life with Patrick is like. Anytime we go out in public, people are rushing to be the ones to do something for him, and then by extension, me. Now that I've been outed as his girlfriend, people are trying twice as hard to be nice to me. It would be insulting if it wasn't so funny."

"Insulting to offer you free champagne?"

"Zoe, these people would never have looked at me twice six months ago," Emma said. "I was a nothing in thrift store clothes. Now I'm in designer clothes and on the arm of a millionaire superstar, and suddenly everyone wants to be my friend."

"I'm sorry," Zoe said softly. "Are you okay?"

"Oh, I'm not complaining. Patrick and I laugh about it, he can totally relate and said he knows how weird it is. I think in some ways it makes him feel better, because there weren't many people who could identify with how he felt before. Not that I'll ever be as famous as him," Emma said. "But the sudden limelight on your life, everyone being nice to you for their own selfish reasons not just because you're a nice person, it's weird. I'm glad he and I have been able to bond over it."

"Well, I'm happy to tag along, if it's going to be more like this." Zoe toasted her sister with the champagne glass as two attendants arrived to begin their pedicures. She had barely been on vacation twenty-four hours at this point and couldn't believe the difference a day could make. From spending twelve to eighteen hours in a kitchen to getting a foot massage she knew she couldn't afford on her own, life seemed to have flipped upside down in a minute.

Chapter 4

JJ was settled at the bar at an exclusive restaurant in Beverly Hills, patiently sipping a beer while Patrick posed for selfies and talked to fans. They had spent the afternoon golfing, and were meeting the girls here after their afternoon of pampering and shopping. He found himself looking up every time the door opened, hoping to see Zoe's face. It was weird that he would miss her, he was used to spending his day at work and not spending every minute with her. However, even when at work, he could stop in and grab a meal so he never went a full shift without seeing her. And he was now banking on ending each day with her, which was quickly becoming the best part of his day. Smelling the day's specials on her skin, hearing about the odd requests that she had encountered, and sharing his experiences had become a key part of his daily wind down.

The door opened again, and he did a double take when a stunning woman came in, followed by Emma. At first glance, he hadn't even realized it was his Zoe, but when his eyes met hers, he saw the shy insecurity she kept hidden from everyone else. She was in a tight red dress that opened on one side, exposing a toned leg and heels higher than he had ever seen her in. Her pixie cut was styled differently, her hair swept to one side rather than toward the back of her head, and a slight curl added to the ends. Her eyes popped under the sweep of hair, and he would swear her skin glowed in the soft light.

"You look amazing," he greeted her, planting a soft kiss on her cheek. "You too, Emma."

"Thanks," Emma grinned at him as she took her place under Patrick's arm.

"I feel a little ridiculous," Zoe whispered to him. "We went to a store and Patrick's friend Maria met us. The next thing I knew, I had a new wardrobe and was having my hair and makeup done before being stuffed into this dress. I feel like an imposter."

"Darling," he said slowly, pulling her closer. "You are stunning in a bathrobe with no makeup on. You outshine these Hollywood types in your hideous Crocs. But like this, I'm afraid I'm going to have to fight off a stampede of men."

"Really?" She relaxed slightly under his arm, meeting his gaze.

"It's all I can do to stay here for dinner and not throw you over my shoulder and race to the nearest dark corner I can find," he told her. "And I promise I don't have much restraint when it comes to you, so don't push me."

She laughed and leaned into him, surprising him with a soft kiss in public. "Thank you."

"No, thank you," he said. "I plan to remember this night forever."

"Did you guys have a fun day?"

"We did, we played golf and then sat in the hot tub for a while. Then Patrick had his assistant drive us here so we could all ride home together in a car service. Did he meet you outside to take the car home?"

"Yes, he was right out front," Zoe nodded.

JJ caught the bartenders' eye to order glasses of wine for Emma and Zoe, glad Patrick had thought to plan ahead so no one had to worry about driving them all home later. They talked quietly about their day as they waited for the rest of their group for dinner, and JJ found himself putting a possessive arm around Zoe when Zane and Liam arrived. After spending the day golfing with them, he had a good sense of their womanizing ways, and he wanted to make it very clear that Zoe was off limits. Once Natalie arrived and was introduced around, the larger group made their way to a private table nestled in the corner of the restaurant. Close enough for people to catch sight of the major celebrities who dined there, but far enough that they could all relax without a constant barrage of fans at the table.

He pulled out a chair for Zoe, carefully placing her between himself and Emma, with the three newcomers across the table. "Have you staked your claim yet, or did you need to mark me with your scent?" She teased him as he sat down, leaning over to whisper in his ear.

"I just want to make sure Liam and Zane know you're taken," he responded.

"Am I?"

He met her teasing gaze with a serious look of his own, waiting to respond until she recognized that he meant what he was going to say. "Forever."

She let out a shaky laugh, breaking eye contact, but he knew that he had gotten through to her. Whatever had happened in her life to make her think he would pass her over for someone else or do anything other than show up for her every day for the rest of her life, he intended to overcome. The sooner the better, if he had anything to say about it.

***

The few days in Los Angeles flew by, and before he knew it, JJ found himself on a private plane headed to Las Vegas. Zane, Liam and Natalie were all going to the same event as Patrick, and flying was easier than driving since Patrik and Emma were heading back to Vermont after the weekend. Flying private was a new experience, and one he would happily replicate any day of his life. No security lines or five-dollar bottles of water, crowds and crying babies, just them and the small flight crew. The flight was short, and they were whisked to a private entrance at the Wynn and checked into their Villa suites in the actual rooms. Patrick had opted to book a two-bedroom for the four of them, knowing Emma and Zoe would want to be together. The other three celebrities had their own suites and disappeared with promises to catch up shortly.

"We have a massage room," JJ said in wonder as the clerk left the room. "Our own private massage room. Zoe, I'm offering my services right now."

Patrick laughed. "The hotel will send a masseuse up; we just need to let them know when. We should probably schedule before the other three make their calls, because there is no doubt they will all take advantage."

"I wish I could offer to split this with you, but my salary wouldn't cover a night here," JJ said. "I owe you a few beers."

"The studio is putting us up, so no worries. They wanted us all here for the event, and this is part of it."

"I definitely went into the wrong business," Zoe said from the door to the balcony. "This is crazy."

"What's on the agenda?" Emma asked as she came out of the bedroom where she had been putting her bags.

"Dinner up here," Patrick said. "We already arranged for that, it's easier than going into public with the four of us. Then they have a private room if we want to do a little gambling before the concert. Tomorrow night is the big studio event, and then we have the fundraiser before we fly home. I chartered a plane for us all heading back, so we can take the red eye and not be miserable."

"Will you marry me?" JJ asked Patrick, laughing when his friend hit his arm.

"How quickly you dropped me to marry him," Zoe said in a teasing voice. "But I don't blame you, I don't come with fancy suites or private jets."

"No, but you do come with other benefits that I enjoy," he said, pulling her out onto the patio to enjoy the view together. "Do you want me to detail them now that we're alone?"

"You're ridiculous," she sighed. But then she snuggled closer to him, and he grinned to himself, knowing things were going in the right direction.

***

After an amazing dinner, the group spent an hour losing money to the casino before heading to the concert. Patrick had pulled JJ out of the gambling for a quick detour to meet the headline act, a favor he could never repay, and he was both nervous and excited as they took their seats. They were directly in front of the stage, ushered in from backstage when the lights were dimmed before the main act so no one immediately noticed the movie stars in their midst.

The first few songs passed in a blur, with Emma, Zoe and Natalie all dancing and singing along to the well-known songs. After the third song, the lead singer looked at JJ, who nodded, feeling a surge of nerves pass through him. It was perfect that he was in Vegas when he was putting it all on the line, and he had no idea how Zoe was going to react.

"My man," the singer pointed down at JJ, who saw Zoe's jaw drop. "How you doing tonight?"

"Great," JJ yelled back.

"I heard you have a little something to say," the singer sat down on the stage directly in front of them. "Which one of you pretty ladies is Zoe?"

The entire group pointed at her, and JJ had to stop himself from laughing at the mixture of horror and excitement that was on her face. She met his eyes and grabbed his wrist. "What's happening?"

"This is the love of my life," JJ said into the microphone held out to him. "And tonight, I'm going to marry her."

The crowd erupted around them, even their own friends cheering while looking confused. Zoe had to put her lips next to his ear for him to hear her. "What are you doing?"

"I love you," he said, pulling back to look in her eyes. "Marry me. Tonight."

Chapter 5

The music thundered in her ears, and she became hyper aware of everything around her. The crowd screaming, the band staring at her waiting for a response, her sister grabbing her arm, and JJ's soft blue eyes staring right into her. The blue eyes that reflected his honesty, his loyalty, and his love for her. As she stood transfixed, he pulled a ring from his pocket and dropped to his knee in front of her, never letting go of her hand.

The ring was perfect, he had clearly paid attention when she had talked about how she couldn't wear elaborate jewelry in the kitchen. Rather than a large stone standing out, the band was flat, with stones inlaid around the circumference. One large diamond was set inside the band, with diamonds encompassing as far as she could see.

He grinned up at her, and she had to strain to hear him. "I know you're scared, but trust me. Marry me. Let me love you forever. Remember the question you promised I could ask and you had to be honest answering? This is it. Will you be brave enough to let me love you and prove I'll be with you always?"

She pulled on his hand so he was standing, close enough so she could whisper in his ear. "Is this a joke?"

"I would never joke about the rest of our lives," he said into her ear. "I'm very serious. Say yes."

"Yes." The word escaped her mouth without her brain fully comprehending what she was doing. If she had given herself a chance to think and for her brain to stop the words, she wouldn't have said it. But her heart spoke first, and she was both elated and terrified to listen to it for once.   As soon as JJ put her down from swinging her around in a celebratory hug, Emma grabbed her.

"What is happening? Are you really getting married tonight?" Emma looked as dumbstruck as she felt, but it was as if she had lost all control over her body as her head started to nod.

Patrick gave her a brotherly hug, and then his friends grabbed her to do the same.

"You sure about this guy," Liam asked on a laugh. "Because I'm still available."

"Thanks, but the Hollywood life is not for me," she said.

He grinned back at her, wincing from the elbow that Zane sent him. "That's okay, I'm not quite done sowing my wild oats. He seems like a solid guy, congrats."

JJ grabbed her back, pulling her into his arms to dance to the song being performed. A slow love song, the crowd around them holding up phones as if they were lighters, and everyone around them smiling. It was the most surreal moment of her life, and she couldn't be one-hundred percent sure that it was really happening. Until JJ kissed her, and the crowd went wild again, and the band wrapped up the song by congratulating them one more time. Then JJ took her hand, and they were all swept out again by security, as if the whole thing had been orchestrated from the start.

"When did you come up with this plan?" she asked as he pulled her through the dark recesses of the backstage area.

"Months ago," he responded over his shoulder. "I know you love that band, and that song reminds me of us. I'd love you no matter what, even if you said no to marrying me. I'd just keep asking you, and loving you anyway."

"JJ, this is crazy," she said, trying to stop walking. She managed to pull him to the side, their friends pausing just ahead to wait for them. "We can't get married."

"Oh, we are. You already said yes. Very publicly."

"But this is crazy!"

"Is it? Or are you scared?"

"Of course it is. We aren't even dating." She crossed her arms, trying to look less rattled than she felt inside.

"We most certainly are. You're my best friend, and I'm yours. I look forward to seeing you every day, and I miss you when I'm not with you. And I know you feel the same, because you can't manage to hide the happiness on your face when I come in to see you for lunch," he said. "And you can't stay away from me at the end of the day. We laugh together, we share everything, and there is no one else that I want to spend my time with. I have loved you since the day we met, and this has always been my goal. I know you can't say it, I know you can't even admit it to yourself, but I know you feel the same. This is the best way for me to prove myself to you, that I'll never hurt you, and I'll never leave you. And our marriage will work, because our love is stronger than anything else."

"You can't know that," she bit back tears, unsure where they were even coming from.

"I can," he promised. "I would never do anything to hurt you. I know you're unsure and scared of love. I know there is more that you need to tell me about your past, and what has made you this way. But I also know that I love you, scars and all, and you feel the same deep down in your heart. This is what we are destined for, but maybe I'm pushing a little because I need to know you trust me."

"Trust you enough to get married on a whim in Vegas?"

"It's not a whim, I've been planning for a long time," he said, pulling the ring out. "I had this made for you three months after we met. I have always known that you're it for me, and that it would take something drastic to get you to agree. But now I have to ask you again, trust in me. Trust in us."

She took a shaky breath, staring at him and seeing her sister's concerned face at the end of the hall. These two people were all she had in her life, and despite her best efforts not to rely on JJ, she had started to a long time ago. When she had a bad day, he could make her laugh. When she was scared, he made her feel safe. Trusting him with her fragile heart would be the biggest gamble she could take, but he knew her well enough to know that this drastic move was the only way she could make the jump. And she knew if she said no and walked away right now, he would forgive her. He would continue professing his love and showing her every day how much he wanted to be with her, no matter what happened tonight.

"If you're really not sure, or want to say no, that's ok. I know I'm moving fast, but I don't want you to feel pressured. I just ask that you look into your heart, and answer with whatever it says." He looked uncertain for the first time that night. Or ever, she realized. "Do you think there is a chance that you love me, but you're scared? For this one moment, I'm asking you to just listen to your heart and nothing else, and tell me what you want to do."

"Let's do this," she whispered.

"You sure?"

"Yes. We're in Vegas, and I have no idea why I keep saying yes, but let's go with it," she said. "And on the bright side, now I'll finally find out what JJ stands for."

He laughed as he started walking with her towards their small group. "We'll see about that."

***

An hour later, she was in a brand-new white dress that Patrick had produced out of thin air. Natalie had redone her makeup and come up with a blue garter from somewhere, and Liam and Zane had gifted her a bracelet as something new.

"You still need something old, and something borrowed," Emma fretted, looking around the room. "Let me go see what I can come up with." She left the room, and Zoe could hear her talking in the living room of their suite, JJ's low voice responding.

"He seems like a good guy," Natalie said. "You're lucky, congrats."

"Thanks, he really is. I'm not quite sure how all this happened, we really aren't even a couple."

"Really? Seeing you two together I assumed you had been for a while. Between you two and Emma and Patrick, I'm starting to feel a little sorry for myself."

"You must have people falling all over you," Zoe objected. "You're the woman all men want."

"In their fantasies, sure," Natalie responded. "In reality, not so much. I've tried dating other actors, people in the industry, and just regular guys. But who I am in real life and who I am in public is a big difference, and that's hard for people to realize. Or live with."

"You'll find someone," Zoe squeezed her new friend's hand. Another odd moment to add to this night of surreal life, her consoling a gorgeous movie star about her love life.

"JJ has something," Emma announced as she came into the room. "But he's going to give it to you at the chapel. He said it will cover both the old and the borrowed, so we're all set. You ready?"

"No," Zoe admitted. "I'm terrified. Why am I doing this?"

Emma sat in front of her, taking both her hands. "You love him. He loves you. I know that's hard for you to see, but it's true."

"This is just a fluke," Zoe said, trying to convince herself. "When we get back to real life and he realizes he's trapped with me forever, things will change."

"I don't think so," Emma said. "But I can't predict the future, and neither can you."

"People don't stay for me," she said softly. "I don't know why, but everyone leaves me."

Emma wiped a tear from her eye and then pulled her closer. "I know it felt like I left you, but I never did. I always wanted my sister back, and I would have done anything to find you. And I think JJ feels the same way about you."

"Even my mom doesn't love me," she tried again. "My father was gone before I was born. I've never had a relationship last longer than a month. How loveable could I really be?"

"Your mom is wrong, and we both know our dad is rotten. And maybe you were waiting for the right guy all along," Emma said confidently. "But if you really don't want to do this, you don't have to. We support you no matter what, and if this doesn't feel right, we can leave right now."

"I can have a chopper here in ten minutes," Natalie said, pulling her phone out. "Just say the word if you want to escape."

"No," she said, taking a deep breath. "Let's go."

They filed out of the room, and when JJ's eyes met hers, she felt comfortable again. Her second thoughts and doubts were all still there, but much quieter. This was the craziest thing she had ever done, but as they got in the elevator, he squeezed her hand and smiled at her. A limousine was waiting at the private exit, and they piled in before the car sped off down the street. Minutes later, they pulled into a long driveway. The Chapel of the Flowers sign caught her eye as they went behind the building to a private entrance.

JJ stepped out, then reached back to offer her a hand. "We made it just in time," he told her. "I booked us for the last wedding of the night."

"When did you do this?"

"The day Patrick told me that he was able to get us to the concert, it all came together," he said. "I was a little worried about the timing, but it all worked out perfectly."

An attendant pulled open the door to a chapel, and it took her breath away. A glass ceiling appeared to give way to the night sky above, soft lighting making it appear the stars were within the room. Wood beams and flowers graced the walls, bringing a garden into this space. It was calm and perfect, and everything she had never realized she would have wanted. "This is amazing," she wondered, glancing around in wonder.

"I thought you would like it," JJ said, sounding almost shy.

"Like it? I want to move in."

"I have one more thing for you," JJ said, pulling a plush bag from his pocket. "This was my grandmother's wedding ring. I put it on a chain so you can wear it as a necklace. My grandparents were married for seventy years, and I thought it might bring us some good luck if you used it as your old and borrowed."

"JJ," she felt tears prickling her eyes again. "You're too much."

"In a good way, of course," he laughed, moving behind her to clasp the necklace. "Patrick is going to be my best man, but he can give you away if you want."

"No, I'll have Emma walk with me." She turned to get a reassuring smile from her sister. "Thank you for the offer, Patrick."

"No problem," he grinned at her. "Happy to be a part of this."

"See you at the altar," JJ smiled at her, walking away with everyone but Emma.

"Are you sure about this?" Emma asked, moving in front of her.

"No," Zoe laughed. "This is all crazy, right? Who gets married in Vegas on a whim?"

"If it's a whim, then we shouldn't be here," Emma said. "But if you think there is a chance of happiness, that's a different story."

Zane, Liam and Natalie were settled into the first pew to observe. Patrick and JJ stood confidently at the altar, chatting with the minister. An attendant approached, handing her a bouquet of flowers and asked if they were ready, switching on music when she nodded her agreement. Linking arms with Emma, Zoe took a deep breath and started the walk down the aisle.

JJ's eyes never left her as she walked, and she was shocked to see him wipe a tear with his sleeve. Emma gave her a hug as she handed her off at the end of the aisle, moving to stand next to Patrick to watch the ceremony. Her life was about to change forever, and she felt a surge of panic, unsure how she had gotten here.

JJ took her hand and smiled at her. "Relax. I've got you."

And for reasons she would never understand, she believed him.

Chapter 6

"Good evening and thank you for choosing our Chapel to exchange your vows," the minister said. "If you're ready to begin, I believe you are choosing to exchange the traditional vows?"

"Yes, please," JJ answered. He hadn't expected any of this to work and wanted the ceremony to go as quickly as possible to get a ring on Zoe's finger. She took his breath away as she walked down the aisle, and he held tight to her hand to keep her from running away at the last second. This was a big risk he had taken, but months of being stalled in the same place had forced him to take drastic measures. He knew what he wanted, and he believed that she felt the same, but needed a little nudge to admit it.

"Do you, JJ, take this woman to be your wife?" The minister's voice boomed through his thoughts.

"I do."

"Wait," Zoe held up her free hand.

His stomach dropped, thinking she was about to back out, but he forced himself to stay calm. "What's wrong?"

"You can't use a nickname to get married."

He laughed, the sound ricocheting off the beamed walls. "Whatever you say." He nodded at the minister, who cleared his throat.

"Do you, Jeremiah, take this woman to be your wife?"

"Jeremiah?" Zoe whispered, smiling at him.

"Yes, and yes."

"Do you, Zoe, take this man to be your husband?"

His heart skipped a beat as he waited for her to respond. "Yes," she said softly.

The minister walked them through the vows, and before he knew it, was congratulating them and inviting them to kiss. He smiled at his now wife, then swept her into his arms and dipped her, kissing her to the chorus of cheers from their friends. She looked dazed as he met her eyes, but a slow smile slid across her face before he tilted her back to her feet.

"Mrs. Monahan," he said slowly, savoring the words.

She narrowed her eyes at him. "I didn't say I would take your name."

He laughed, tucking her hand into his elbow to start their walk down the aisle together. "We can cross that bridge when we get home. This weekend, we just enjoy being newlyweds."

Everyone crowded around them, offering hugs and congratulations. JJ watched as Emma hugged Zoe tightly and the two had a quiet conversation, looking serious until both smiled and wiped away tears before hugging again.

"Should we do a late-night snack," Patrick asked. "Or do you two want to be alone?"

"Snack?" Liam looked horrified. "Drinks. We need drinks, and a club to celebrate."

"That's not our speed," JJ said quickly. "I think we'll head back to the hotel."

"Got you," Zane said with a wink. "Nat, you with us? Patrick?"

Both declined, but they all piled back into the limo so that they could be dropped at the hotel before the two guys headed out for the night. JJ kept a hold on Zoe's hand as they rode home, feeling as though they both needed the reassurance. Feeling the two bands on her finger was surreal, the original he had given her earlier and a thinner matching band that he had slid on during the ceremony. She was his wife, despite all her refusals to accept his love or admit her feelings. He was committed to making their life together happy and wanted to make sure she knew how seriously he was taking this.

When they got back to their private floor at the hotel, JJ was surprised when the attendant indicated that he and Zoe should go into a different room than the suite they were sharing. Patrick and Emma were snuggled together in the hallway, grinning at them.

"It's our treat," Patrick said. "You two should have some privacy to celebrate your wedding night."

"Don't be ridiculous," Zoe objected. "This isn't real."

"I believe this says otherwise," JJ said, holding up their wedding certificate. "Thank you, Patrick and Emma. This was very thoughtful, even if my wife is acting like a brat."

"I'm not a brat! This is just unnecessary," Zoe pouted.

"The hotel moved your stuff over for you," Emma explained. "I guess we'll see you in the morning? Zoe, will you be alright?"

"Yes," Zoe hugged her quickly. "I'm sorry, this was just a lot. Thank you both for being so thoughtful."

They said goodnight to Natalie before JJ opened the door to the suite that they had been moved to. The room was decorated in soft white and pink, flowers on every surface, and a bottle of champagne sat on a table along with a plate of chocolate covered strawberries. A note card next to the treats offered congratulations from the hotel staff, and JJ stifled a laugh at the sight of the bed covered in rose petals.

Rather than let Zoe get caught off guard by the romantic elements of the room, he turned and swept her up into his arms.

"What are you doing," she cried, almost hitting him in the face with the bouquet she still held.

"I need to carry you over the threshold," he said. "Have you never watched a romantic comedy?"

"That would have you bashing my head into the door frame, so please don't do that."

"Never." He walked carefully through the door, kicking it closed with his foot. Rather than placing her on her feet immediately, he carried her to the king size bed and then seemed to surprise her when he placed her gently down rather than tossing her onto it. They stood there, staring at each other, for a heartbeat before she rested her head on his chest.

"This is crazy."

"No, it's not," he assured her, holding her. "This was coming no matter what. I knew the day I met you that I would marry you, and it's been a challenge ever since for me to figure out how."

"JJ," she sighed. "You don't want to be married to me. I'm a mess."

"You're my mess, and I love it. I'm also here for you, and not leaving." He kissed her softly, trying to wipe the look of worry off her face. "Do you want me to open the champagne?"

"Sure," she said. "I'm going to take a quick shower."

"Want help?"

She swatted him with her empty hand and laughed, stepping away from him. He watched as she carefully placed the bouquet on the nightstand, angling it so that the flowers faced the pillow where she would later sleep.

She emerged from the bathroom minutes later, wearing soft cotton pajamas, hair still wet and her face free from makeup. "You are the most beautiful woman I've ever seen," he said, handing her a glass of champagne.

"You're ridiculous. We were just with Natalie Cloud, who is legally the most beautiful woman alive."

"Not like you, though." He sat on the couch, patting the cushion next to him. "Come sit for a bit, Mrs. Monahan."

"I still didn't say that I would change my name," she said. "But before we get to that, we need to discuss something."

His stomach dropped, and he carefully placed his flute on the table in front of him. "What's that?"

"Jeremiah. What is your middle name?"

"Luke."

"It is not," she laughed.

"It really is," he said. "Jeremiah Luke Monahan."

"Junior?"

"No, you've met my dad, remember?"

"Oh, that's true. Frank, right?"

"Yes." He bit the top off a strawberry and watched her brain at work, as she ran through the options.

"You're just going to have to tell me." She sighed. "I can't figure out how you got JJ from Jeremiah Luke."

"This is how we're going to spend our wedding night? Talking about the origins of my name?" He pulled her closer, kissing her softly on the neck and feeling her shiver as he did.

"Yes, we'll get to the other stuff later. But I want to know."

"You're killing me," he said. "It's not a favorable look, which is why I didn't want to tell you. But if you insist, you can't hold it against me later."

"I promise," she said quickly.

"I was a wild kid. Couldn't sit still in school, didn't want to focus on anything other than playing sports or having fun. Always getting into trouble without trying," he said. "The twins were younger, and had each other. Colin was more studious, and disciplined, and I drove him crazy. I always had to be doing something, even if what I was doing wasn't nice."

"I can't imagine you being mean," she protested.

"I don't think I meant to be," he said. "But I was. And one day at school when I was particularly mean to a classmate, someone called me 'Jerky Jerm'. That only made me meaner, but it stuck. Then it became JJ."

"Why keep it now? You've moved to a different area, you could have come in and started fresh if that nickname bothers you," she asked. "But for the record, I don't think you're a jerk at all."

"Thanks," he smiled at her. "When I was a senior, I got caught up with a bad crowd. Drinking, smoking, causing havoc around town. I was spray painting on a local business when I got caught by the sheriff. He cuffed me, dragged me back to the station in the backseat of his car, and scared the life out of me. I sat there for hours, sweating because I didn't know what was going to happen. I was supposed to go play football in college, get out of this little town finally, and now it was all on the line."

"What happened?" She grabbed the champagne bottle and refilled both of their glasses.

"He came back and talked to me through the door. Asked if I liked the accommodations," he said, remember the day clearly. "I said no, and he pointed out this was where I was headed. I might think I was going to college, have a big life ahead of me, but if these were the decisions that I was going to keep making, it would all end. Asked if I thought the college I was going to would still take me with a rap sheet."

"Oh no," she said.

"I tried to be cocky at first, play it off like it didn't matter. But then he told me that he was just like me as a kid, and then the right cop got a hold of him. Said that bad choices as a kid shouldn't shape our future, but that if I kept going on the path I was on, it would. I wouldn't be able to play college ball, or even go to college. I'd end up stuck in that town forever, probably as a resident of the county for a time," he said. "It was like my whole life flashed before my eyes, one where I could go and be successful, and the other where I was going to be one of the townies that my friends and I made fun of."

"You obviously made the right choice," she said.

"He let me sit there for a few more hours to let it all sink in," JJ explained. "By the time he let me out and told me that he wouldn't charge me if I went and cleaned the paint off in the morning, I was so relieved. I cleaned up my act, finished high school and went to college. I planned on majoring in business, but halfway through school I realized I wouldn't be there without that one night. I switched my major to criminal justice and the rest is history."

"It's amazing the influence a good person can have on our lives," she said softly. "And the bad ones."

"Yeah, it really is. I can't imagine what my life would have been like without that night. Even the kids at school couldn't figure out if I was pranking them by suddenly trying to pay attention and be nice to people," he laughed. "They thought it was some kind of long con I was running."

"But I have to ask again," she said. "Why go by it now? Why not just have people call you Jer?"

"Because it's a lesson I need to remember every day," he told her. "That even the people who look like they are beyond help might have a second chance inside of them. And to myself, to be mindful of how I'm treating people."

"I do have to say," she said quietly. "You've been amazing to me. Especially when everything happened with my father, and when Emma came back into my life. The last year has been rocky, and you've been the one constant for me. I really do appreciate it, no matter what happens between us now."

"You mean the next fifty years of marital bliss?"

"Seriously," she said. "If this all goes horribly wrong, I want you to know how much it has meant to me. I honestly think we should get this annulled. Our friendship is so important to me, and this is just crazy."

"It's not crazy," he said. "It's exactly what we were headed for, I just took the second guessing out of the equation for you."

"But now I'm second guessing, and I think you're a little nuts."

"You love me, I know you do. I know you can't say it, and that's alright, you'll get there. But I love you, and I know we are meant to be together. If you can't trust in your own heart right now, please trust in mine," he said. "You know I would never do anything to hurt you. Let's see how this goes."

He watched the emotions cross her face as she struggled through it, knowing that the commitment went against every fiber of her being. He didn't know why, and it wasn't important tonight. Tonight, he wanted to celebrate their marriage in a way that they could both look back and with happiness. Even though she was sure it would fall apart, he was equally as confident that they would last, and creating these memories for her was important. With that in mind, he switched on a song on his phone and stood, offering her a hand.

"Will you please dance with me?" His heart skipped a beat as she stood slowly, unfolding herself from the couch before stepping into his arms. She fit perfectly, and he pulled her close, swaying her slowly around the living room to what he considered 'their' song, before softly kissing her and leading her to the bedroom.

Chapter 7

"It's not real," Zoe heard herself explaining to Emma. "All of this, it's just a fantasy for him. He thinks he's in love with me, but he really isn't."

The two sisters were enjoying breakfast together while Patrick and JJ hit the local golf course before the movie event that evening. JJ had woken Zoe up early, wanting to make sure she didn't mind him leaving her alone. She had encouraged him to go, anxious to break down the last twenty-four hours with her sister. Despite her willingness to go through with the wedding, she felt her darker side filling her with doubts. Of him, of their odd relationship, of their future. The dark clouds had billowed in suddenly and without warning, and she didn't know which way to turn.

"I think you might be underestimating him," Emma said. "I think this is real for him. Did you know that he asked me right before we went into the concert?"

"He what?" She froze, a bite of French toast halfway to her mouth.

Emma nodded. "He pulled me aside and told me he planned to marry you last night. And that since we don't have a dad, and your relationship with your mom is difficult, he didn't have anyone to ask for a blessing other than me."

"And you gave it to him?"

"Of course I did! Zoe, I cried, it was so beautiful. And thoughtful," Emma said. "He really does love you."

"We barely know each other." Zoe hated the pouting she felt herself doing but couldn't stop it.

"That's not true, and you know it. You've been inseparable for two years now," Emma pointed out. "And I'm pretty sure he's always made it known that he wants to be with you. You guys know each other in all the ways that matter. He's a good person, you're a good person. You laugh together, you look out for each other. What more could you need?"

"Marriage is more than that," Zoe said. "You and Patrick are all of those things, and you love each other."

"We do, and I can't wait until he asks me to marry him, if I'm that lucky," Emma looked dreamy thinking about it. "I think about our future, having babies with him, growing old with him. It's all I want."

"I don't do that with JJ," Zoe said.

"You don't let yourself do that with JJ," Emma argued. "Or with anyone, and I don't know why that is. Obviously, you and your mom had major issues, and it's affecting everything else. You mentioned on your wedding night that you felt like no one stays with you, and that's not true. I never would have left you if we weren't kids and I had control of the situation, and I don't think JJ will ever leave you. Zo, you need to move past your fears of abandonment. We can talk about it, or you should do therapy, or you could talk to JJ. Get it behind you so you can start living your life."

"You make everything sound so easy."

"And you sound like a bratty little girl," Emma chided her. "I was essentially homeless six months ago, and now look at my life. I wouldn't trade anything that got me to this point, with you back and with Patrick. I had to be open to being hurt when I came looking for you, and when I fell in love with him. Sometimes you have to take big risks to get great rewards. You've kept yourself in a little bubble for the last few years, and JJ is the only person that you let in there. Other than me, of course, but that's different. You've trusted him for a long time, and I see your happiness with him. You just need to let yourself see it too."

"Why did you have to get so wise," Zoe said. "I'm the big sister, you should be coming to me for help."

"And I did," Emma said. "You gave me good advice and let me cry all over you. Now it's your turn to come to me."

Zoe considered her sister, looking so happy and confident in her life now. Loving Patrick had given her a glow, and she knew that it made Emma feel secure for the first time in a long time. As desperately as she wanted that feeling for herself, life had taught her that it was safer to only count on herself. No one could hurt her if she didn't expect anything from them, and no one could leave her if she never let them in. It was a hard way to live, and the people of Windsor Peak had started breaking down her defenses the second she set foot in the town. Making her soft enough that she suddenly found herself married to the one person who could hurt her more than anyone else, and that terrified her.

"Have you talked to your mother recently?" Emma's sudden change in topic startled Zoe, and she splashed a spot of coffee onto her shirt.

"No," she said. "Why do you ask?"

"No reason," Emma said as she reached over and grabbed her hand, giving it a gentle squeeze. "You'll always have me, I promise. And I think if you let yourself be open to the possibility, you'll always have JJ. Give yourself a chance, please."

***

Two days later, Zoe climbed aboard a private jet with JJ, Patrick and Emma, headed back to Vermont. They had attended two glamorous events over the two nights since the wedding, and the days had passed in a blur. The first night at a gala where movie stars were three deep at the bar, JJ had told her he was going to pretend it was their wedding reception. He insisted on dancing to every slow song the band played and feeding her a bite of the dessert that was served, much to the entertainment of their table. Fortunately, they were sitting with people she had gotten to know over the trip, so it was less embarrassing. Natalie had even whispered to her at one point that she was a little jealous of how in love JJ was with her, and she had to fight back the urge to explain that he couldn't possibly be serious. It was only a matter of time before he decided to leave her, but she didn't want to burst Natalie's bubble.

They had attended a fundraiser for a horse rescue that Patrick worked closely with, where Patrick, Zane, Liam and Natalie had been the biggest stars in attendance. Others from the night before who had worked with them in the past had attended as well, but the four celebrities who had helped bring attention to the horse rescue mission were the focus. Fortunately, that had Emma hanging back more with Zoe and JJ as Patrick met volunteer after volunteer. He hadn't wanted to leave until he had met everyone who had come out to see them, and from the look on his face, it had exhausted him. Yet he had insisted

58

that they fly home directly after the party, so they could all be home the next day.

Once the plane was in the air, Patrick let out a big yawn and laughed. "Sorry, guys, but I'm exhausted. All that handshaking and selfie-taking really took a toll on me. Do you guys mind if I take the bed?"

"Seriously? It's your plane, buddy. Take anything you want," JJ laughed.

"Not my plane, the studios," Patrick said. "But thanks. Emma, want to come?"

"I'll be right in, I want to take a quick shower," Emma said. "You guys all set?"

"Absolutely," JJ answered for both of them. "We'll cuddle up on the couch and watch a movie. Have a good night."

"I'm going to shower after Emma," Zoe said. "You can put on whatever you want to watch, and I'll join in after."

"I can wait," JJ offered. "I'm not ready for reality yet, I can't believe this trip is over so fast."

"I know, I feel like we just flew out to Los Angeles, and we're already back to it. You don't have to work tomorrow, do you?"

"No," he shook his head. "We need to move, so it's a good thing I told them I wouldn't be back until Tuesday."

"Move?" She stopped digging in her carryon bag to look at him.

"Yes, move. I know you're attached to your place, but mine is bigger. If you'd rather, we can stay in yours and look for something bigger that's closer to town than mine?"

She sat back on her heels and stared at him. "We aren't living together."

"Oh, but we are. We're married now, remember? I'm going to live with my wife," he said slowly. "But I'm game on where it will be."

"Why do we have to move? You already spend most nights at my place."

"That's different. I want to have my stuff mixed in with your stuff. I'd like to get a dog, assuming you aren't allergic. I want to split chores and bills, and all the ugly stuff that will cause us to fight, like when I leave my dirty socks on the couch."

"It's not like the laundry basket is that far away," she said, lost in thought. "But this is crazy. We can't just up and move in together."

"Zoe." He waited until she looked him in the eye before continuing. "I want to move ahead in our relationship. I'd like to have kids one day. Not anytime soon, before you freak out, but in the next five years. We are going to have a long life ahead of us, the sooner we get the kinks worked out, the better."

"This isn't kinks," she said, fighting off hysteria. "This is my life."

"It's our life," he said gently, sliding to the floor to take her in his arms. "I want to make it a beautiful one. Just think about it for now, we can decide in the morning after you've gotten some sleep."

She heard the bathroom door open and saw Emma slip into the bedroom, so she jumped to her feet and grabbed her toiletries and clothes. "I'll be right back." She practically ran the short distance to the bathroom, closing the door and resting her head on the back of it before setting everything down. Once she was in the shower, she waited for the panic or the tears to come. Neither happened, instead she had a quick vision of JJ's clothes hanging next to hers in the closet, his toothbrush next to hers on the sink. She even let herself daydream for a minute about a blond-haired, blue-eyed baby that would look just like him, before shutting that down.

The fastest way to make him realize that he didn't want to be with her was to show him what life would actually be like. Not the fun of ending the night together, or the occasional relaxation of watching a movie or playing cards. It was easy to think you were in love when you could go your separate ways after an argument, but when he was stuck with her day after day, surely, he would see why no one stuck around for her.

She pulled on her yoga pants and a t-shirt before heading back out, finding him snoozing on the couch. He had paused one of her favorite movies on the large TV before falling asleep and pulled out a blanket that was folded next to him. She was always cold, he was always hot, and this was his way of looking out for her. She studied him for a minute, this gorgeous man who was now her husband. He had his feet up, long legs stretched in front of him, one arm along the back of the sofa and his head tilted back. His phone was still in his hand, so she gently took it and plugged it into the cord next to him before settling onto the couch next to him. After a minute's hesitation, she pulled the blanket over herself and tucked into him, his arm automatically falling down to envelop her. A tired yawn escaped her lips before her eyes closed, putting to rest her panic over the next steps in their relationship.

Chapter 8

JJ helped Patrick load the luggage into the SUV that they had left parked at the airport, surprised at how energetic he felt after a night on the plane. He had expected to be tired and ready to lounge all day, but he was rested and ready to make some big life changes. "What are you going to do today?" he asked Patrick, closing the hatchback after the last bag.

"Most likely, lay on the couch and watch movies with Emma," Patrick replied. "After we check on the horses and stop over to see my dad and Stella, of course. And probably check in with Kendra and Shea, see how they are feeling."

"Due dates are coming up quick," JJ said.

"They are," Patrick nodded. "I can't wait to have some new babies to spoil. What about you? What's up for the day?"

"House hunting, hopefully," JJ admitted. "I'm going to try and talk Zoe into looking at some places."

"Moving already? This really isn't a joke to you, is it?" Patrick leaned on the back of the car and studied him. "I know you keep saying it's serious, but I just keep waiting for the other shoe to drop."

"No other shoe," he shook his head. "I'm very serious. I don't know how to convince her of that, or anyone else for that matter."

"Just keep doing what you're doing, man. Show her and the world that you're committed, and you aren't going anywhere."

"That's the plan," JJ grinned. "Let's get on the road so I can find her dream home. I already started looking online and have been texting with Kendra's friend Julie, the real estate agent. I think I have a good lead on something she can't resist."

"Good luck," Patrick said as he pulled the keys out of his pocket. "I'll be rooting for you."

***

"Oh, wow," Zoe whispered as Julie led them into the kitchen of the house that JJ had found online. A huge Viking stove was caressed by her, then she turned and surveyed the room. JJ knew the enormous granite island, double stainless sink and massive refrigerator were the ways to her heart. When he saw this Craftsman style house listed and saw the kitchen, he had been ready to buy it sight unseen. But he wanted his new wife to be a part of the decision. Patrick had helped him by rushing everyone home the night before so that they could be one of the first to view the house, and he had already told the agent to alert him if any other offers went in.

"We can't possibly afford this," Zoe said. The stars in her eyes were replaced with sadness as she opened the door to an enormous walk-in pantry.

"The owners started remodeling and then hit some financial issues," Julie explained. "The rest of the house needs a lot of work; the kitchen is the only room completed. That being said, the price is great, and they are hoping for a fast sale."

"We can afford it," JJ said. "I don't know exactly what you make, but I know what you pay in rent. What we pay combined between my mortgage and your rent, we can afford this."

"What about your house?" Zoe turned to him. "You would need to sell that, right?"

"I have people who would rent it quickly," Julie interjected. "Or that would sell fast. Your house is in a great neighborhood, and close to the school."

"We can do this, if you want," JJ said. He took Zoe's hand and made sure she was looking at him when he spoke. "Do you want this house?"

"I do," she said. "It's so perfect. Still walking distance to the restaurant and town, and this kitchen is a dream. But what are we doing, buying a house together? JJ, this is crazy."

"We have two choices, as I see it," he answered. "I can buy it, and we can both live here until you get adapted to the idea of being together forever. Then we can figure out how to do it again so we both own it. Or you can take a leap of faith with me, and we can do this together. Make this our home."

She stared at him for several minutes. "This is crazy."

"So is getting married in Vegas the same night that I propose."

"JJ," she rolled her eyes. "I know this is all a game to you, I don't want to make a huge decision like this on a whim."

"None of this is a game to me. I love you, and that's why I married you. I plan to live a long, happy life with you. I'm not going anywhere," he said forcefully.

"Do you want to see the rest of the house?" Julie asked tentatively, breaking the tension and their staring contest. She was pointing down a hall, but JJ could only stare at Zoe. If she wanted to pitch a tent out back and live in it, he would be on board.

"I don't think we need to," she said slowly. "I think this is our house."

"I would suggest doing an inspection, at least," Julie insisted. "There is a lot of work to be done."

"No, it's fine. Jake can come by quickly for a look, he's a contractor and would be doing the work," JJ said. He pulled his phone from his pocket and held it up. "Mind if I call him to come now?"

Julie shook her head, and JJ quickly dialed Jake's number. After a quick conversation, he texted his friend the address and put his phone away. "He'll be in here in a few minutes."

"Honestly, this house could be falling down around us, and I would still want this kitchen. I never would have thought to have navy cabinets, but these are just stunning. Especially with the white counters and all the stainless," Zoe marveled. "And all this storage. Plus, the pot filler. I think I'm in heaven."

"I'll be in heaven with you cooking for me in here," JJ grinned at her. "I can't wait to see what kind of magic you'll work in here. But maybe you should take a look at the bedrooms and the bathrooms, just to be safe."

"Where you'll work your magic?" Zoe teased him, and he laughed as the agent turned away.

"Absolutely, anything for you," he pulled her close and planted a kiss on her head.

"Honestly, I could live anywhere," Zoe said. "The apartment I had in Paris when I first moved there barely had running water and was overrun with critters. This will be fine."

"I want to show you one thing," JJ said, tugging her towards the kitchen door. They stepped out onto a large back porch, overlooking a large lawn with the mountain in the background. "I was thinking this has enough room for some nice rockers, and maybe we could put in a patio with an outdoor kitchen for you. And a firepit, so on the odd nights we are both off, we could relax out here."

"That sounds amazing," Zoe said. She leaned against him slightly, and he wrapped an arm around her shoulders, enjoying the peace together.

"I think we'll be happy here," he said as he saw Jake's truck approach. "Together." He kissed her quickly before jogging outside to get his friend. Avoiding eye contact and the time for her to deny their future felt wrong, but he needed to stay optimistic about this next step. If she agreed to buying this house, he decided, it would be the little bit of proof he needed that she was as all-in as he was.

***

Two hours later, he was sitting on Zoe's couch as she paced back and forth in front of him. They had signed their offer officially with the real estate agent, confirming it was the only one the seller had received so far. Jake had given them a quick estimate of the cost to finish the work on the house, and Julie expected the seller to respond quickly. The goal was to close on the house in two weeks if they could get the bank working quickly enough, but they wouldn't be able to do anything until the seller responded.

"This is dumb," Zoe said. She stopped and stared at him for a moment before starting her pacing again. "We shouldn't be doing this."

"Yes, we should. You love the kitchen; we both love the area that the house is in. The repairs will take some time, but Jake said he could prioritize the most important ones. Mainly, the bedroom and master bath, so we can live there comfortably while he does the rest." JJ leaned forward, putting his elbows on his knees as he studied her. "You love that house."

"I love that kitchen," she admitted. "I'm not even sure I noticed the rest of it."

"In the meantime," he said, waiting for her to look at him before continuing. "We need to decide where we want to live until we can close. I'm happy to move in here if that would be easier for you, but my house is bigger."

She stared at him for so long, he was sure she wouldn't respond, then suddenly dropped into the chair behind her. "We're married."

"We are."

"And you want to live with me."

"I do. Very much."

"We can't do that here," she finally said. "It's too small. You take up a lot of space with those shoulders."

He laughed; glad she wasn't arguing with him about living together any longer. "They don't take up that much room."

"They do," she insisted. "You should probably walk through the doors sideways, make sure you don't knock the walls down."

"Okay, so it's settled. My house it is. That will make it easier when we move into the new house, we'll have already emptied this one." He stood, clapping his hands together. "Do you have any boxes?"

"Now?" She gaped at him, then looked around the room in a panic. "We can't do all this now."

"How about this? Why don't you pack the essentials, and then when we both have a couple days off, we can get the rest of it. I'll invite everyone here to help pack, we can make a party of it."

"This is nuts," she sighed. "How is this my life?"

He pulled her to him, wrapping her in his arms as he laughed. "Because I'm the luckiest man alive, that's how."

She pushed him lightly but laughed with him. "You're a full-blown lunatic. And I'm not sure what that says about me, that I'm going along with all of this."

His phone rang, and he pulled it out to see his mother's picture flash on the screen. "Wait until I tell my mom that her new daughter-in-law just called her baby a lunatic."

She gasped and grabbed for his phone, knocking it out of his hand. "Did you tell her we're married?"

"Not yet," he said, grabbing the phone from under the couch. "I called and this is her calling me back. Want to tell them in person instead?"

"No! I mean yes. I mean, don't tell her now," she hissed as he hit the button to accept the call.

"Hey, Mama," he said, smiling into the phone. His mother's enthusiastic voice greeted him and asked about the trip, and he laughed as Zoe sank onto the couch and covered her eyes. He switched the phone to speaker as he responded. "We just got home this morning. It was an unforgettable trip to say the least. Want to have dinner so we can tell you all about it?"

"We?" Her voice rang out from the speaker. "Zoe too?"

"Yes, Zoe and I can meet you and Dad for dinner if you're free."

"Are you sure you're not too tired? That long flight overnight must have been exhausting." Her motherly concern had him picturing her putting a hand to his forehead when he coughed just once as a kid.

"Not nearly as bad when you fly private," he told her. "Listen, we are in the middle of something, but can you meet us at Fireside at six? I'll call ahead and get a table."

"Sure, honey. We'll see you there, I can't wait. Tell Zoe I said hi," she said.

"Hi," Zoe responded weakly from the couch.

"Oh, honey, I didn't know you were right there," she exclaimed, sounding more excited. "I can't wait to see you tonight and hear all about the trip."

"Looking forward to it," Zoe said, unable to resist his mother's enthusiasm.

He hung up the phone and glanced at his watch. "I'll call and reserve a table; you should get moving. We'll have to leave in a couple hours for dinner, and I want to get your stuff settled in first."

"You make it sound like my clothes are pets, or people," she laughed.

"Speaking of, want to go to the dog rescue tomorrow and see what they have?"

"No," she responded over her shoulder. "One step at a time was our rule, and we've somehow gone about two hundred steps at once. No dog yet."

"Got it," he replied, smiling at her as he lifted the phone to his ear again. He knew when to pick his battles, and the dog could absolutely wait until she was more comfortable. Once they were settled into the new house, maybe. As he had the thought, his phone rang again, showing the realtor's name on the screen. Five minutes later, he walked in on Zoe throwing things in a suitcase as she muttered under her breath in French.

"If you're here to help, you can do that drawer," she said, pointing behind him.

"Happy to help, my love," he said. "But I also came as the bearer of good news."

"What?"

"Our offer was accepted," he reported. "We can close as soon as the bank is ready. I'll call Erin at the bank and let her know we'll fill out the application online tonight, so she knows to look for it in the morning."

"Wait." Zoe held up a hand, then realizing it was full of leggings, threw them into the suitcase. "We got the house?"

"We did," he nodded. "We just need to do the financing, but I'll drop off a check tomorrow for the deposit if that's alright with you. I don't mind covering it."

"That's fine," she waved her hand. "I never thought I would own a Viking stove. This is maybe the most exciting moment in my life."

He stared at her, then caught the quick twitch of her lips that suggested she was hiding laughter. "Oh, I'm going to make you take those words back."

"We don't have time now," she warned him. "Not if you want to get all this to your house and still have time for me to shower and be ready to go."

"I have nothing but time," he promised her as he moved closer to her. "Now that we live together, I have time before your shower. In the shower. After the shower. And at bedtime. More than enough time to convince you that I should outrank the stove."

Chapter 9

Maggie Monahan was exactly what Zoe would picture when envisioning a perfect mom, and she had envied JJ when he first introduced her to his parents. Maggie's hair was neatly cut just shy of her shoulders, more white than blonde now. She was wearing an adorable skirt with daisies on it, coupled with a pink sweater set. As an elementary school teacher prior to retirement, she couldn't help but still dress brightly, as though she had to keep the attention of twenty third graders. Laugh lines circled her eyes, which were bright and full of joy when she saw her oldest son approaching. JJ's father, Frank, was a towering figure with a big laugh that made everyone around him feel at ease. They both hugged their son before embracing her as well, a feeling she had yet to get used to. Not just being hugged by JJ's mom, but any mom.

"It's so good to see you both," Maggie gushed. "I feel like it's been months since we last saw you."

"It was two weeks, Mom. The cookout at Patrick's house, remember? Or were you too busy peppering Patrick with questions about Hollywood to recall seeing us," he teased her.

Maggie hit him lightly on the shoulder before leaning closer to Zoe to stage whisper. "I don't know how you put up with him."

"Me neither," Zoe laughed, rolling her eyes at JJ acting wounded. "He's a lot to handle."

"I blame myself," Maggie said. "The oldest is supposed to be the easiest, but between Colin and the twins, I was just too busy to keep him out of trouble."

"I was never trouble," JJ argued. "Adventurous, maybe."

"Sure, if that's what you want to call it," Frank said with a wink to Zoe. "I think they're ready to seat us now."

Zoe felt JJ's hand on her back as she followed his mom to the table and had a sudden longing for exactly what she was experiencing right this moment. A mother-in-law who would make up for her own mother's deficits, a father-in-law who would offer advice without judgement. A man who adored her the way that Frank did Maggie and treated her as well as JJ did his own mom. Which, she had to admit to herself, was exactly how he currently treated her. It was her own stubbornness that had prevented them from moving ahead in their relationship, and it was that same self-doubt that had her waiting for the other shoe to drop. All she had to do was trust that he wouldn't leave her, and this could be her life. If only she could find a way to trick her mind into believing.

She sat in the seat that JJ had pulled out for her, feeling his heat as he took the chair next to her and draped his arm along the back of her chair. She kept her hands on her lap, fiddling with the napkin that she had draped there, realizing that Maggie had so far missed the ring on her finger. As though sensing that was her sudden nervousness, JJ cleared his throat and looked to her before he started speaking.

"We have some news we wanted to share," he said. Maggie's eyes brightened and darted between them, but before he could continue, the waiter interrupted asking for drink orders. Once they had full water glasses in front of them, and cocktails on the way, JJ started again. "As I was saying, we have some news."

"You're engaged!" Maggie clapped her hands together and said it loud enough for other diners to look over with smiles.

"No," JJ said quickly. "Even better. We just got married in Vegas."

"What?" Zoe watched the emotions run across Maggie's face rapid fire, as she turned to her husband and then back to them. "You got married? Without me?"

"I'm sorry, Mom." JJ reached over and squeezed her hand. "It was spur of the moment, if we had known of course I would have had you there."

"Oh, I'm sorry. I'm being selfish," she said, dabbing at her eyes. "The most important thing is that I have a new daughter! Zoe, I couldn't be happier to have you as part of our family."

"Welcome to the family," Frank smiled warmly at her. "I hope you're prepared."

"She'll be fine," JJ grinned at her. "She puts up with me every day."

"Tell me all about it," Maggie said. "Do you have pictures?"

JJ pulled out his phone to flip through pictures as he told the story to his parents. Zoe listened, smiling when it was appropriate, but suddenly feeling as though her world was spinning a little. Looking at Maggie's open, loving face across the table made it even more profound how badly she could screw up not just JJ's life, but his amazing family. She had no idea how to be a loving daughter, never mind daughter-in-law, and this part of it hadn't really clicked for her yet. Up until this moment, she had let herself live in JJ's optimistic fairy tale bubble, but the thought of learning to love them and then losing them all made her chest hurt.

"I'm just going to run to the ladies' room," she said, pushing her chair back. Both JJ and Frank stood as she did, and JJ's concerned face forced her to keep it together. "Be right back."

Emma answered on the first ring, thankfully. She needed her sister to talk her down from the fear that was clawing its way into her body, and no one could do it like she could. "Hey, Zoe. I thought you were going to dinner?"

"I am," she whispered. "I'm in the hall by the bathroom. We just told his parents that we got married and I'm completely freaking out. Talk me out of leaving right this minute."

"You can't leave," Emma said gently. "That's your husband. And it's JJ, who you trust. Just breathe and tell me what's freaking you out."

"His mom," she admitted. "She looks so happy, and I can't help but think that I'll screw that up somehow."

"Not to mention, it's probably a reminder of what you never had growing up," Emma guessed.

Zoe sighed. "She's everything you could imagine if you pictured a perfect mom."

"No one is perfect," Emma said. "I'm sure she had bad days, especially when they were younger. Imagine a young JJ?"

Zoe laughed, and wiped her eyes at the same time. "Why do I have to get like this?"

"Because you're human," Emma said. "And you're an emotional person. Who has had a less than ideal life and is scared of happiness. But I think you could have it, if you let yourself."

"Running out the back door would probably be a mistake, then. Ok, thank you. I'll pull myself together and go back to the table." Zoe took a deep breath and said goodbye to her sister before putting her phone back into her pocket. Her step faltered when she approached, but the warmth in all three sets of eyes put her at ease as she sat back down.

"We were just catching JJ up on his siblings," Maggie told her. "His brother Colin is coming to town soon, so you'll finally get to meet him. You've met the twins, right?"

"I have," Zoe nodded. "They came to karaoke with us one night and come into the restaurant quite a bit."

"Probably looking for free food," JJ said as he buttered a piece of bread and put it on her plate. "Don't give it to them."

"They probably learned that from you," Zoe laughed. "But they always insist on paying."

"Good," Frank nodded. "Make JJ pay as well."

"Dad." JJ pretended to be wounded. "You would deny me all these amazing meals?"

"You need to stay in shape for your job," Frank teased. "Zoe, maybe more salads would be good."

She nodded, playing along with him. "Grilled chicken too, nice and plain."

"You two are brutal," JJ said. "But fortunately, I know there is zero chance you would ever make me plain chicken. Besides, I work out almost every day to make up for it. I'm probably in the best shape of my life, working out with Patrick and crew."

"You got lucky there, having Mike available to train you," Zoe nodded. "I can see the difference in the Burrows men since they started working out with him."

JJ raised an eyebrow at her. "I think what you're saying is you need me to take my shirt off."

She laughed and took a sip of her wine, feeling herself relax finally as Maggie chided her son about suggesting he would remove his clothes in a restaurant. "You should have seen them when they were little," Maggie said. "We could never go out to eat, they were all so impossible to keep still."

"I can imagine, since he still can't." Zoe said, nodding at JJ, who was talking to his father about his workout.

"JJ showed us the pictures from your wedding while you were in the bathroom," Maggie said, leaning closer across the table. "You looked beautiful, honey. I really can't tell you how happy I am for you both. I promise we will try not to overwhelm you, so you can adjust slowly to being a part of our big, noisy family. If I remember right, it's just you and your sister? Has your mom passed away?"

"No," Zoe said. "But she's not in my life."

JJ was watching her as she spoke, and fortunately seemed to realize she needed a change in subject quickly. "I almost forgot to tell you; we bought a house."

"You certainly have a lot of news," Frank laughed. "Where is the house?"

JJ pulled his phone out suddenly and frowned at the screen, then looked at Zoe. "Mind if I go take this? Can you tell them about the house?"

"Sure," she agreed, surprised. He rarely let his phone interrupt meals, so it had to be important for him to leave the table. She watched him walk away and then turned back to his parents, seeing the same concerned look on their faces. Wanting to distract them, she decided to start talking about the house. "JJ found the perfect house, although I can't remember much more than the kitchen. Someone had started renovations on the place and then lost their funding, so the only part that's done is the kitchen, and it's gorgeous. It's still close enough to town to walk to work, but closer to the mountain. Do you know where Overlook Park is?"

They both nodded. "We started playing pickleball recently and that's one of the few courts that's usually available," Maggie said.

"It's near there," Zoe said. "Just a few streets over."

"That's a great area," Frank said. "Not that there are many bad spots in Windsor Peak, if any. Best decision we ever made, following JJ up this way after we retired. Most people go south, we did the opposite."

Maggie laughed. "You wouldn't be able to tolerate the heat down south. This is better for us."

JJ returned to the table just in time to hear his mother's comment, and laughed. "I'm glad you're up here, and secretly happy that the twins followed you. Very different from how we grew up, but I like it. And we can always visit Boston, it's just a short drive."

"We get so many visitors up here, we don't need to go down very often," Maggie said. "We have a wedding coming up for one of your cousins, so we'll all have to make the drive that time. And maybe we can get Colin to consider settling down one day."

Their entrees arrived, and Zoe took the distraction as an opportunity to lean over to whisper to JJ. "Everything okay?"

He nodded, but she noticed the tenseness in his shoulders and the slight frown on his face. "Yes. I'll tell you about it on the way home."

"Not the house?"

"Oh, no," he said. "Sorry, it's nothing to do with us. Everything is fine."

She studied him as he accepted his plate of prime rib from the server, and then accepted her short rib risotto plate. Inhaling the scents, she made a mental note of what she guessed the ingredients would be before she took her first bite. She tried to never copy another chef's menu, but always derived inspiration from dining out, and her plate looked perfect. JJ was back to joking with his parents, so she decided to enjoy her meal and not let worry take over again.

An hour later, they were stuffed and happy and hugging his parents in the parking lot. Zoe found herself agreeing to a day of shopping in the near future with Maggie and Finley and heard JJ setting up a time to golf with his dad. It was all so normal, and even knowing that people had these relationships with their parents, it still caught her off guard to be thrust in the middle of a family like this.

JJ opened her car door for her before getting into the driver seat and starting the car. The warmth of the day had left with the sun, and the sudden blast of air conditioning had her shivering. He reached over and pushed a button to turn on the heated seats and smiled at her. "Even for you, I can't handle turning the heat on at this time of the year."

"I'll warm up in a second, it was just that blast of cold that got me," she said, snuggling into the warmth of the seat. "What was the phone call about?"

Chapter 10

JJ carefully turned onto the main road after seeing his parents turn out of the parking lot safely before responding. "It was the station. There was a robbery at the gas station just outside of town, the desk officer just wasn't sure how to send the details out to everyone. He's still new."

"Was everyone okay?"

"Yes, luckily," he sighed. "We try and talk to businesses to educate their staff never to argue or try to fight back. Insurance will cover losses, but it can't replace their life. No job is worth giving your life for, especially a single mom working a second job at a gas station."

"Is that what happened?" Zoe gasped, putting her hand over her mouth.

"Yes," he said grimly. They so rarely had anything of the sort happen in their neck of the woods, and the thought of this young woman being terrified had shocked him. "She's okay. They took her to the hospital just to be safe, but the guy had a gun, so it could have been way worse."

"Oh, that's so scary."

They drove in silence until he pulled into his driveway, and he realized she had been staring at him for the last few minutes. "You said no job is worth giving your life for, but you risk yours."

"I do," he said slowly, putting the car into park. "Yes, in practice. It was certainly more dangerous when I worked in

Boston. Here it's more small things and peace keeping than violent crimes."

"But there are times when you are in danger," she said matter-of-factly.

"That's true in any job," he argued. "You could cut yourself fatally or suffer severe burns."

"Burns from cooking wouldn't kill me," she laughed. "They just might give me some hideous scars you would need to look at."

"A grease fire could," he said. "And for the record, I'd love you anyway, scars and all."

"Okay, enough about this death talk. This is getting dark."

"Just so you know, I have good life insurance. Financially, at least, you'd be okay if something did happen to me. You could stay in the new house and not worry."

"JJ," she said, sounding horrified. "Please stop. Nothing is going to happen to you."

"First of all, I love how upset you are at the thought of it," he said. "Proves how much you love me. Secondly, it's just a fact of life. Yes, my job in theory is dangerous. Do I think it is in Windsor Peak? Not really. But it's a reality with my line of work that I'd rather us accept, talk about, and then move on from. Like when Jake went to war for the first time, he had to put a plan in place for Charlie and make sure his brothers had the knowledge to get what they needed."

"You aren't going to war, you're looking for a bicycle thief and keeping the kids from drinking underage," she said, crossing her arms. "I'm done talking about this. If you need me to know things on the very, very long shot that something was to happen to you, write it down."

He nodded, reaching over for her hand. "I will. I'm sorry, I didn't mean to upset you. I promise I'll stick around for many more years to annoy you."

She huffed out a sigh as she stared out her side window but held on to his hand tightly as he drove the rest of the way to his house. This was their first night at home, and doing something so mundane as returning from a dinner with his parents together was secretly thrilling. He was still finding it hard to believe that they were married, and in the process of buying a home together, planning for their future together. He hoped that one day he would stop worrying about her walking away from him, but every sign indicated that she wanted to be with him as much as he wanted her. If only she would admit it, then he could fully relax and settle into this new phase of his life.

***

JJ had slipped out of bed early the next morning, before Zoe had moved. She was usually up with him early, but the time difference and the travel had seemed to tire her out more than she admitted. Plus, he knew she had been on an emotional roller coaster since they got married, so it was best to let her sleep. He brewed a pot of coffee and left her a note taped to the handle, then headed to the Sheriff's office to check in. At the last second, he ran into the bakery to grab a dozen donuts, knowing his staff had worked overtime to cover for him on his vacation.

"Welcome back, JJ," Piper called from behind the counter. "I heard the news, congrats. I'm so happy for you and Zoe."

"Thanks," he grinned at his friend. "Emma wasted no time spreading the word, I guess?"

"She sent me pictures that night," Piper laughed. Emma was her employee at the bakery, and they had become close friends. Piper had quickly become a part of their close circle of friends in town. "What can I get you?"

He ordered the donuts and threw in some muffins, which she boxed up for him. He glanced around her shop as she did, noting the older lock on the front door and the lack of a security camera. "Everything been good around here?"

"Yes, it's been great. Business really picks up over the summer, when we get all the hikers and tourists in town. It makes up for the college kids who go home, that's for sure."

"No issues?"

"Nothing," she said, giving him a curious look. "Anything I should be concerned about?"

"There was a robbery last night at the gas station by the highway," he told her. "I just want to make sure our local businesses are aware. Please, if anyone comes in with a weapon demanding money, just give it to them. Don't try and fight back."

"I won't," Piper had gone pale at the thought of it. "We close pretty early; I think it would be harder for someone to walk in here mid-day and hold me or Emma at gunpoint."

"But you come in earlier than most," he pointed out. "And you're often alone for the first few hours. A camera in here and by the back door, plus some upgraded locks might be a good idea."

"I'll see if Jake can swing by and do the locks," she said. "And I'll hop on Amazon when Emma gets here to find some cameras."

"I don't want to scare you," he said. "I bet this was a one-time thing. But I just want to make sure you know and have a plan if something were to happen."

"Hopefully the worst thing I have to call you about is when the teens come in for cookie samples and won't leave," she said with a grin. "That's about as bad as it gets."

He paid for the treats for his office and started the short walk, greeting neighbors and friends along the way. He stuck his head into the general store and talked to the owner, warning him of the events the night before. All the other stores were still locked up tight, and nothing looked amiss, so he continued to the precinct. The desk officer lit up when he saw the pink boxes, jumping up to help carry them to the break room.

"Hey, boss," his assistant Mary called out. "I heard a rumor about you."

"Of course you did, Mary," he said. "You are the central figure in most gossip circles in town."

"Oh, you take that back," she said. "I just have a lot of friends, and they like to tell me things. Want to know what I heard?"

He held up his left hand, showing the room his new ring. "It's all true."

"You really did get married in Vegas?" Mary looked shocked. "Does your mother know?"

Mary was a grandmother and the town crier, as well as his dedicated assistant, and she was amazing at all three things. "She does. I can't believe she didn't call you last night after dinner."

"I can't either," she said. "I'm going to find my cell phone so I can text her right now. Actually, no. First, I need all the details."

He gave the office the brief version of his elopement, then got them to all go back to work. Grabbing the last blueberry muffin, he went into his office to catch up on the paperwork and read through the messages left for him. He flipped through the copy of the report from the incident at the gas station before grabbing the phone to call the officer in charge of the investigation. If there was any risk to Windsor Peak, he wanted to be aware before it arrived.

The quick rundown was exactly that, the officer had little to share. The woman who had been working stated that it was a male voice, but that he wore a face mask. She was too panic stricken to note any details of either the man or the gun and couldn't recall if he had arrived in a car or by foot. The cameras were barely operational, an issue that JJ had addressed with the same manager months before when Kendra's ex had started appearing around town. Unfortunately, the owner had told his employee that it wasn't a priority, and they didn't get enough traffic to justify upgrading the system. JJ made a note to visit the owner himself and implore for an upgrade for his staff safety, as well as the aid it would provide insurance and investigators.

His cell phone distracted him mid-morning with a text from Desmond in his sibling group chat, chastising him for getting married and not telling anyone. His sister and brother Colin chimed in, and soon his phone was dinging every few seconds.

Finally grabbing the phone, he sent a quick response asking Des and Finley to meet him for lunch at Windsor Palace and was able to finish his work in some degree of quiet. Mary helped by taking his cell phone to scroll through the pictures of the wedding, which he was sure she would forward to herself and spread around town before the end of the day.

He left early for his walk to the restaurant, taking the time to go into each of the shops along the way to talk to them about safety. Inside the pizza place and the coffee shop, he got caught up answering questions of patrons about the clerks' injuries, so clearly word had spread. He just hoped that his town would hear his message and keep an eye out for any potential danger.

When he ducked into the Palace, Kendra was behind the bar and his siblings were seated at the door closest to the kitchen. He knew it wasn't a coincidence, especially since half the tables in front of windows were open, and the hostess would have utilized them before the one they were at. Waving to Kendra, he greeted Finley with a kiss to the cheek and returned a fist bump to Des before sitting. The twins were five years younger than him and had moved in with their parents when they finished college, so he saw them often. They were clearly twins, both with their father's auburn hair and their mom's hazel eyes.

"Is she working today? We were hoping she could come eat with us," Finley asked before he had fully settled into his chair.

"Am I not good enough anymore?"

"I've been alone with three brothers for my entire life," Finley rolled her eyes. "You provided me with a sister, and I'm supposed to ignore it?"

"I'll send her out," Kendra said as she walked past.

"I can't believe you got married," Des said. "You aren't much older than us, and I'm nowhere near ready to get married. I can barely afford my own life, never mind someone else."

"You wouldn't have to support someone just because you marry them," Finley said with an eye roll. "You could easily marry someone who's way better off than you."

"What are the odds of that, in Vermont?" Des challenged. "Besides, I never meet anyone."

"That's your fault, if you got out from behind the computer maybe you would. My friends from school all liked you, but it's too late for that now."

"My job is behind the computer," Des said. "And your friends were a little immature."

"What are you saying?" Finley glared at her twin with fire shooting from her eyes.

"Not to make this about me," JJ interrupted. "But isn't this lunch about me?"

"Oh, right. Tell us everything," Finley said, turning her attention to him. "I'll deal with him later."

Before he could start, Zoe came through the door, and his day immediately felt better. She came to their table and leaned on the chair that he had tried to pull out for her, shaking her head.

"Sorry, I can't sit. We just got a huge takeout order for the bank, and I need to work on it. But I'll try and come back out later," she said.

"Mom said that we were going to have a girl's day soon," Finley said excitedly. "I can't wait."

"I'm looking forward to it," Zoe said, smiling at his little sister. "I'll try to come back before you leave."

Kendra took Zoe's spot, dropping an appetizer tray on the table. "Your wife made this for you," she said, smiling at JJ. "Congratulations."

"Thank you," he said. "How are you feeling?"

"As though I could pop at any second," Kendra responded, rubbing her pregnant belly. "You're certified to deliver this baby, if need be, right?"

"I'd rather not," JJ laughed. "But yes, they train us for all emergencies."

"Des, I've been meaning to talk to you," Kendra turned her attention to his brother. "I'll be out of work for a few months, and I know you haven't bartended in a while, but any chance you'd want to fill in a few nights?"

"That will certainly solve the issue of meeting girls," Finley said.

"I'd love to help, let me figure out the logistics. My parent's house isn't far, but adding that time on at the end of a night might be tough," Des said. "I can talk to you about what nights and hours you're looking to fill."

"If you want to, the apartment upstairs is open," Kendra said. "I can give you a great deal as an employee."

"Really?"

"How many bedrooms is it?" Finley asked at the same time as her twin.

Kendra grinned at her. "Two. It's a good size, if you guys want to take a look after lunch, I'll bring you up."

"That would be fantastic," Finley said. "We need to move out of our parents' house."

"I don't think she said anything about you moving," Des said. "This could be my bachelor pad."

"Oh, like when you thought we could go to different colleges, and had to transfer because you missed me? I think we'll stick together for now," Finley said. "I'll grab you when we're done, Kendra."

Kendra agreed and moved back to behind the bar, rubbing her back as she walked.

"I have a feeling you'll be needed here soon," JJ said to Des. "She looks ready to go."

Finley waved a hand. "Enough about Des. I want to see the pictures and hear all about your wedding. The one we weren't invited to."

JJ groaned but handed over his phone and started telling his siblings about the wedding. He watched the kitchen door through their meal, hoping every time that it opened that Zoe would come out, but she never did. His brief glance at her hadn't been enough, and he realized that no matter how much time he spent with her, it would be too short. A difficult situation to remedy when he had piles of work on his desk and she was working twelve hours a day, but he would find a way.

Chapter 11

Weeks flew by, and before Zoe knew what was happening, her stuff was being moved into their new house. They had met at the bank early in the morning, signing all the paperwork and accepting the keys to their new house, but it still felt weird. Living with JJ since they returned from Vegas had gotten more comfortable, although it was still weird to think of him as her husband. She had realized they had spent more time together than apart prior to their trip, and not much had changed between them. Now they were financially linked together, and giving up their individual homes, so it felt like a huge step.

Her landlord had been shocked when she told him that she had gotten married and had agreed to let her out of her lease with no notice in exchange for catering a small dinner party he was hosting. JJ's house was being emptied by his friends into a large truck, which they had been almost done with when they had returned from the bank.

"When are you listing this house?" Mike asked as he walked by with a rolled-up rug under one arm.

"My brother Colin might want to move in," JJ answered. "I'm waiting for him to make a decision."

"I didn't know that," Zoe said, feeling strangely upset at the lack of information.

"Sorry, love," JJ kissed her. "He just texted me this morning, asking what my plans were. We were rushing to get to the bank, so I haven't even answered him. We can talk about it in person when he gets to town."

"The mysterious Colin," Jake Burrows said as he walked by with a chair. "I feel like I know him, even though we've never met."

"You'll bond with him over the military," JJ said. "You'll like him."

"He's planning on staying here?" Dan stopped, carrying a lamp.

"He's not sure, so he doesn't want to get a long-term rental. And living with my parents is a no go for him, he'd rather stay in Boston," JJ said.

"Is that all you're carrying?" Jake called to Dan. "You serious?"

"Hey, the rest of the furniture in that room is staying," Dan responded. "Not my fault you guys took all the heavy stuff."

Zoe walked away from the guys bickering and teasing each other to walk through the house one more time. Although she could easily come back if they had forgotten something, she didn't want to miss something major, like the coffee pot or her shampoo. Satisfied that everything had been packed and was ready to go, she grabbed her bag and walked to the driveway.

"I'm going to head over to the house, get the door open and ready for you guys," she said as she opened her car door.

"Wait," JJ said from the back of the truck. He hopped down and ran towards her, tossing something to Mike as he went. "I'll come with you."

"You need to drive your own car there," she said. "I can just meet you there, it's not a big deal."

"First of all, it is a big deal," he said. "We are going to the first house we own together. Where we are hopefully going to spend the rest of our lives. Secondly, Mike will drive my truck over."

She rolled her eyes as she got into the driver's seat. "You could have driven."

He hummed along with a song, a half a second late on almost all the notes, the entire drive. By the time they pulled into the driveway, Zoe was frazzled and having second thoughts about all the decisions she had made. He wasn't intentionally driving her crazy, but she hated feeling unsettled, and that was the best description of the day so far. She stomped toward the front door, spun around when JJ grabbed her elbow from behind. She slipped and would have fallen if he hadn't been there to catch her, and he easily swung her up into his arms a second later.

"What are you doing? Put me down."

"I'm carrying you across the threshold," he said. "You might want to put your arms around me, I'd hate for the neighbors to call the police thinking I was carrying a hostage inside."

"JJ, this is crazy," she said, while still slipping her hands around his neck. "You don't need to do this, it's so old-fashioned."

"Maybe I am too," he said. He was trying to get the key into the door, and she felt herself slipping, so she held tighter to his neck until he turned the doorknob. He carried her through the door before carefully setting her on her feet, but not letting go. Instead, he stared into her eyes for a moment before kissing her softly. "I'm really happy to be here with you. I know this doesn't feel real to you yet, but it does to me. And I'm excited about what will happen here."

She wanted to tell him that she was excited too, and that she was looking forward to their life together. Having a home, one that she loved, and sharing it with him. Feeling safe, and secure, and knowing that he would always show up for her. It all threatened to spill out, but she was saved by the beeping horn of the truck as it pulled into their driveway. Settling for a kiss and feeling relieved that she hadn't allowed the floodgates to open, she pushed him toward the door.

"You'll have to show them where everything else goes, I'll take care of the kitchen," she said. As soon as she was behind the door, she allowed herself to sag against the counter. Why was this so much harder for her than everyone else? She knew she deserved to be loved, that her past didn't define her, but years of therapy hadn't prepared her for the fear that love could bring.

***

Zoe had just tucked away the last pot when she heard an excited cry from the front of the house, and she ran toward the sound. Jake was standing by the front door, looking pale and as uncertain as she had ever seen him look.

"What's wrong?" Patrick was at his side, watching his brother carefully, Dan joining them.

"Shea just called," Jake said. "She's in labor. I have to go. We're having a baby."

"Come on," Dan said. "I'll drive. Patrick, can you and Mike return the truck and then you and Emma meet us at the hospital?"

"Absolutely," Patrick nodded. "Emma, can you drive my car, and I'll go with Mike?"

"Don't worry about me," Mike said. "You guys go, I'll return the truck and find a ride. Keep us posted."

Emma turned to Zoe, wonder in her eyes. "Are you alright here?"

"Yes," she said, hugging her sister quickly. "Keep us posted from the hospital."

Emma rushed out with Patrick, chasing after Dan and Jake's speeding car in Patrick's SUV. JJ laughed as he watched them go, shaking his head. "They'll probably all get speeding tickets on the way."

"They should have asked you for an escort," Mike said. "You guys good? I'll take this back now, then I can get to the gym to get a ride home."

"Want me to follow you?" JJ offered.

"No," Mike said. "You enjoy your new house with your beautiful wife. I'll see you guys later."

Suddenly alone, Zoe stared at JJ and the stack of boxes taking up most of their living space. They both burst out laughing at the same time, as he moved closer to hug her.

"We'll get through it," he said. "I bet we didn't really use this stuff all that much anyway."

"The kitchen is all unpacked," she said. "So at least I can make us dinner for our first night here."

"I'll make sure the bed is set up and get sheets on it," he said. "And find some towels, so we can shower later. Most everything else can probably wait a bit, right? I'm exhausted."

"Yes," she said. "We have our clothes and can make coffee, so we're alright. You might want to see about hooking up the cable before the next football game, but I did make sure the Wi-Fi works."

"My wife is so efficient," he chuckled as a phone chimed. "Any idea where that could be?"

They both searched, and when she found hers, it bore yet another text from her mother, demanding that Zoe call her. She had been ignoring her calls and texts for months now, but they were ramping up. Why she couldn't just block her mother and move on, she would never understand. She had happily closed the door when her biological father had turned up suddenly, wanting to meet Emma once she had linked up with Patrick. The small glimmer of hope that had resided in her as a child that her dad would show up and be a wonderful person had been dashed when it was clear that all he wanted was the money and celebrity that Patrick could offer. Somehow turning her back on her mother was that much harder, even though the relationship had never been good. Looking up, she saw the same unhappy look on JJ's face that she was sure she wore.

She snapped out of her fog as JJ picked up his car keys. "I have to run to the station," he said, still distracted by his phone. "Text me if you need me to grab anything at the grocery store on the way back. I promise I'll be back by seven for dinner."

"JJ," she called as he opened the door. "You just said how exhausted you are, can this wait?"

"Sadly, no," he answered. "Another armed robbery, this time at Clarks General Store. I need to go down there and see what happened."

"Oh no," she said. "I hope it wasn't their son working behind the counter. I know he does that a lot on weekends."

"I know," JJ said grimly. "I'll fill you in later. Love you."

The door closed behind him, as if he already knew that she wouldn't be able to answer with the same words. They just didn't come as easy to her as they did him, and she knew why. The source of that was still texting her, making vague threats about showing up in Vermont. Her mother had never gone out of her way for anyone when it didn't benefit her, so there was no chance she would arrive now. Putting her phone down, she headed to her happy place to start a sauce for dinner. Their first meal in their first home together should be special, and she was determined to celebrate it and not freak out. At least not right away.

***

Zoe's phone pinged nonstop from the time JJ left the house, with updates from Emma at the hospital, Linda at the restaurant checking in on a special offer they had scheduled for the week, her mother still insisting on a phone call, and from local friends about the incident at Clark's. She answered all, leaving her mother's unread, and spent the hours in the kitchen. It was where she found the most comfort and peace, and before she knew it, she had made way more than what she and JJ could eat in a week.

As she started packing up containers to freeze and drop off for Shea and Jake when they returned from the hospital, she couldn't help but think about the odd turns her life had taken lately. When she had left France and virtually fled to Vermont, all she had wanted was a quiet life and a well-run kitchen. One in which she wouldn't be subject to a tyrants emotional meltdowns, or worry about challenging his ego with a well-made dish. Although she had learned a ton from her mentor and from being in France, her mother's arrival had led to the ultimate destruction of that part of her life. And now she was threatening to do the same to her life in Windsor Peak.

Although she kept waiting for the other shoe to drop with JJ, a part of her was also terrified to lose him. And if Marise turned up, he would see that even her own mother didn't love her, so why should he? Not to mention, her own behavior around her mother was unlike what JJ was used to with his own parents and might change how he saw her, even if her mother didn't ruin things. Making the phone call might be the only way to keep her at bay, and as much as she hated the thought, losing the life she had built in Windsor Peak would be way worse.

"It's about time," her mother sniped when she answered the phone. "I've been trying to reach you for months."

"What do you need?" She couldn't help but get cold, just hearing her mother's voice made her feel angry.

"Mon cher, you are too busy for your only relative?"

"I have a sister," she bit out. "As much as you would like to pretend that's not true."

"Ah, and how is your darling papa? Has he come back to cause problems?" The sounds of a lighter came over the phone, and a deep inhale followed. Her mother had always been a smoker, and apparently that hadn't changed.

"What do you want," Zoe ground out.

"I want to see you," Marise said. "It's been too long."

"It's been years since we last saw each other, and that seems to have worked out well for both of us," Zoe said. "Did you have a bad breakup? No one else to turn to?"

"That's not what it is," Marise said with a sigh. "You act like I always chose men over you."

"That's because you did," Zoe retorted. "Every chance you get."

"This is what I get for raising you," Marise murmured. "All those years sacrificing and working two jobs to give you what you needed."

"All I needed was a loving parent," Zoe snapped. "I never asked you for anything. You were never there to ask anyway. There must be a man out there who can pay attention to you now, so you can leave me alone. We both know you have no issues in that area."

"Oh, you're still bitter about France? That was not my fault."

Zoe laughed, but not in a happy way. "Sure, it never is. And I'll forget what a crappy mother you have been my entire life. You've never done anything for me or gone out of your way for me. Not once. You tore my sister away from me and lied to me for years. Then ruined my life in France with your actions. I'm done with letting you destroy my life."

"I wasn't taking that man's other daughter into my house," Marise said cruelly. "If you had known about what happened, you never would have let that go. And I did help you, remember when Hoyt showed up and you were looking for answers? You called me, and I gave you them."

"I didn't know they would come with a price," Zoe said. "Listen, I'm busy. I don't have time for this. You wouldn't like this town, and we have no reason to see each other. I have to go."

"Never time for me, I get it. If you remember I'm alive, maybe you'll call me again," Marise's accent grew thicker as she piled on the guilt. "Only one parent, and I sacrificed everything for you. But pretend I don't exist."

"You sacrificed nothing," Zoe snapped. "I see parents here who actually love their kids and have made sacrifices for them. Who want to be a part of their kids lives, not use them as a prop or ignore them when they aren't important to the story you're selling. Try the pity party on someone else, Marise. I know who you are."

She hung up the call, although it took three tries because her hands were shaking so badly. She could hear her mother's voice still going on the other end, having switched fully to French to scream at her. Flashbacks of her childhood, spent wondering which mother would come home that night, were running through her head. Sinking to the floor of the kitchen, she wrapped her arms around her legs and rested her head on her knees, willing the memories to stop.

Chapter 12

JJ drove home faster than he normally would, upset with himself for being late to their first dinner in the new house. Zoe would understand and likely have planned for this to happen, but he had completely lost track of time while at the Clark's house, and then at the station. The young officer who had responded to the call was still shaken up, and he had wanted to make sure he was alright before he left. The surge of adrenaline that went into your bloodstream when faced with a dangerous situation got you through the incident but could leave you feeling shaky and overall bad when it ended. He understood how the other cop felt all too well.

Pulling into the driveway beside Zoe's car finally put a smile on his face. Seeing the lights warming the Craftsman style house from the inside and knowing this was his home, with his wife, brightened his mood instantly. This was everything he had ever wanted, and he couldn't let a bad day sour their first night together.

"Honey, I'm home," he called as he hung his jacket on the rack in the foyer. "Where are you?"

Silence met his ears, but the lights and soft music, as well as Zoe's entire being, suggested he would find her in the kitchen. The smile instantly dropped from his face as he saw her crumpled on the floor near the stove.

"What's wrong? Are you hurt? Did something happen?" His eyes ran over her, quickly computing that she was breathing, no sign of blood, and she didn't appear to suffer from any trauma.

But as he ran his hands over her checking for injury, her tear-filled eyes met his.

"I'm okay," she said softly.

"You aren't," he answered. "And I need you to tell me what happened."

"It's nothing," she said, wiping tears from her cheeks.

"Zoe." He waited until she looked up again and met his eyes. "I'm here. I'm your husband. I love you. Please tell me why you're crying."

She took a deep breath, and he was sure she would shoot him down again. She was the queen of diversion; he had learned over the years. Anytime he got close to seeing the inner sanctum of her emotions and thoughts, she shut it down and distracted him. But this time, she surprised him.

"My mother called."

"Oh," he said, unsure what that meant. He knew they had a difficult relationship, but she rarely spoke of her. "And that went badly?"

"Yes."

"Will you tell me about it?" He turned so he was sitting next to her, rather than squatting in front of her. Stretching out his legs, he tried to get comfortable on the floor.

"I will," she said. At his shocked look, she let out a small laugh. "I know, I'm surprising myself too. But let's do it with a glass of wine and a more comfortable place to sit."

He stood quickly and helped her from the floor, then pointed to a bottle of red that was uncorked on the counter. "This one?"

She nodded, and he grabbed two glasses and followed her to the small deck off the kitchen. They had brought the two rocking chairs from his house and placed them there, knowing they needed bigger furniture for the outdoor space, but wanting to wait to make any decisions on new purchases. He poured the two glasses and handed her one before settling into with his own glass.

"My mother is a selfish person," Zoe said. "Always has been. She's a little weird, almost. It's like she doesn't have the gene to connect with people on a human level, but she thrived off attention from men. They would be short relationships, if you could even call them that, but she seemed to base her self-worth on the men who were chasing her. She was always distant from me, never a mom who I could run to with a scrape on my knee, or an issue with a friend. The only place I could find those things was when I was with Emma, and her mom."

"How old were you when Emma's mom died?" JJ was familiar with the idea of Emma's mother having Zoe come stay with them for the summers, but Zoe usually evaded talking about her childhood.

"Fourteen," she said. "But I didn't know. I was already pretty wild, and when Emma and Gwen suddenly disappeared from my life, I got worse. My mother didn't see to care what I did or where I was, she was just happy not to have to deal with me."

"That's terrible," he said.

"You know about my father," Zoe said. "I never knew of him until this year, when he showed up. The only true thing I think he said to me was that he was surprised when my mom came on to him the night I was conceived. I have to wonder if it was a checkbox for her to fill out, or a task to accomplish. Get pregnant, check. Or maybe it was a mistake, she just wanted him for the satisfaction of taking him away from someone else, and I was a side effect."

"You never felt like she cared about you at all?" JJ couldn't imagine feeling that way. His mother was the opposite, she was involved in everything her kids did, and he swore she could read their minds.

"No," Zoe shook her head. "Never."

"And your dad never made any effort to be there? Did he know about you?"

"She said that he did," Zoe answered. "I guess a part of me always hoped she was lying, and that he would show up to save me. But that never happened, and when he did finally turn up, he wanted nothing to do with me. He was only here for Emma, and really, for Patrick."

"Not all men are like that," JJ said gently. "We don't know his story, but some dads do stick around. Some men stick around."

"The rational part of my brain knows that," she said. "I see your dad, and Ben Burrows, and I see what it should look like. But when my own parents don't stick around or want to take care of you, it does something to you."

"I'm sure it does. I can see that in you, the difficulty trusting and the independence."

"I knew from a very young age that I had to do everything on my own. It's how I started cooking, really. I had to learn to make myself something when she forgot I was around and left me at dinner."

"Wait, she left you alone as a little kid?"

"I don't think it was intentional," Zoe said. "She just would get into her own head about work, or whatever else was going on in her life, and forget about me. She'd come home, look surprised to see me, and then be satisfied that I was fine. By the time I was twelve I was essentially living on my own. She gave me money so I could buy groceries, school supplies, and clothes, but I rarely saw her."

"Still, that's neglectful," JJ was furious, but tried to keep that out of his voice. He had never met her mother and hoped he didn't now, because he would have a hard time being nice to the woman.

"Anyway, I got a little wild as a teen," Zoe said. "Not that she noticed. But I was drinking and smoking. Doing all the wrong things, and she started making it clear that when I turned eighteen, she was done with me. I had already lost Emma and Gwen, and honestly, I thought it was because of something I did. Knowing my own mother couldn't stand me made me feel that even more. How could anyone love me and stay if my own mother couldn't?"

She kept her eyes averted from him, but he could see the tears still on her face. He placed his wine glass on the table and stood, then took hers and placed it next to his. Scooping her up from the chair, he sat back down with her on his lap. She tried to push him away, but it was clear that wasn't what she wanted, and she leaned into him.

"First, I think you are person most deserving of love, more than anyone else I've met. You are kind, and generous, and thoughtful. You look out for the people around you, and always give rather than take. I love you, and I'm staying," he said. He dropped a kiss on her head as she burrowed her face further into his neck. "Second, your mother sounds like a person who has something wrong with her. I try not to think of people as bad or good, even though my first instinct is to hate her. But I have to let myself believe that somewhere inside, there is a decent person, who has her own struggles."

"Don't defend her," Zoe whispered.

"No, I'm not. I think she was a terrible mother, and I hate how she treated you. How she made you feel. If I could go back in time and take you away from her, have you experience the over-the-top love that my mom gives, I would," he said. "Although that would be weird now."

She let out a half-laugh, half-sob. "You would not have liked teenage Zoe."

"You don't know that," he said. "And who you were as a teen is indicative of your situation. Just like your mom's behavior could be from something you don't know. What matters is that you were able to overcome it, and she wasn't. That's the difference between you two."

They sat in silence for a few minutes, and he could feel the tension leaving her body. He rocked them slowly on the chair and they watched the last of the sun set behind the mountain, which immediately turned the air around them a few degrees cooler.

"I need to make dinner," she said. "I can't believe how late it is."

"We can just do something easy," he suggested.

She stopped at the door and stared at him; one eyebrow raised. "It's like you don't know me at all. Do something easy? When have I ever done that?"

He laughed and stood to follow her. "Okay, what's on the menu?"

He did his best to distract her with his attempts to help in the kitchen, at least making her laugh at his tendency to always be exactly where she needed to go. At one point, the song they had danced to after their engagement played on the Alexa, and he managed to grab her for a quick dance. She had sighed but leaned heavily on him, and he knew that she had taken comfort from it.

"Tell me about what happened," she said, pushing him away at the end of the song. "But do it from the seat at the island, where you're out of my way."

"You wound me," he griped, kissing her on the cheek before moving to where she pointed. "I'm guessing you mean at the store."

"Yes," she nodded.

"Same robbery as the gas station," he told her. "Guy waving a gun around, demanding cash. No one saw how he got there or how he left, the teenager behind the counter had been so terrified he hadn't noted much at all. You know the Clarks, right?"

She nodded, so he continued. "They were beside themselves and shut the store down for the night. Said they wanted to bring Ethan to the hospital to be checked, but he refused to go. He denies that the guy did anything other than scare him, and he's already kicking himself for not fighting back. I had to have a long talk with him about that, but he's worried the kids at school will tease him."

"For not getting shot? That's ridiculous," she said.

"That's what I told him," JJ said. "I told him the best thing he could do for his classmates is to let them know how he handled it. That way, if one of them is in the same situation, they won't try something heroic."

"How were his parents?"

"They were already calling security companies when I left," he said. "Having cameras installed tomorrow, as well as a panic button. I told them the chances of the guy returning are probably low, but they'd rather be safe."

"I agree," Zoe said. "I always feel better when I get to the restaurant first and all the alarms had been set."

She plated the food and gestured for him to stay sitting, carrying both plates to where he sat. They ate the chicken and pasta dish, delicious in it's simplicity, sitting side by side at the island. When they both finished, he stood to wash the dishes while she finished her wine.

"Movie or bed?" he asked as he rinsed the last bowl.

"Movie, unless you're exhausted," she said.

"I wasn't suggesting going to sleep," he laughed. "But movie it is, you go ahead and pick one out."

The worry and stress of the robbery left him as he followed her to their family room. Just being around Zoe relaxed him and knowing that he could do this every day for the rest of his life made him grin like an idiot. She met his eyes and laughed, rolling hers, as though she knew exactly what he was thinking. For once, though, she didn't object to his optimism about their future, so he took that as a win.

Zoe woke with a gasp that had JJ nearly jumping out of his skin next to her. "What? What is it?" he demanded.

"I just realized we went to sleep last night and never thought to check on Jake and Shea," she groaned. "We should have texted someone at least."

"We had other priorities," he said, pulling her close. "They'll understand."

"We need to do it now," she argued.

"My phone is right here," he said. Grabbing the phone off the nightstand, he shot a quick text off to his group chat with Jake, Patrick, Dan and their friend Mike, asking for an update. "Happy? I'm sure one of them will get back to me shortly."

"She can't still be in labor," Zoe said. "That's a long time."

"Not really, for a first baby. Or maybe she did have the baby, and they just didn't want to wake anyone up." His phone pinged and he grabbed it, laughing when her head got in the way so she could read it first.

"Oh, she just had the baby an hour ago! She's a champ," Zoe said. "Let's get showered and go see them."

"She might want a little recovery time," he warned her.

"It will take us a while. I know you need to eat, and we have to stop and get a gift. We won't get there for hours, knowing you."

"Sure, blame me. But when you're reading every single card in the store to choose the right one, I'll be reminding you of this."

She stuck her head back out from the bathroom door to respond. "Can you remind me after you've started the coffeepot?"

"I can see why you aren't a sous chef," he yelled from the bedroom. "You like giving the orders. But yes, I will."

She laughed and turned on the shower. They had been living together at his house for the last few weeks and had gotten more comfortable with each other. However, it felt way more permanent now that all of their stuff was mixed together, and they had gone to sleep last night under a roof they both owned. She washed her hair as she told herself to stop worrying and laughed when JJ came into the bathroom carrying a mug.

"I didn't want you to have to wait," he called out. "Or make the dangerous trek to the kitchen without caffeine. I'll be scrolling through TikTok until you're done in here."

An hour later, they had finished breakfast at the small diner in town and were headed to the store where they could grab a gift and a card. JJ was driving, and Zoe noticed his attention to everything that was happening on Main Street as they drove through. He waved to everyone and stopped to lecture a young boy about the dangers of crossing the road without a crosswalk.

"The Harvest festival is coming up," he said to her. "Are you and Kendra planning to do a booth again?"

"I am," she said. "With Linda. Kendra will either be eight hundred weeks pregnant or home with a newborn, so we took the task on. We'll keep it simple, do some squash soup, maybe a finger food with maple theme, and something kid friendly."

"She should get a food truck," he suggested. "Make things easier on you, you wouldn't have to cook everything early and figure out how to keep it hot."

"We've been talking about ways to expand into catering," she admitted. "A food truck was one option, or some better equipment to keep the food warm or cold. It's definitely something that's been on the back of my mind for a while now."

"Are you interested in doing that? Starting your own catering company?"

"Not on my own, no," she said. "I don't want to compete with Kendra, but I see ways that we could make improvements or expand beyond what can be done in the restaurant. I wouldn't mind being more involved with the efforts there."

"And being out of the kitchen?"

"Not truly," she answered slowly. "But maybe I would do more menu designing and less cooking on the line, if that makes sense. I don't want to work ten-to-twelve-hour days for the rest of my life or be on my feet when I'm older."

"If you were to have a baby," he said, sounding hesitant. "I would think it would be easier if you were in more of a managerial role."

"It would," she said. "Not that I'm agreeing we need to have a baby right now, so don't get ahead of yourself. But yes, if I were to have a family, I wouldn't want to be at the restaurant all the time. After my experience as a kid, I wouldn't want to bring a baby into the world unless I was sure I had the time to spend with it."

"I think you'd make the time," JJ said confidently. "You'll be a great mom."

"Maybe," she cautioned him. "One day."

"I hope our daughter looks just like you," he said, reaching for her hand.

"You're insufferable." She couldn't help but laugh, he was so impossible and yet he always knew how to make her feel good.

"That's why you love me."

***

They entered the maternity suite at the nearby hospital slowly, then realized the people in the room weren't even aware of them. Patrick and Emma were seated by the windows, next to Ben and Stella, who held a newborn. Dan and Kendra were sitting near the foot of the bed, a chattering Calle bouncing on her feet trying to get her cousin Charlie's attention. JJ cleared his throat, and they all turned to look at them.

"Hi," she said, waving shyly.

JJ was more effusive, as always. He went straight to Shea, who was in bed with Jake sitting next to her and handed her flowers before kissing her on the cheek. He shook Jake's hand before hugging him and waving for her to come closer.

"Congratulations," she said, handing Jake the gift bag she held. "We are so happy for you guys."

"Thank you," Shea said. She was beaming at them while it appeared tears were threatening.

"Are you okay?" Zoe asked, hugging her friend. Shea was normally a ray of sunshine, and seeing her cry always put Zoe on edge.

"I'm perfect," Shea said, wiping at the tears. "Ignore those. I'm hormonal and exhausted. But my life is perfect. Go, meet the baby."

Stella stood, handing the small bundle to Zoe while Jake oversaw. "Meet Isobel Stella Burrows," he said. "Named for my two moms. We'll call her Izzie, at Calle's request."

"She's beautiful," Zoe whispered, tracing a finger on the baby's face. "So tiny."

"Trust me, she didn't feel that way," Shea laughed. "And she took her sweet time coming out, I'll be using that against her when she's a teenager."

"You were a champ," Jake insisted. "I think I'm tough, and I couldn't do that."

"Still have a pregnant woman in the room," Kendra laughed. "And your brother, who has never experienced a childbirth before."

"He did pass out at the class, didn't he," Jake grinned. "Can I come to the birth?"

"No," Kendra and Dan answered together.

"Jake, leave your brother alone," Ben said. "Stella, let's take the two other kids home before they both get stir crazy."

The grandparents left with Charlie and Calle in a blur of hugs and kisses for everyone, and the room felt quiet without them. Zoe couldn't stop staring at the small face sleeping in her arms and jumped when Izzie's eyes opened and the baby let out a whimper.

"She must want her mom," Zoe said, rushing to hand the baby to Shea. Within seconds, the baby was back to sleep and the room went back to talking quietly.

Zoe was touched by how gentle Jake was with his wife and new baby, constantly checking on them and staying close in case they needed him. Dan was rubbing Kendra's shoulders, while Patrick held Emma's hand. The three brothers were clearly in love with their significant others, and it made Zoes' heart happy to see her sister comfortably a part of such a wonderful family.

"Are you guys pretty settled in?" Emma asked, bringing Zoe back to the present.

"Somewhat," she nodded. "We have a lot of unpacking to do, and tons of work to do on the house."

"But our contractor just had a baby," JJ laughed. "That might be delayed a bit."

"Just a little," Jake said. "I already applied for permits, so once they came in, we should be good to go. Plans are all ready for you two to look at, and I can get a crew in there as soon as the town signs off."

"No rush," Zoe said, horrified. She hadn't realized that her comment could cause him to worry, and he surely wanted to be home with his new baby.

"It's not a problem," Jake assured her. "The first thing that has to happen is the demo, and my crew is more than capable of banging down some walls and pulling up floor without me."

"He moves fast," Patrick said. "He was done with my house in way less time than I thought it would take."

"And that's about twenty times bigger than ours," JJ laughed. "No gym or media room to worry about at our house."

"Good thing you have mine," Patrick said. "I'd hate to see you lose your six pack now that you're married."

The men all started ribbing on each other in their good-natured way, and Emma grabbed Zoe's attention while they were distracted. "Are you guys' free tonight? Want to come up for dinner?"

"We both took the whole weekend off to get settled in," she answered. "That sounds perfect, I feel like I've barely seen you since we got home from Vegas."

"Your life has been a little off kilter," her sister laughed. "It will be good to catch up. Anything new and exciting with you?"

Zoe thought about the phone call from her mother the night before, but decided she didn't want to bring that darkness into this happy room. "Nothing major. We can talk later."

"Sounds good," Emma said. "We should get out of here, Shea looks exhausted."

They both watched as the new mom stifled another yawn and stood at the same time. "We should go," Emma said. "Let you guys get some rest. We'll come back tomorrow."

"We're going home tomorrow," Shea answered. "Come by the house tomorrow afternoon. We can put the football game on and have a little welcome home party for Isobel."

"Are you sure that's not too much trouble?" Kendra looked worried.

"Not at all. I plan to sit with my feet up, and I know Stella will love it," Shea said. "JJ and Zoe, you come too, please."

"We will," JJ said. "Thanks."

"And feel free to bring food," Jake said, smiling at Zoe. "If it's no trouble."

"None at all," she answered. "Happy to."

***

"Do you need to stop at the store for anything?" JJ asked, pulling the SUV out of the parking lot.

"No, I think I'm good. Emma said they planned to order Thai food, I told her that sounded perfect," she said. "I don't know what I'll do for tomorrow, so I'll make a plan and then run out in the morning."

"I want that," JJ said suddenly. "All of it. The babies and the dogs and all that happiness that was in that room. I want it all."

"I know," she said softly. "I don't want to be the reason you don't have it."

"You're the person I want it with," he said loudly. He reached for her hand and squeezed. "Sorry, that came out more aggressively than I intended. I just needed you to know that my long-term game plan has all of that for us. And whatever I can do to help you get on the same page, I'll do it."

"I'm not sure how we went from the grocery store to here," she said slowly. "But I know what you're saying. And I appreciate how patient you have been with me. I'm trying."

"I know you are," he said. "Please, keep trying. I know we can be happy together for the rest of our lives. I just need you to believe that."

"JJ, no one can promise that."

"I didn't," he argued. "I stated it as a fact. I know it will take work. I know there will definitely be days where we can't stand each other, and huge fights that we'll be questioning our decision. But I also know that when I'm in a room like that, you're the person I want to share it with. When I get bad news, you're the one I go to. And when I have something good to share, I want to tell you first so I can see you smile. Tell me that you don't feel the same."

"You're my best friend," she said.

"And you're mine. That's how I know this will work."

"There's so much you don't know about me," she couldn't stop herself from saying. "It could make you not like me."

"No, it couldn't," he said, shaking his head. "There's plenty of things you don't know about me, too. We have time. And we have the right foundation. You couldn't scare me away if you tried."

She let herself believe his words, even knowing the doubt would return at some point. But for now, she was going to believe that this one person could love her unconditionally and stay. Even though no one ever had before, this day was about new beginnings and happiness, and she couldn't let her insecurities ruin it.

Years before, she had taken a rock-climbing class, thinking it would be a fun hobby. One she never ended up having time for, but she had loved it at the time. The instructor's words had stuck with her, even in situations that had nothing to do with hanging off the side of a mountain. *Never look down*, she had said. *Looking back where you came from makes it too hard to focus on where you need to go.* That was the attitude Zoe was going to embrace, she decided, letting JJ's optimism warm her heart.

Chapter 14

JJ was busy reviewing the safety plans for the upcoming Harvest Festival when a sharp knock on his office door snapped his attention away. The door opened quickly, and his brother Colin's face appeared with a grin.

"Hey, boss man," Colin said. "You are a hard man to get in to see."

"Clearly," JJ said drolly. "I bet it took you less than two minutes of charm to convince Mary to let you back here. I could have shot you, startling me like that."

"Oh please." Colin crossed the room to give him a quick hug before settling into the chair across from the desk. "I needed to see my big brother, and I knew the best place to find you was at work."

"Needed to see me why?"

"Because I've been gone for a while? What do you mean?" Colin looked puzzled, so JJ relaxed.

"I thought you had gotten yourself into some kind of trouble," JJ admitted. " The way you said that."

"Me? Trouble? Never." Colin grinned at him. "You must have me confused with Des."

"He's been doing some growing up," JJ said. "He's working at Windsor Palace a few nights a week, and he and Finley moved into the apartment right above it. Our baby siblings are finally growing up."

"Yeah, I'm having a hard time being back in my parent's house when the twins are living alone," Colin admitted. "It's a little weird being the only one there. And having my mom do my laundry."

JJ laughed. "Mom is probably so happy. She cried when they moved out, and Dad had to take her to the spa at Stowe for two days just to get her to relax."

"I need to find a place fast," Colin said. "If I'm there longer than a week, she'll never let me go."

"My house is already sold, it went fast. If you had responded to me, I would have held on to it for you. But I think the apartment that Zoe rented is still open, if you want me to ask. Kendra's friend Julie is a realtor, I saw her post about it yesterday."

"That would be amazing, let me know how to get in touch with her. Not that I don't love Mom and Dad," Colin said. "But I'm twenty-eight and need my own space."

"You're back for good, then?" JJ studied his brother, curious if this was a move he was doing for necessity or because he wanted to. Colin had been traveling for years, exploring the world, and settling down didn't seem to be in his nature.

"I think so," Colin said. "I promised myself that when I was considering ordering room service in a great city that I would cut back. I was in Paris and picked up the phone to call for dinner, and realized I was done."

"Just like that?"

"More or less," Colin shrugged. "It's getting old. All the flights and hotels, not knowing anyone for more than a few weeks at a time. Being away from all of you."

"We missed you too," JJ said. "What about work?"

"I'm a consultant, I can do that from anywhere. I told my firm that I wanted to work remote for at least six months, and then I'll reconsider," Colin said.

"I still have no idea what it is that you do," JJ admitted.

"I help companies that are floundering," Colin explained. "Help them find their marketing angle, improve sales techniques, and get rid of people who aren't pulling their weight. I go in and look at the overall company and messaging and help them fix what's broken before they collapse."

"Sounds interesting, and a little lonely," JJ said.

"Little bit, but I have no complaints. I had a home base in Boston until last week when I gave up my lease, and my company offers consistency. And it's not like I've ever had a hard time finding a date," Colin laughed. "Little harder with language barriers, but I've made it work."

"My brother the heartbreaker," JJ smiled at him. "Try not to burn through all the women in Windsor Peak in your first week back."

"Speaking of, I need to meet your wife," Colin said. "I can't believe you got married without me."

"I had to take the opportunity when it presented itself," JJ said. "When you meet her, you'll understand. She's amazing."

"I'm sure she is, if you are happy with her. When can I meet her?"

"She was going to Burlington today to do a presentation at the University of Vermont," JJ said. "She won't be back until late. She's off tomorrow, why don't you come by after work, and we can throw something on the grill. Bring Mom and Dad if you want."

"Sounds good," Colin said, starting to stand. "Oh, before I forget, text me the realtor information. I'm going to see if I can meet up with her while I'm in town."

JJ sent him the number and his brother walked out into the busy office, greeting someone across the room as he did. Since his phone was already out, he sent a quick text to Finley and Desmond, asking them to come over the next day, and then went back to work. The recent robberies had him on edge about the Harvest Festival, when hundreds of tourists would flock to his small town, and he needed to make sure people were safe.

***

Four hours and two phone calls with the mayors office later, he was starving. Pushing back from his desk, he stretched and decided to walk to the bakery to grab a quick sandwich before his afternoon meetings. He walked the short distance, greeting familiar faces as he went, and smiled at Emma when he entered the small storefront.

"Hey," he said. "How are you? How's the baby?"

"She's amazing," Emma grinned. "We all fight over who gets to hold her. I don't think anyone has put her down yet. We need her cousin to arrive, so we have two to spoil."

"Any sign that Kendra is ready to pop?"

"Not yet, but she said labor was fast with Calle, so it could happen at any minute," Emma said. She stopped talking as her boss came through the swinging door from the kitchen carrying trays of cookies.

"Are those all for me?" JJ asked as Emma grabbed one to place on the counter before both women began refilling the display case.

Piper smiled at him. "No, the high school gets out in a half hour, and they will fill this space in seconds. It's amazing the selling power of a warm cookie."

"I believe that," he said. "Bag up a couple for me to have with my sandwich, before they get here and eat them all."

Piper put a few in a bag and passed it to him, then leaned against the counter. "I've been meaning to call over to you. I have a little problem."

His senses went on high alert, quickly surveying the room for potential danger. "What is it?"

"There's a stray dog that lives in the alley behind the building," Piper said. "No huge danger or threat, but I just feel horrible for her. I've tried calling animal control a few times, and they are swamped. I heard they just took a bunch of cats from a hoarder's house, and they have their hands full. I've been feeding her and would just take her home, but my dog doesn't want a roommate."

"Want to show me?" He left his sandwich and cookies by the register and followed her through the kitchen to the back door.

As soon as Piper opened the door, the tiny mutt appeared, looking happy to see her. She was dirty and matted, but friendly and clearly in need of human companionship. Piper looked at him as the dog jumped on her legs, and he reached down and scooped the puppy up.

"Hey there," he said, stroking her small back. "You've been outside for a while, huh?"

"She looks like it," Piper agreed. "She's here curled up on the porch when I get here in the morning, and I worry about what will happen when it gets cold. I left this little blanket here for her, but that won't be enough."

"I'll take her with me," JJ said. "I'll figure it out."

The dog continued to wiggle and try to lick his face as he walked around the building and met Piper on the front porch to grab his food. "Thanks for that, I can't have her inside or I'll get dinged by the Board of Health. I don't know how they know, but they always sense when a rule has been broken."

"No problem," he said, pulling out his wallet and taking out some cash. "This should cover it."

"No," she waved the money away. "On the house. Thanks for taking care of her. I was going to ask Emma to take her if I couldn't figure anything else out, but they've got their hands full with all the rescue horses and now babies coming. I didn't want to add more to their plates."

"I doubt she would have minded, but I'm glad you told me," JJ assured her. He glanced down at the puppy again, laughing as she lunged at his face. "I think we'll take a quick visit to the pet store for a leash. And a bath."

"Good plan," Piper said, waving as they headed down the street.

He knew he looked ridiculous, carrying a tiny, dirty ball of fluff in one arm and his lunch in the other hand. His uniform was getting filthy as she tried to climb his chest, and he switched hands to keep her away from his holster. Fortunately, the small pet store was close by, and he made it there without incident. The owner, Ralph, cringed when he saw JJ and pointed at the self-wash stations set up in the back of the store.

"Give that one a bath if you want," he offered. "Looks like it's been a while."

"You could say that," JJ laughed. "Would you mind grabbing me a collar and a leash that will fit her so I can make it out of here with some of my dignity left?"

He placed his lunch on the nearby shelf and placed the puppy gently in the sink. She immediately began shivering and trying to climb out, whimpering softly. He made comforting noises as he tested the water temperature, and then started gently washing her. It took a long time to get all the dirt and grime off her, and he was surprised to see how cute she was under it all. He pulled her out and wrapped her in a towel, using a drying station to dry and brush her quickly before putting the new collar on.

"There we go," he said. "Now you look presentable. You almost look like a lab now."

She barked happily at him as he clipped the leash on, and they made their way to the front of the store. The owner, Ralph, who JJ had known for years, was waiting at the register.

"I didn't know you had a dog," Ralph said.

"I don't," JJ answered. "Piper found this stray in her back alley and was worried. I told her I would bring her into animal control, but she needed a bath first."

"You can say that again," Ralph agreed. "I heard the shelter is overrun right now, from what I hear. You may have some sway to find her a spot, but it might be hard. I might be able to help find a foster if you need me to."

"I could probably foster her," JJ said. "I'll see how she does the rest of the day."

"Looks like a young lab," Ralph said, peering over the counter at her. "You want some balls, and something for her to chew on. Keep her busy, she needs to burn energy."

"Want to get everything I could use, and I'll grab it on my way home?"

"Sure," Ralph agreed. "Here, take a chew toy with you now, this will keep her happy for a while."

"You sure you and Julie don't need another dog?" JJ asked, half joking.

"Two dogs and a cat are the limit," Ralph said. "Trust me, we can barely find room for ourselves on the couch as it is."

"I just gave my brother Colin Julie's number, he wants to look at Zoe's old apartment," JJ told him. Ralph and Julie had been married for as long as JJ knew them, and they were both regulars at the town meetings.

"Great, she's been wanting to get that rented out," Ralph said. "I'll let her know when I see her."

He paid Ralph for the items he was taking and reminded him again about the precautions he was asking store owners to take in light of the robberies. Ralph pointed out the new cameras he had installed, as well as the new locks on the front door. Satisfied, JJ took his lunch, and his new companion, and finally headed back to the office.

Now he just had to figure out how to tell Zoe he had gotten them a dog, and hope she agreed to it.

Zoe arrived home from the trade show she had been invited to demonstrate at, feet exhausted from standing all day, but thrilled with how things had gone. She considered her cooking to be an art form, and practicing with the elite chefs who had come to participate had been a thrill. She loved her job at the Windsor Palace, but making the same menu daily got old. The day had inspired her to talk to Kendra about ways they could expand their offerings without overwhelming the staff.

"We're in here," JJ's voice called from the living room as she opened the door.

"We?" She questioned as she hung up her jacket by the door and left her bag on the small table underneath.

"Don't kill me," JJ said, grinning at her as she walked in. The small yellow dog let out a friendly bark before jumping off JJ's lap to run around her feet.

"Who is this?" She sat on the floor and buried her face in the soft fur, laughing when her face was covered in kisses.

"Okay, why am I suddenly jealous of a dog? I'd like a greeting like that," JJ said. "Piper found this girl in the alley behind her store, and she was a mess this morning. I got her washed up at Ralph's store and he sent me home with enough supplies for ten dogs."

"We have a dog now?" Zoe looked at him in surprise. "I thought we had agreed to wait?"

"Is that alright? We can just foster her if you're not ready, but the shelter has no space at all. And look at how cute she is, I thought you would love her. She can come to work with me most days, and Ralph suggested crate training when we are both out," JJ said. "She loved running around out in the yard and came right back when I whistled. And she's friendly."

"A few weeks ago, I was single, renting an apartment, and living alone," Zoe said. "Now I suddenly have a house, a husband and a dog."

JJ grinned at her. "Next time can I outrank the house? I know you just mean the Viking, but still."

"I'll try," she said.

"You're okay with keeping her?"

She laughed as the puppy licked her face again, hugging her and enjoying the warmth and energy the dog brought into the house. "What are we naming her?"

"I had some thoughts," JJ said. "Mostly centered around food. Hot Dog. Blondie. Vanilla ice cream. Spaghetti."

"You have issues," she laughed. "None of those work. Also, before we name her, are you sure we can keep her?"

"I called the Vet, he said they had no reports of a lost dog and had me swing in to see if she had a chip. No chip, so he thinks she must be part of a dumped litter, or who knows what could have happened," he said. "But no one is looking for her. He was thrilled that I was going to keep her rather than drop her at animal control, I guess they have way too many dogs right now."

"Who's your favorite athlete of all time?"

"Tedy Bruschi," he answered quickly.

"From the Patriots?"

"Yes," he nodded. "Came back from a life-threatening stroke, and not only did he recover, but he went back to playing football. Taught me that anything is possible if you put your mind to it."

"Wow," she said. "I had no idea. I'll have to look him up, but that would be a good name for her. Tedy."

"Tedy," he smiled. "I like it."

The doorbell rang, causing Tedy to showcase her bark and make them both laugh. "It's pretty late," Zoe said. "Did you know anyone was coming over?"

"No," he shook his head. "But it's probably Colin. I told them to come tomorrow, and he's an idiot so he probably thought I said today."

JJ stood to go to the door, but she waved him back down. "I've got it."

She flipped on the outside light before pulling the door open and stopped short when she saw her mother standing on their porch. "No," she said automatically, going to close the door.

"Don't be ridiculous," her mother snapped. "Open the door."

"You can't just show up here. This is not okay."

"I'm your mother," Marise said. "It took almost forty-eight hours to give birth to you. I can do what I want."

"Please leave," Zoe whispered. JJ could come around the corner at any minute, and she knew he didn't have it in him to send her mother packing. What had been an amazing day was suddenly on her top ten list of worst days, and she needed her mother to leave so she could shower and go to bed. Forget this happened entirely.

"I drove all this way," Marise said. "I'm going to see my daughter."

Zoe heard the sound of paws on the wood floors and winced when Tedy stuck her nose out the door and then jumped on her mother's legs. Marise, true to form, winced and pulled away, causing the puppy to fall. "Come back in, Tedy." Zoe opened the door wider for the dog, and her mother pushed her way in.

"This is a nice house," Marise said. "But it looks much better from the outside than in. You have a lot of work to do here."

"Yes, we know that."

"We?" Her mother's interest immediately caught, and Zoe kicked herself for the slip. Before she could cover, JJ came out of the living room, smiling and looking as handsome and welcoming as ever.

"Hi," he said. He put his arm around Zoe and pulled her closer, sensing her need for support. "I'm JJ."

"JJ," Marise purred. "So nice to meet you. I wish I had heard anything about you before this very moment, but my daughter likes to keep her secrets."

"Mom, I had a long day," Zoe said. "Can we please pick this up tomorrow?"

"You aren't going to invite me to stay?" Marise pouted and started her poor-me act.

"No," Zoe said quickly, before JJ could open his mouth. "As you so kindly noted, we have a lot of work to do. We just moved in here, and none of the spare bedrooms are set up. As a matter of fact, they are filled to the brim with all our stuff until we unpack. I'll call over to the Inn and get you set up with a room."

Marise sniffed, as if the local resort was beneath her. "I suppose that will do," she said.

It was all Zoe could do to keep her calm, and to stay focused on just getting Marise out of the house. "I'll stop there in the morning to see what it is you need to discuss so urgently. The sooner we can get you back to Canada the better."

"Well, that's a horrible thing to say to your mother," Marise gasped, putting a hand over where her heart should be. "I just came all this way to see you."

"Mother, JJ isn't buying what you're selling. Save it." Zoe crossed to the door and opened it wide, waving with her arm. "See you tomorrow."

She slammed the door and then leaned against it, closing her eyes. Suddenly, she wanted nothing more than to be alone, in darkness, where no one could see her or judge her. Before she could take any steps toward the bedroom, she felt JJ's arms wrap around her.

"That went well," he murmured against her hair. "You okay?"

"She's insufferable," Zoe said. "I can't believe she just showed up here. I'm supposed to drop everything for her, when she couldn't give me the time of day my entire life."

"Come, sit," he urged. "I'll give you a foot rub while you drink a glass of wine, and we can discuss."

"JJ, I'm not in the mood for this."

"For what?"

"For you to be perfect," she said. "I'm sorry, but it's true. I need to go sulk and be alone."

She saw the hurt flash across his face as he took a step back from her. His eyes darted around the small entry way, everywhere but at her, and then glanced at his watch.

"The guys were going to watch the Thursday night game at the Palace," he said. "I think I'll go meet them."

"I'm sorry," she said. "I didn't mean to hurt you."

"And I didn't mean to offend you just by being who I am," he snapped.

"That's not what it was," she argued.

"What was it then? I'm not perfect, and you know that," he said. His shoulders were rigid, and his hands clenched, so she knew he was upset.

"I can't explain it," she tried. "But sometimes I just need space."

"Space." He shook his head and stared at something over her head for a moment before grabbing his keys and stormed through the door, slamming it shut behind him. The quick burst of temper was rarely seen with him, he was usually so composed and in charge of his emotions, but it wasn't the first time she had seen it. In previous relationships, she had been drawn to hotheads who liked to throw things and have massive tantrums. Part of the draw to JJ was how reasonable and even tempered he was, even when upset. She knew she would be the one to apologize, because she already knew that she was in the wrong, but first she would take some time to have a good sulk.

The puppy had hidden under the console table, looking terrified by the raised voices and loud noise of the door. Completely forgetting her own irrational anger and emotions over her mother, she dropped to the floor and reached for her. Before she knew it, she was crying and Tedy was trying to catch the tears as they rained down her face. One added benefit to having a dog, she realized, was that they made it very difficult to feel true sadness for any length of time.

One hour and one pint of Ben & Jerry's later, she shut off the Real Housewives reunion and picked up her phone. An hour of sugar and the absurd behavior of grown adults on the TV had reset her mind. She sent a quick text to JJ apologizing, hoping it would clear the air so he would come home before she fell asleep. Going to bed angry would be unlike him, and she knew it would throw off her sleep and everything about the next day.

It was still off putting to think of him as her husband, or to recognize that she was married at all. JJ had been a staple in her life since she moved to Windsor Peak, and his constant presence had been a gift. She had been able to get herself out of the funk she had been in and felt horrible at how she had treated him. Pushing people away was natural for her, especially when she was hurting. JJ had never done anything but support her, and she needed to adapt to allowing that if she wanted their relationship to work.

As hesitant as she still was to believe that love could happen as naturally as it had with them, she had to admit to herself that she did want it to work. She looked forward to seeing him and had been relying on him emotionally for a long time. He was always the person who could put a smile on her face, and they never tired of things to talk about. She either had to embrace it and trust him with her whole heart or break his.

She had tried to picture her life without him in it, and she couldn't. He had somehow become so deeply enmeshed with her life, that everything she thought of, he was there. He visited her at the restaurant so much that Kendra had put a small table and chair in the kitchen for him. They shared friends, and other than a rare girl's night, they socialized together with the same group. They even volunteered together, enjoying working together on town clean ups or charity events.

Leaving the small town would be the only answer if she were to lose JJ, and both thoughts caused her stomach to churn. As much as she tried, she couldn't conjure up an image of herself back in Montreal, or in another city anywhere in the world. She wanted to be here, with her sister and the friends she had made. But JJ was a huge part of her life in this town, and if he decided he didn't want to be with her, it would all come crashing down around her.

Chapter 16

"You going to snap out of it soon," Patrick asked. "Or should we just ignore you?"

"Ignore me," JJ answered.

"Come on, man," Mike said. "This isn't like you at all."

"I'm allowed to be in a bad mood, aren't I?" JJ nearly snarled at his friend.

"Sorry," Mike said, putting his hands up.

"Talk to us," Patrick said. "It will help."

"Where are Dan and Jake?" JJ asked instead.

"Jake is in baby heaven with Isobel, and will probably never leave her side again," Patrick said. "And Dan is obsessing about every sound that Kendra makes. He's convinced she's going into labor at any second, and she is hoping he's right. She told me earlier that she's at least seventy-two weeks pregnant by now. I didn't do the math, but that feels wrong."

"Where is Emma?"

"Piper asked her to come over tonight," Patrick said. "Sounds like she was having a rough day. Must be a full moon or something."

"I just had a fight with Zoe, okay? Nothing life shattering," JJ said. "She wanted to be alone, and I thought I could spend some time with you two and not be under inquisition. I really don't want Des to overhear us." Desmond was at the far end of the bar, having slapped some beers in front of them before devoting his time to a woman sitting alone at the end of the bar. He would occasionally glance around and get drinks for people when needed, but his charm and focus was entirely on the woman smiling coyly at him.

"Not a problem," Patrick said. "We need to figure out Mike's love life anyway. And what is wrong with the Patriots? Lots of problems to solve that aren't you."

"I already told you who I need to be fixed up with," Mike said. "I don't know why you don't listen."

"You've facetimed with her a few times," Patrick pointed out. "And you barely spoke to her. Made her nervous."

"I did?" Mike paled at the thought.

Patrick laughed. "No, but it made me nervous. You just went mute every time she came onto the screen."

"She's so beautiful," Mike said. "It's not normal."

"She's also smart and funny," Patrick said dryly. "Important things to remember when you see her again."

"I know all that," Mike argued. "I listened to every word she said. I felt like a creep, hanging out just watching her. I just didn't know what to say."

"How about 'hey, I'm Patrick's friend Mike that you've talked to on Facetime'?" JJ suggested.

"I'm not taking advice from you while you're pouting," Mike said.

Patrick pulled out his phone. "Want to facetime her now?"

"No," Mike said quickly. "I feel like I should prepare better next time. Maybe have some topics to discuss. See what her thoughts are on electric cars, or what she likes to read."

"Yes, I'm sure she's dying for someone to ask her about electric cars," JJ said, rolling his eyes.

"I should have just proposed to her," Mike said. "That clearly works out well."

"It was, until tonight," JJ said.

"What changed?" Patrick asked.

"Her mom showed up."

Patrick took a sharp breath, causing both men to look at him. "I've heard about her from Emma. She doesn't sound great."

"I wouldn't know, Zoe shoved her out the door so fast my head spun," JJ admitted. "What she's told me so far, I probably would have pushed her out myself. But there must be a reason that she showed up here, it's not like she lives next door."

"Not your problem to solve," Mike said. "Sometimes you have to step back and let the other person work through it on their own. I know you're a problem solver by nature, but this is her mom. Let her figure it out."

"That's good advice," Patrick nodded. "You can be there for her, but don't try to tell her what to do."

"I didn't," JJ said. "I just offered to rub her feet and listen."

"Hey, if you're giving foot rubs, I'm in. " Mike started to pull off his sneakers.

"Not you," JJ knocked his foot off his chair. "My wife doesn't have nasty feet."

"I don't either," Mike said.

"It's still weird to hear you say that," Patrick said.

"What?"

"Wife," JJ and Mike said in chorus.

"Weird for me too," JJ admitted. "But I like it."

"Just feels so fast, but I guess it really wasn't. You guys were basically in a relationship for the last two years," Mike said. "Even though I don't think Zoe knew that."

"She was in denial," JJ said. "Trust me, if Zoe didn't want me around, she would get rid of me. I know her well enough to know that she wouldn't just tolerate me. She can tell herself that it's not real all she wants, but I know how she feels."

"Emma says the same thing," Patrick said. "She thinks Zoe is happy, and that she should be with you."

"Emma wants to be with me? That could make things awkward. Are we talking sister-wives?"

"Why do I even try to help him?" Patrick asked Mike.

"No, I'm glad to hear that I have Emma's stamp of approval," JJ said. "Any chance you'll be my brother-in-law soon?"

"I can't imagine being with anyone else," Patrick said, closing the subject.

They sat in silence for a few minutes, watching the game and sipping on their beers, before JJ's phone chimed. They all turned to look at it, and JJ turned the screen so only he could see it. The short and sweet text from Zoe apologizing came through, and he pulled his wallet out to throw money on the bar. "I'm out," he said, clapping his friends on their backs. "Thanks for this. I'll talk to you guys tomorrow."

He paused at the end of the bar, catching his brothers' eye. "I'll see you tomorrow," he said.

"You walking?" Des asked, glancing back at the beer on the bar.

"Yes, Dad," he said.

"Wouldn't want you to have to arrest yourself," Des responded, making the woman laugh.

"Want to introduce me to your friend?" JJ challenged, causing his brother to glare at him.

"I'll see you tomorrow," Des said, dismissing him and turning back to the woman.

JJ walked home quickly, scanning the streets as he went for anything out of the ordinary. Although they had a few days without any incident or reports of anyone unusual in town, he had a sense that the robberies weren't over yet. Something to worry about tomorrow, he decided, as he turned down the street to his house.

Seeing the lights still on quickened his step, and he was relieved to see Zoe still awake on the couch when he walked in. Tedy barked but remained where she was, settled on Zoe's lap.

"I'm sorry," Zoe said immediately. "I shouldn't have jumped all over you like that."

"You're allowed to want some space," he answered. "I'm sorry if I was too in your face about it. I just wanted to make sure you knew I was here to support you."

"I know that," she sighed. "I already feel terrible, don't make it worse."

"Not my intention at all," he said, settling in on the opposite end of the couch. "Do you want to talk about it, or no? I still want to hear about your day, if you'd rather do that."

"I think I would," she said. "If you don't mind, let's shelve my mother for the night. Today was amazing, right up until she rang the doorbell."

"Tell me about it," he encouraged.

"Burlington does this event, Cooking on Lake Champlain, every year. Restaurants from all over the state come and set up tents, and do tastings," she said. "Kendra and I have never done it, we're so small it doesn't make a lot of sense. But the alumni director at Le Cordon Bleu found out I was working here and asked me if I would attend for them. Do some demonstrations, work with other alumni to both promote the school and where we are working currently."

"How many of you were there?"

"Six," she said. "Most of them are working in Montreal, a couple came from Boston or New York. I was the only one representing Vermont, so the pressure was added."

"I'm sure you did great," he said. "I wish I had come with you."

"You would have had to take the day off," she said. "And probably been bored. But to work alongside these chefs and talk about what we cook, bounce menu ideas off each other, it was amazing. It really got me thinking of things that Kendra and I could be doing."

"Like what?" he asked, loving how enthusiastic she looked when she talked about her art.

"Catering, or even cooking classes at the restaurant. I'd love to have a freezer full of family meals that busy moms could pick up on their way home, rather than having to order off the menu. Just pop it in the oven and relax," she said. "I made a bunch and dropped them to Jake and Shea, and she was thrilled. I have more for Kendra and Dan when the time comes."

"People would love that," he said. "Even visitors could take your cooking home with them, when they head back from a weekend of skiing. I bet you would sell a ton."

"I think so too," she said.

"Any thought to doing it yourself? Open a shop right downtown, where you can teach classes and sell the food? Plus you could cater," he suggested.

"I don't know," she admitted. "The business side of things really overwhelms me, and Kendra has been so good to me. I think it would be better to work with her and expand, let Dan deal with the extra things that she and I would rather avoid."

"That's a good plan," he agreed. "Maybe she could make you partner, at least for the new plans."

"I was looking at our building, and I think we could rent out the empty space right next door," she said. "Make that into a place where I could hold classes and we could sell the meals or run the catering out of. Then the restaurant can operate as normal, and I could partner with her in the new venture. Kind of a new business but also an expansion, if that makes sense."

"It does," he said. "And I think you're brilliant."

She blushed slightly and ducked her head. "That's a stretch."

"How did you end up at Le Cordon Bleu? That must have been a difficult school to get accepted to," he asked.

"Not so difficult," she answered. "Although for me, having given less than I should have in school, it was probably a long shot. I had started working as a dishwasher to make some extra money, and one night they had someone call in sick. They were in desperate need of someone to do prep work, so I volunteered. I was always cooking for myself and loved it and was quick to pick up what they were teaching."

"I'm sure you were," he agreed.

"One of the sous chefs took me under her wing, taught me how to do some more difficult techniques," she continued. "Then suddenly I was working the line alongside them, and the owner came through."

"How old were you?"

"Seventeen," she answered. "About to start my last year, and really not sure what I was going to do with my life. There was no way my mother was going to pay for me to do anything, and she had made it clear that I needed to be out when I graduated. I didn't have the grades to get a scholarship anywhere, so I figured I was going to work in the restaurant full time after I finished school. Which would have been fine."

"Your mother really wasn't going to help you in any way?" He couldn't imagine his mother kicking him or any of his siblings out, even now as adults.

"No," she shook her head. "She was done. And honestly, I couldn't wait to be away from her. I had enough naivety that I thought life would be so easy. I figured I basically lived alone as it was, so what difference would it make? But I didn't factor in things like rent and utilities, never mind something like tuition."

"That's a lot to take on at eighteen," he said.

"Well, one night I got very lucky," she said. "The owner of the restaurant was a James Beard award winner at a young age, and so talented. She owned a few spots and really hadn't been in the kitchen when I was there before this one night. She came in to test out some new dishes and work with us, and whatever I did that night impressed her."

"I'd imagine nothing less," he said, smiling at her.

"She came back the next night, and the one after that. Kept asking me to do different things, or to watch her and then recreate the dish. The fourth night, she had me come in early, right after school. I was so nervous," she said. "I thought I was going to get fired. Instead, she asked me to pick out anything I wanted from the kitchen and make her a dish. I didn't know what to make of it, but I did. After she ate every bite, she asked me to come and sit with her."

"She must have loved it," he guessed.

Zoe nodded, blushing slightly. "She did. Said that I reminded her of herself at a young age, but that she was nervous that I was better than she was. She asked about my plans for the future, and then said she was torn. As much as she wanted to keep me working in her kitchen, she knew that was selfish. She offered to send me to school, pay for everything, if I would agree to work for her after for two years."

"Wow. That's not a bad deal at all, she could have asked for way more," JJ said.

"I know," Zoe said. "What I didn't know at the time was that she was going to spend the time I was in school getting a restaurant set up in Paris and have me go there. Those two years were brutal, especially compared to school."

"Brutal how?"

He watched as the light went out of her eyes slightly, and she seemed to close down right in front of him. Finally, she shook her head and glanced at him. "That's a story for another day. Right now, I'm exhausted and still have to make good on my apology."

"Oh yeah? I knew our first fight would end up being worth it," he said. He stood and herded Tedy into her crate before scooping her into his arms, easily carrying her to the bedroom. He knew she was trying to avoid something difficult, but he decided to let it slide for now. She had already opened up to him more in the last few months than she had in their years of friendship, and he didn't want to push too hard and have her pull fully away from him.

Chapter 17

Zoe was up early the next morning, prepping everything for JJ's family to come that afternoon. He had told her not to worry, that they could throw burgers on the grill, but that was impossible for her. This was the first time they had hosted anyone at the house, and now these people were her in-laws, making it even more intimidating.

The freak out over suddenly being part of a large family took her mind off where it wanted to go, which was to stew over why her mother had turned up. She never did anything if it didn't suit her needs, so making the trip all the way down from Montreal was very out of character for her. Maybe a few days to stew at the Inn would be enough to send Marise back to Canada without whatever drama she came to town for.

Pushing the thoughts aside, she marinated meats and prepared trays of appetizers that she carefully stored in the refrigerator. Tedy sat patiently by her side, seemingly convinced that she would begin dropping him bites of food at any moment. By the time JJ rolled out of bed and came sniffing out a cup of coffee, she was nearly done and the kitchen showed little signs of all she had prepared.

"You're up early," he said, hugging her from behind. He planted a kiss on the nape of her neck before reaching above her for a coffee mug.

"Early? It's nine thirty. That's nearly mid-day."

"It's Saturday," he argued. "And my wife kept me up late, not my fault."

"Oh, that's where we are already? Blaming me for everything?" she teased him as he sipped his coffee.

"I thought that was the point of marriage? Have someone to blame for things. 'Wish I could go tonight, but the wife wants me to stay home and watch Survivor with her.' It's a built-in excuse to be on the couch instead of out running around," he explained. He reached down to pet Tedy, who was trying to climb onto the chair with JJ.

"Does that include the golf game you have on the calendar for Tuesday?"

He coughed out a laugh. "No, I think I'll keep that. But if for some reason I decided I hate golf, or it was going to rain, then yes."

"That's not going to happen anytime soon," she said. "At least the part where you hate golf. The rain, yes."

"Bite your tongue," he chided her. "We have just a few short weeks left of nice weather, and then we'll start seeing snowflakes. The Harvest Festival is next weekend, and it's as if the weather knows that it needs to be cool by then."

His phone beeped from the counter where he had dropped it, and he groaned. "That is probably going to be work, and I don't want to look at it."

"Want me to check?" she offered.

"Yes, please. If it's work just make something else up instead."

"Are Patrick and Emma coming today?"

"Oh, I didn't invite them," she said. "I thought this was just your family."

"No reason for your sister not to be included," he said. "I'll mention it now."

He typed and put the phone down, watching as she finished the last dish and stuck it in the refrigerator. She quickly washed the last few bowls and stacked them to dry, then surveyed the kitchen. It was spotless, exactly as she liked it.

"Happy?" JJ asked.

"Very," she said. "I just need to make sure the rest of the house is clean. Maybe you can try to tire Tedy out before everyone arrives?"

"Sure, I'll throw a ball for her outside," he agreed. "You sure you don't need my help in here?"

"Positive," she nodded. "It's helping calm my nerves."

***

Maggie and Frank arrived first, carrying bottles of wine and trays of cookies that she had baked. Frank disappeared again as Maggie met an enthusiastic Tedy and returned carrying a small sapling in a planting bucket. He handed it to JJ and signaled to Maggie to explain.

"We weren't sure what to get you as a housewarming present," she said. "And we still owe you a wedding gift. Rather than combine them, we went to the tree farm and picked this out for you as a housewarming. If you plant it now, it will have a chance to settle in before spring, when it should really start growing. This tree grows best when it has a chance to settle in quietly, and not have to endure the stress of a hot, dry summer.

153

It flourishes with sunlight and will grow strong and tall here. You'll be able to watch it grow, while your marriage is growing alongside it in this house. We hope that you'll have the patience to nurture this sapling into a healthy tree, and your relationship into a happy marriage."

Maggie wiped her eyes while Frank protectively put a hand on her shoulder. "It's not your wedding gift, despite what Maggie made it sound like. We hope that you'll see this tree growing and remember you are starting out fragile too and hoping to build strong roots. Give yourselves a chance to grow into something great. Marriage and living together isn't always easy, and sometimes bowing under the pressure would be the simpler way. But stand tall, fight together, and play fair."

"Wow," JJ smiled at his parents. "You came prepared."

"We just want you both to be happy," Maggie said. "I love you so much, and I already love Zoe. We remember what it's like to be newlyweds, with a new house and adapting to life together. It's a challenge, but one that will lead to great things."

"Can you excuse me for a minute? I just need to check something in the kitchen," she said. Her emotions were in overdrive, and she needed to escape as quickly as possible. She saw the question in JJ's eyes, matched in Maggie's, but she fled the room. She could hear JJ distracting his parents by offering them a tour, so she leaned against the sink, forcing herself to slow her breathing.

His parents were everything she had ever wanted as parents. Having them embrace her and welcome her to their family, and offer such support and loving advice, was almost too much. Her feet wanted to run to the backdoor, and just keep running. Get far, far away before anyone else could break their way into her heart. It was enough that JJ had worked his way in, and of course Emma, but she hadn't expected to feel this way about JJ's family. Their casual get togethers over the last few years had been fun, but now they were treating her like a family member. It was hard to wrap her head around having such a loving family accept her just as she was.

She heard JJ take his parents into the garage, and then saw them come out the back door to the yard. JJ had clearly done that to give her a minute alone, and she was touched by the thoughtfulness. Grabbing the buffalo chicken dip out of the refrigerator, she stuck it in the preheated oven and got a tray ready to place it on. The doorbell rang, and JJ was still engaged in the yard, so she wiped her hands and went to open it.

"Hi," she said, expecting it to be someone she already knew. But the man on the other side of the door had her catch her breath from surprise. "What are you doing here?"

"Me? What are you doing at my brother's house?" He demanded.

"You're at the wrong place," she said, trying to close the door. "This is my house."

"Oh, wow. You're JJ's Zoe?"

"Yes," she said slowly, opening the door again. "Who are you?"

"Colin," he answered. "His brother."

"Oh." They stared at each other for a moment and then she fully opened the door. "I guess you better come in."

"How did this happen? The last time I saw you, you were in Paris," he said.

He was as tall as JJ and took up more space than she realized in the small front hallway. His hair was brown and neatly cut, eyes hazel and inquisitive as ever. The same handsome customer who had witnessed her downfall in Paris was now her brother-in-law, and that was going to take a minute to wrap her head around.

"I moved here," she said simply. "JJ and your parents are in the backyard."

"Wait," he said, reaching out as though he was going to grab her arm and then dropping his hand as if he had second thoughts. "Are you okay? This is weird, but it's not like we dated. I just asked you out a few times."

"A few?"

"Okay, a lot. But I can't be faulted for admiring a beautiful, talented woman," he said, smiling winningly at her.

"You can't do that," she said. At his quizzical expression she went on. "You can't flirt with me here, with JJ."

"Does that mean I can flirt with you in other places when he's not around?"

"No," she said quickly. "Don't flirt with me at all."

"He'll think it's weird," he said. "I have always hit on his girlfriends. It's a competition thing between us, he's always flirted with mine too."

"Well, not anymore," she bit out.

He studied her, then grinned. "I like this. That you're protective of him. That's nice."

She heard herself nearly growl at him before stomping into the kitchen, waving at the back door. "They are outside. I need to finish cooking this dip."

He disappeared, and as soon as the back door closed, the doorbell rang again. Thankfully, this time her sister and Patrick were on the other side, and Emma pulled her in for a fierce hug.

"Why do you look stressed?" Emma demanded.

"I'm not," she said. Hugging Patrick quickly, she led them both into the kitchen.

"I want to see what you did after we finished moving things in," Emma said. "But first, why the face?"

"Because I was born with it?"

"No, Emma's right," Patrick said. "You have a look, like you're annoyed at something. Did JJ mess up already?"

"No," she sighed. "His brother Colin just got here; I had never met him. Or apparently seen pictures of him. Right before I left Paris, he would come into the restaurant I worked at every night and ask me out."

Emma and Patrick looked at each other and then burst out laughing. "Oh, that's something my brother's and I would do," Patrick said. "Hit on the same woman, I mean."

"Did you go out with him?" Emma asked, looking horrified. "That would be really weird."

"No," she said. "I was miserable at the time and had a horrible boss. I never had time off, and I was too stressed to be interested in any fun. Plus, he wasn't my type, he was always so perfectly dressed and smooth."

"Yes, handsome and well-dressed are a total turn off," Emma laughed. "Sorry, honey. I love you because you're hideous and sloppy."

"Hideous? Millions of people disagree," Patrick said, pretending to preen in the reflection of the microwave.

JJ came in from the back door, with his parents and Colin behind him and laughed when he saw Patrick. "You admiring yourself again?"

"My love just called me hideous," he explained. "I was checking to see if she was right."

"You're impossible," Emma said. "Hi, I'm Emma, Zoe's sister. You must be JJ's brother."

Colin greeted Emma and Patrick, and the three of them convinced JJ to take them on a tour. The doorbell rang again, and JJ's father excused himself to open it, knowing it had to be the twins.

"They will be late for their own weddings," Maggie whispered to Zoe. "It's my fault, I spoiled them."

"No, they are amazing. You did a great job with all of them," Zoe said. "Des seems to be happy working at the Palace, and they both seem to have settled into the apartment nicely. Do you miss them at home?"

"I do, but it's also nice to have some quiet," Maggie said. "Now we have Colin there, but I don't think he'll stay long. He's been out from under my thumb for so long, he's not adapting well to being with us. Although he doesn't tend to stick around anywhere for long, he could decide to move to Hawaii next week and I wouldn't be surprised."

The two women set up the tray with the snacks as they chatted, and soon the family was settled around the living room, all talking over each other. Zoe sat with Emma on one side and JJ on the other, avoiding Colin's gaze. He appeared to be doing the same, talking to the twins quietly on the other side of the room. When the doorbell rang again, everyone stopped talking and glanced around, as if wondering who they had started without. JJ stood to answer, and Zoe felt a pit grow in her stomach, already sensing who was on the other side.

Chapter 18

"Why would she come here?" Zoe slammed a dish down so hard into the sink, JJ winced at the noise. "And in front of your family! I'm so embarrassed. That was terrible. She ruined everything."

"She didn't," he said, daring to approach her slowly and take her in his arms. "It was fine. You know my mom can talk to anyone, and she had her trapped most of the day."

"She shouldn't have had to do that," Zoe insisted. "It ruined her day."

"No, it didn't," he said. "She told me how much she enjoyed getting to know her, and she was still a part of all the other conversations. My mom has a gift, she can somehow talk to everyone all at once."

"It was so weird," Zoe said.

"I think it was fine and the day was a success," JJ said, stepping back from her. "Wouldn't you?"

"It was nice," she said, still sounding put off.

"Colin said he knew you in Paris? You never mentioned that," he said.

"Oh, it was nothing," she said, turning to start washing dishes.

"Small world, I guess." When she didn't turn to look at him, he moved to lean on the counter next to him. "Why do I feel like something is weird with this?"

"What do you mean?" She studied the bowl in her hands.

"You seemed to avoid talking to him at all," he pointed out. "Which is odd, because he's the only one you had never met before."

"Huh," she said. "I didn't avoid him."

"What am I missing? If you knew him in Paris and he happens to be my brother, I would think that would have been a source or a story," he pushed. "Or at least a casual catch up, since it's obviously been a few years."

"We weren't friends," she said. "Nothing big. We knew of each other a little, that's all."

He frowned, sensing that she was lying to him. Colin had been quieter than usual, seeming more reserved and almost to the point of uncomfortable around Zoe. If he didn't know better, he would think they had a romantic past that they were trying to hide. Although he really didn't know better, getting some answers out of his wife or brother suddenly felt more important. Before he could ask again, his phone rang from across the room.

"Saved by the bell, I guess," he said. "One second."

He grabbed the phone and moved into the other room for quiet, groaning to himself when he saw the incoming call was from the station. It wasn't going to be good news; he already knew that in his gut.

"Hey boss," Jeff Nicols, his second in command, greeted him. "You might want to come in."

"What's happening?"

"Break in at one of the houses by the ski resort," Jeff said. "We think it's the same guy who did the robberies at the gas station and Clark's. No one was there, luckily, it's a vacation rental. But looks like the guy might have been there a few days, so we might be able to get a lead on him."

"I'll meet you there," JJ said. "Text me the address. Did you call the State Police as well, so their lab can come?"

"Already done. I'll see you in a few." The phone beeped, indicating Jeff had hung up.

JJ stuck his head in the kitchen, letting Zoe know he had to run in to work, and left quickly. It was only as he was driving to the site of the break-in that he realized why Zoe had looked so relieved when he told her he had to go. He definitely needed to get to the bottom of the history between her and Colin, and it needed to happen fast.

***

The house was in better shape than he had anticipated. Jeff had limited the number of people allowed inside before the crime lab arrived, and now they were standing in the processed kitchen surveying the room. It was neat, with a few dishes stacked in the drying rack and the trash empty. The room and dishes had been dusted for fingerprints, leaving a fine black powder everywhere.

"The rest of the rooms are as neat as this," Jeff reported. "The bed in the guest room looks slept in, it's not made as nicely as the others. The towel in the bathroom was a little damp. And little things are out of place, the cleaner is waiting outside but already told me of a few things she saw through the window."

"Like what?" JJ asked, looking through the doorway to the living room that was just about done being searched.

"The TV remote was on the coffee table. A book that was on the table next to the armchair shouldn't be there. The rug by the back door was folded over a little, and it wasn't in the last pictures that she took," Jeff said. "She took detailed pictures of each room after she was done cleaning to send to the owner."

"That's good for us," JJ said.

"Yeah, but she's freaking out. She cleaned it Monday after the owners' friends left, and she's worried she left the door unlocked. Apparently, the owner has already called her ten times, demanding answers."

"I'll call them when we're done here," JJ promised. "Let her know I'll deal with it. Where do we think he got in?"

"The back door. There is some damage to the wood frame, like a screwdriver or something was used to pry the door open," Jeff said. "They didn't have great locks or security here, probably because they aren't here much. I'll show you."

They walked around the outside of the house, studying windows as they went, and examined the door. It was probably left unlocked after the first entry, allowing the person to come and go as they pleased. JJ was relieved there was no broken glass or seemingly any damage to the house, which should please the owners. When the crime lab finished, they turned the house over to the cleaners to get rid of the dust and JJ headed back to the station. After a quick phone call with the owners and a check in with Jeff to make sure the report would be done, he fired a text off to Colin telling him to meet him at the Palace.

Des was working behind the bar when he arrived, and there was a healthy crowd. JJ made his way to two empty barstools, staking the second out for Colin, and gestured to Des to bring two beers over. Des tore himself away from the redhead he had been talking to, clicking the tops off the bottles as he walked over.

"Who are you meeting? Zoe's not here," Des said. "I thought you two were in for the night."

"Colin is coming down," he said. "I had to go into the station, so thought I would stop in for a drink before I head home."

"Okay," Des said slowly. "Is there more to this, or can I get back to it?"

"Go back to your flirting," JJ said. "Nothing happening here."

"I feel like you're lying, but I'm going to roll with it," Des said, backing away with a grin. "If you guys get into a fight here, Kendra will blackball you for a month. Don't do anything stupid."

JJ was done with half of his beer by the time Colin rolled in, looking unbothered by the demand from his older brother. He crossed the room slowly, seemingly stopping by every person before reaching his brother.

"Hey," he said, sliding out the bar stool. "That for me?"

"If you get it before I finish this one," JJ answered. "Took you long enough to get here."

"Mom and dad live outside of town," Colin said. "We were together all day. You couldn't have talked to me about whatever the issue is then? You had to make me drive all the way back, so this better be good."

"Did you sleep with my wife?"

Colin choked on the sip of beer he had just taken and coughed for a full minute before meeting JJ's eyes. "No."

"Then what was that about," JJ said. "You two barely spoke to the point of it almost being rude."

"I didn't want to make her uncomfortable," Colin said. "I used to flirt with her. A lot. I asked her out every day for about three months, and then she left Paris. She was caught off guard when she saw me and told me that I couldn't flirt with her in front of you. Or at all."

"When did she tell you that?"

"She answered the door when I got there," Colin explained. "We had a quick conversation before you guys came back inside. It's really not a big deal at all. We'll be more comfortable next time, I'm sure."

"How did you know here in Paris?"

"The restaurant that she worked at was right down the street from where I was staying," he said. "I was there as a consultant on US advertising for a clothing line, and they put me up in a little place on the West Bank. Everyone raved about this place but said the head chef was a nut. He was known for chasing staff out of the kitchen with knives, firing people for nothing, just crazy. I went out of curiosity, and it was one of those open kitchens. Zoe caught my eye."

"I'm sure she did," JJ said. "But that's over now, right?"

"I wouldn't hit on your wife," Colin said. "Even if I do think she's hot. I was just a little off today because she was so nervous about it, and I even told her that my natural instinct is to flirt with everyone. I can't help myself. I don't even know if I would call it flirting, it's more my charm."

"Keep your charm in your pants," JJ said. "Nothing happened between you two?"

"Nothing," Colin shook his head. "The night she left the restaurant I would have at least given her a hug, but she was gone before I knew it. I felt bad for what I had witnessed, and I think the last thing she needed was a hug from me anyway."

"What happened?"

"She hasn't told you?" Colin looked shocked, and picked up his beer to swig before responding. "Not my place. Ask her, and if she doesn't tell you, I will."

"You're my least favorite sibling," JJ said. He stood and pushed the empty bottle of beer away from him. "And you're buying, since you're not helping me at all."

"Hey, you invited me here! Are you really walking away?" Colins voice trailed off as JJ headed toward the door, wanting to get home before Zoe fell asleep.

He drove home quickly and was happy to see lights on in the backyard, indicating she would be outside with Tedy. The dog tended to resist coming inside when she had her last potty break of the day, as if knowing it meant it was time for bed. He found Zoe sitting in a rocking chair on their porch as Tedy ran wildly around the yard, using up any last bit of energy she had.

"Hey," Zoe said softly. "What happened at work?"

"A house was broken in to, it looks like that might be where our suspect has been staying," he said. "No one was there tonight, and I don't know that it will give us any good clues as to who this guy is. He's one step ahead of us at all times."

"Maybe he's already moved on to another town," Zoe said. "I can't imagine it makes sense to stay in a small town after committing a crime."

"Could be," JJ said. He picked up the ball that Tedy had dropped at his feet and threw it out into the yard. "I talked to Colin."

"Oh, really," Zoe met his eyes briefly and then turned away. "He must have told you nothing ever happened between us."

"He did," JJ said. "Told me about how he used to hit on you, and you shot him down, so thank you for that. I very much appreciate you not falling for my playboy brother."

"Anytime," she said with a soft laugh.

"He also mentioned that something dramatic happened on your last night in Paris," JJ said. "Want to tell me about it?"

Chapter 19

Zoe's hands felt clammy suddenly, and she had the sensation of being at a higher altitude. Air seemed in short supply, and she was breathing funny, like when she went hiking on some of the higher peaks around the state. She had visited a town in Colorado once and had gotten altitude sickness so badly she had passed out in the hotel lobby, and she vaguely wondered if that was happening again as black spots started appearing in her vision.

Suddenly JJ was there, holding her head down between her knees. "Just breathe," he said. "Focus on my voice. Or on Tedy."

The dog was going crazy, trying to lick her face and get onto her lap. After a few minutes she was able to breathe easier and sat up slowly. Tedy immediately climbed onto her lap and offered her warmth and weight, as if knowing she needed the support.

"Is this not something you want to talk about," JJ asked her softly.

"No," she said. "It really isn't. But I should tell you, and then we can be done with it. I'm guessing Colin said something to you?"

"Yes, but that it wasn't his story to tell," JJ admitted. "He thought I should hear about it from you."

"He's right," she nodded. "I should have told you already. But when I don't think about it, it's nothing, you know? And you've seen much worse, so I don't think you'll be shocked by it."

"Try me," he said.

"When I was thirteen, my mom had this brute of a boyfriend," she said. She saw the confusion on his face but kept going. "He was a total meathead. American, former football player. Eric was his name. I hated him and avoided him as much as I could. One day I was home studying with a friend and thought they were going to go out. Only the plans they had were canceled and Eric didn't want to go anymore, he wanted to stay home and have my mom wait on him."

"Did he live with you guys?"

"No, thankfully. He just stayed over some nights, but mostly seemed annoyed that she had a kid, and I felt like I was in the way," she explained. "Anyway, I went to the kitchen to get something, and realized my mom had run out. Eric was standing in the living room, acting funny, but I just ignored him. I grabbed whatever it was we wanted for a snack and was going back to my room as fast as I could, but as I was walking by the couch, he suddenly pushed me down and lay on top of me. He had a fireplace poker in his hand, and he put it right across my neck and told me to be quiet."

JJ made a groaning sound, and she couldn't meet his eyes, she focused on Tedy on her lap. "I don't know what his intention was. My friend came in a minute later and he jumped up, then started laughing like it was a big joke. But for a minute, as I laid there on the couch with his weight on me and the thing across my neck, I was terrified."

"What did your mom do?"

"Nothing," she shook her head. "I told her as soon as he left that night. She accused me of tempting him by what I was wearing, that I shouldn't be prancing around in short skirts. She was always worried that her boyfriends would look at me and not her."

"First of all, that's disgusting," JJ said. "No one should be looking at a teenager like that, other than maybe a teenage boy. But even a teenage boy should be more respectful than to try and force themselves on you. I am going to find this guy and—"

"Moving on," she said, gently squeezing his knee. "From that point on, she was never around. She told me she didn't feel comfortable bringing men around me, and I was old enough to take care of myself."

"Did she stay with the guy?"

"For a bit," she answered. "But it really didn't matter. It was the same cycle of dating and getting what she wanted from them, then moving on to the next. My mother never connected with anyone emotionally, and always had a motive for who she dated. She's a beautiful woman, and she used it to her advantage."

"Still, that's a sad life," he said. "And obviously caused issues between you two."

"Absolutely, we didn't have a relationship from that point on, really. She came to Paris under the pretense of mending fences with me, claiming she had realized what a bad mother she had been and wanted a relationship with me. She really wanted a free place to stay and a wider net of men to shop from. Unfortunately, she landed on my boss as her best option. Antoine was hot tempered and nasty on his best day, and somehow, she thought that was charming. They started dating, and she kept extending how long she would stay. Antoine lightened up in the kitchen, and everyone was relieved. I was just waiting for the other shoe to drop, because she never sticks with one man for long. And I knew that when that happened, he was going to be unbearable."

"What did he do," JJ prodded when she paused for too long.

"She packed up and left suddenly, just left me a note. No indication what had happened between them, just that she was going back home and nice seeing me," she said. "I went to work and had a pit in my stomach, because I knew Antoine would be in a terrible mood if he knew. Turns out, he did know. It was a horrible night, he fired half the staff in the first few hours, and just ranted and screamed all night. It was an open kitchen, and the people in the dining room for the most part thought it was like the show."

"Hell's Kitchen?" he asked.

"Yes," she nodded. "Only it wasn't. It was horrible. Antoine was focused on me in particular and took every opportunity to humiliate me. When we finally closed, he ordered me to take all the trash out. I was second in the kitchen, one step below him in rank, and suddenly I was doing scut work. He stood in the doorway to the alley, smoking cigarette after cigarette, and making comments as I went by. Calling me a whore, saying I was just like my mother. That I must have slept with someone to get this job, because I couldn't cook. Then my last trash run, he closed the door and was leaning against it. He told me that since my mother had left him high and dry, he might as well send her a message. Then he grabbed me, pinned me against the dumpster, trying to kiss me and groping. I think he was probably trying to rip my clothes off, but he was drunk and struggling, although I think he would have succeeded if he had enough time. He was much bigger than me."

"Zoe," JJ groaned. "I'm sorry."

"Your brother came out of nowhere," she said. "He must have been waiting out there, or maybe suspected something since I was gone for so long. He had been in the dining room most of the night and didn't leave when he usually did. Maybe he sensed something was off? I don't know. All I know is that suddenly he hauled Antoine off me and held him against the wall, screaming at him. I am embarrassed to say that I just ran. I ran as fast as I could to get back to my apartment, and then I ran the next morning as far from Paris as I could get. The thirteen year old inside of me who had been terrified when Eric had me pinned down came right back out, and I reacted like a child. I never even stopped to thank Colin, which I feel terrible about."

"Trust me when I say that he would understand," JJ said. "I'm so glad he was there."

"Me too," Zoe said, wiping at tears. "It caught me off guard today when I saw him, I never expected to run into him again."

"I guess you guys never really talked much," JJ guessed. "Or the last name and hometown probably would have tipped you off."

"No," she shook her head. "I only knew him as Colin, and he once mentioned being from Vermont but that was the extent of it. He was always a little flirtatious and asked me out a few times, but he also missed many nights of solo dining when he probably had dates. I would usually tease him about it, and he would laugh and say he would stop if I'd go out with him. But I was constantly working and not looking for romance."

"Thank goodness," he said, kissing her head. "I would have had to deal with some complicated emotions if that wasn't the case. But I guess his interest in you paid off in the long run."

"I'll have to thank him properly, and talk about it with him," she said. "Soon. I don't want him to think I'm ungrateful."

"That's not a problem, we can have him stop by anytime. I'm more concerned about your mother, if I'm being honest. I feel like there's a lifetime of problems there, and something must be going on to make her come all this way," JJ said. "I think talking to her might be important."

She felt herself stiffen, even though rationally she knew that he had her best intentions at heart. He wasn't siding with her mother against her, as much as it felt like that in the moment. "I honestly think we're past any healing. I would like her to leave, and to be able to move on with my life."

"And I want to support you in that," he said slowly. "But I have to wonder if that's the best thing for you. I know you aren't ready to think about having kids, but I'd really like to one day. Whether we had them ourselves or adopted, or even fostered, I'd like to be open to that possibility. And I have to wonder if your doubts are more from the relationship with your mom than anything else."

"I just don't know that I could be responsible for a baby," she said. "I've never been around kids before. And I definitely don't think we're ready to start a family together, this all still feels a little fake."

"Fake?" The disappointment on his face was almost too much to bear. "I'm going to shelve that for now, because you've been through a lot tonight. I have a couple other questions, if you don't mind."

"Okay," she said.

"Did you go to therapy after the assault? Or report it to the authorities?"

"No to reporting it, although I did see a therapist who encouraged me to do so," she said. "I should have at least told the chef who had placed me there, she was a mentor and a friend, and I think she would want to know. But she believed what he told her and left me an angry voicemail before I could talk to her, so I never did."

"That might be worth following up with," JJ said. "Just so you don't have a burnt bridge in your past. Not to mention, maybe you can help someone else avoid the same fate."

"No one else has my mother," she said drolly.

"I can make some calls tomorrow, if you want. I don't want to step on your toes, but if you want to talk to someone, I have a list at the office who will take emergency appointments for victims," JJ said. "Not that we have a lot here, but I was able to get Kendra in quickly to see someone after the incident with Calle, and they met with Calle as well to make sure she was okay."

"Why are you so good to me?" she blurted out before she could stop it. "Honestly. I don't think I'm as good to you as you are to me. I make your life more complicated in every way."

"My dad told me that he knew the night he met my mom that she was his forever," JJ said. "That he walked into this bar with his friends after work, not in any way ready to settle down, and the next thing he knew he was dreaming about weddings. Fortunately, she fell just as hard for him, and they got married three months later. It's been almost fifty years, and they are still just as in love as they were the night they met. Maybe more so."

"That's nice. I can tell being around them how much they love each other."

"You know what it is? They are best friends. They tell each other everything, even when they swear to one of us they will keep it a secret," he said. "They laugh together, and sometimes they fight. They face every problem in their life like a team. They look forward to spending time together, and make the most of it when they do. Things like going for walks after dinner, or spending time doing a puzzle or playing games with all of us. They always show up for each other, no matter what. And that's what I've always wanted."

"I feel like I'm keeping you from that," she said.

He met her gaze, and she would swear he was staring right into her soul. "Funny thing is, I think that's exactly what we have."

Chapter 20

JJ spent several days huddled up with the town executives and business owners making plans for the annual Harvest Festival. The weekend drew tourists from all over the world, as well as fellow Vermonters who drove in for the day. Traffic plans had to be adjusted to maintain safety for the pedestrians, and patrols needed to be increased to maintain the peace. It was inevitable that a few people would have a little too much fun and need to spend a few hours sleeping off their bad decisions in the small holding cell in the precinct. Which meant he needed to staff the building for the full weekend, when his staff all wanted to be out on the street enjoying the food and fun.

When Patrick strolled in late afternoon, JJ used his friend as an excuse to get out of the office. "Whatever this is about," he said, grabbing his cell phone and wallet. "Can be discussed at the Palace over a beer. You game?"

"Of course," Patrick said. "I would have suggested that if you had answered any of my many text messages. And you haven't been showing up to work out at all. Almost like you're avoiding me."

"No," he sighed. "I'm just slammed over next weekend. I look forward to it every year and then desperately want it to be over."

"I hear you," Patrick said. "I agreed to sit at the animal shelter table again this year to help them raise money and recruit adopters. It's always a lot of fun, but my whole weekend ends up being crazy."

"I bet you'll help them empty the kennels," JJ guessed. "Tedy came home with me because they were too full, and it was the best decision ever."

"Emma already suggested that we go down and pick out a rescue," Patrick said. "Don't get her going or we'll have a pack out there."

They settled into two barstools at the Palace, where Des was working behind the bar, and JJ knew that Zoe was in the kitchen. Even if he didn't have her schedule memorized, he could feel the familiar hum of electricity knowing that she was close.

"How's married life?" Patrick asked.

"Good," JJ said. "Zoe still seems a little shocked by the whole idea but I'm looking forward to when she fully embraces her feelings for me."

"Think she'll get there?"

"Yup," JJ nodded. He signaled to his brother to bring them two beers and received a nod in return.

"You're pretty confident," Patrick said. "I really hope you don't get burned by this."

JJ turned to look at Patrick, concerned suddenly. "Has Emma said something that makes you worried?"

"No," he shook his head. "If anything, she's rooting for you guys. She thinks you're perfect together, and fully supported the surprise wedding. If she didn't, she would have stopped it from happening."

"Then where is this coming from?"

"You're my friend," Patrick shrugged. "And I hope that we will be brothers-in-law one day."

"You thinking of popping the question?"

"It's on my mind, that's for sure. Some of it is watching you and Zoe, and my brothers and their wives. Even my dad and Stella are still in their honeymoon phase. I'm surrounded by it." Patrick laughed and took a sip of his beer. "And I know that this is it for me. I just need to make sure that Emma is ready."

"Why do you think she isn't ready now?"

"She's still learning to relax," Patrick answered. "The last year has been a whirlwind, and before that, her life was hard. I want her to have some time to just catch her breath and feel comfortable. When we get engaged, the spotlight will really be shining on her, and I don't think she's ready for that."

"Would you have to tell people? Couldn't you just keep it quiet?"

"And ask her to only wear her ring at home? That's not fair. I don't want to leave her here when I travel, and I don't want her to feel like a secret I'm keeping. I'm proud of her, and I'll be excited to share that she said yes," Patrick said. "If anything, maybe I should take a page from your book. Propose and then get married right away."

"I highly recommend it," JJ said. His eyes went to the kitchen door as it opened, and Zoe came through. She scanned the room and then went to a table near the fireplace, talking with the family before turning to go back to the kitchen. She spotted him as she walked and detoured to the bar.

"Hi," she said. "Hey, Patrick. Where's Emma?"

"She's just about finishing up at work," he said, glancing at his watch. "I'll meet her over there and get a ride home, just had to talk to this guy about some stuff."

"I'll let you get to it," she said. "I just had to discuss an allergy with that family, so I need to go make sure their food is made safely. I'll see you later."

"I'll see you at home," JJ called after her, hearing her laugh in return. He turned back to his friend, taking a sip of his beer before speaking. "I have to keep reminding her of us, helps to make it stick in her brain."

"I think you mean her heart," Patrick said.

"No," JJ shook his head. "Her heart is all mine, she loves me. It's her head that's causing some confusion. But enough about me, what was it you needed to talk about?"

"Natalie," Patrick sighed. His co-star in many movies was the object of men's dreams around the world and had pretended to be in love with Patrick for years to avoid the attention. She had finally backed off when Emma had come into the picture, and the two women were now close friends.

"What about her?"

"She's got a guy who's a little too nutty following her around," Patrick said. "Showing up outside her house, in crowds outside parties she's attending. He hasn't done anything threatening, but it's enough that she's completely creeped out. Her team suggested she disappear for a bit, until we have to go film again. And guess where she has decided to disappear to?"

"Windsor Peak," JJ guessed.

"You got it. She's going to arrive in the next few days, right before the Harvest Festival. I'm going to beg her to stay home that entire weekend, because the less she is seen, the better. But I know her presence could create some extra chaos for you, so I wanted to give you a heads up," Patrick said.

"Any chance she could dye her hair and wear lots of baggy clothes?"

"None," Patrick said. "Although I'll get Emma to try and convince her to dress to fit in here. She's going to be staying with us, at least to start. If she likes it and feels safe, she might look at places to live."

"If she could stay quiet for the Festival weekend, tell her I would really appreciate it," JJ said. "If she needs company, I can send Finley up to talk her ear off."

"She'll have Emma, and she's excited to see my family. I think some downtime will be really good for her," Patrick said. He checked his watch and stood up. "Don't tell Mike. I can't wait to see his face when he comes to work out and she's there."

"Oh, I need to be there for that," JJ laughed. "Make sure to text me and let me know."

"Will do," Patrick clapped him on the shoulder. "I'll see you later." Patrick handed some cash to Desmond at the end of the bar and paused for selfies with the girls that Des had been chatting with before disappearing.

"That just helped me big time," Des said when he came to collect the empty beer bottles. "Now these girls know I'm tight with Patrick."

"Since when?" JJ laughed.

Desmond rolled his eyes. "You want another one?"

"No, I'm good," he said as he stood. "How are things upstairs with you and Fin?"

"Great," Des answered. "It's working out great for me to just be able to pop down here and help out at night, and the extra money is great. Finley seems to be doing well; I barely ever see her."

"Is she home now? Maybe I'll pop up," JJ said.

"No," Des shook his head. "She had some mysterious plans. I'll let her know you were looking for her."

JJ ducked into the kitchen, smiling when he saw the carefully packed to-go bag at the edge of Zoe's workstation. "Is this for me?"

"It is," she said. "I wasn't sure if you were going back to work or home, but I knew you'd be hungry either way."

"I'm going back to the station for a bit," he said. "I left Tedy there and I'm sure she's getting hungry, so I'll just grab some paperwork and go home. You need anything?"

"I'm good," she said.

"Did you drive in or walk?"

"I walked," she answered. "And before you say anything, I am perfectly capable of walking home."

"No need," he said, talking over his shoulder as he started through the door. "I'll be back around ten."

"JJ!" He let the door close behind him, knowing she would gripe about his unnecessary worry, but that she'd also hold his hand as they walked home. Those few minutes, walking together through their sleepy town after dark, was the perfect end to his busy days.

***

Hours later, he pushed aside the safety plans for the festival and clipped a leash on Tedy. The puppy jumped to her feet in excitement, going from sleeping to full energy in one second, and he envied her. His whole body was tired, but his step lightened when he approached the restaurant. As was habit, he was scanning the alleys between each business along the way, and he faltered when he saw a shadowy figure outside the pizza restaurant's kitchen door. They were closed and in clean up mode, so there was no reason for anyone to be lurking in the shadows.

"Hey," he called out, shining the flashlight he carried into the alley. "What are you doing?"

The figure froze, then turned and ran towards the back of the building. JJ started running after, fumbling with his phone to call the station while also trying to manage Tedy's leash. He turned in the same direction they had disappeared, only to see them hop over a fence that separated the back of the businesses from the mechanic's parking lot next door.

"Windsor Peak Police," Officer Sharp's voice came through the phone.

"Nick, it's JJ. I might have just chased our robber away from Slice Girls, they jumped the fence into the parking lot of Bill's Auto. I'm going to go back to check on the pizzeria, can you send someone to check the lot?" The other officer agreed and was calling it over the radio when JJ hung up, retracing his steps back

183

to the kitchen door. The lock held when he tried to open the door, and no one answered when he knocked. He walked around the front, where the workers could see him through the windows, and indicated they should open the door.

"Good evening," he said. "Were any of you expecting someone who would have been picking you up in the alley?"

The three staffers shook their heads silently, all looking at each other in concern. "No, sir." The woman that JJ knew was the owner stepped out of the kitchen. "We decided not to use that door after dark, with all that's been going on. Your warnings, I mean. We take the trash out early and then leave the last bag for the morning. And we all leave together out the front door."

"Excellent, thank you for being so careful," he said. "There was just someone by the back door, they ran when I yelled. I called it in already and have officers looking for them. Do you want me to walk you all to your cars?"

They all nodded, and quickly gathered jackets and purses before heading out the front door. He watched as the owner set the alarm, and locked the door securely before seeing them all to their cars. Waving to them as they pulled out, he frowned when he saw Zoe's back disappearing down Main Street towards their house.

He jogged to catch up with her, Tedy running happily at his side and letting out an excited bark when they got close enough. Zoe stopped when she heard them and bent over to rub the dogs' ears, glancing up at JJ as she did.

"I figured you fell asleep," she said. "Not like you to be late."

"I was here on time," he said. "But I saw someone creeping by the kitchen door for Slice Girls so I tried to run him down."

"You what?" she stared at him, and he couldn't tell if it was shock or something else on her face.

"I tried to catch him," he explained. "I don't know for sure that it was the suspect from the robberies, but it was worth asking him about. The fact that he ran tells me he was up to no good. But I lost him when he jumped a fence, Tedy wouldn't be able to follow me over that."

"You aren't in uniform," she said slowly. "Are you carrying a weapon right now?"

"No," he responded, seeing where she was going.

"You put your life at risk, chasing a possibly armed person, with our dog?"

"I am trained to do this," he said. The defense was weak at best, and he felt bad for even trying. "But you're right. I should have called it in, that's what I would have told anyone else to do."

"Why didn't you?"

"This is personal for me. This is my town, I feel a deep responsibility for everyone here," he said. "Moving here from Boston was a huge change, and I know it's not seen as hardcore police work as what I was doing in the city. But it matters to me," he said. "And I need this threat to you and everyone else out there to be over."

"I don't feel threatened," she said softly. "But I would like you to stay safe. That makes me more nervous than someone waving a gun at me and demanding money. Please just use a little bit of caution."

"I will," he said, leaning over to kiss her. "I am happy that you would miss me if I were gone."

She pulled the leash from his hand and started walking, rolling her eyes at him as she did. "You're ridiculous."

"But you love me, right?"

She reached over for his hand and squeezed it, then laced her fingers with his. "Right."

It wasn't quite the confession of love that he had been hoping for, but it was more than he had gotten. He walked the rest of the way home with a smile on his face, happy to have broken down more walls between them.

Chapter 21

"How come you never talk about your work in Boston?" Zoe asked as they lay in the darkness of their bedroom, just about to go to sleep. She had no idea why it had popped into her head and out of her mouth, but his earlier comment must have been festering within her.

"It wasn't my favorite time," he said after a brief silence. "What do you want to know?"

"Why wasn't it your favorite?" she rolled over, studying his profile in the moonlight coming through the window.

"It was dark, and as you know, I'm not someone who likes that," he said. "I wanted to become a cop to help people, to be someone who others can rely on. Not just to round up addicts and break up domestic fights. Seeing kids living in squalor while their parents were dealing drugs, or trying to kill each other, that can eat away at you."

"I'm sure," she said softly.

"One night I was on a SWAT team," he went on. "We were raiding a house that was known to be a drug haven. People in and out all day and night, using drugs or buying them. We came busting through the doors and the main guy grabs a three-year-old to use as a shield. There were so many kids in this house, all screaming and scared of us. And I felt like a failure."

"Why? You did what you had to do."

"But those little kids, they are going to have that memory forever," he said. "Me, in SWAT gear, pointing a gun at them.

Not really at them, but at the room, you know what I mean. And then hauling their parents away in handcuffs and calling social services to come get them. Imagine what their perspective is of cops now?"

"They were in danger," she said. "You did get them out of a bad situation."

"But I'd rather them see me as someone they can trust," he said. "A safe haven. Not the enemy."

"Is that what made you leave?"

"That was when I started thinking that I needed a change," he said. "Then my partner was killed, and I had to take a leave. After counseling and getting cleared to go back, I couldn't force myself to go back. Everyone said I was fine, but every time I tried to put the uniform on, or pick up my gun, I saw his face."

"Did you blame yourself?"

"No," he said. "We were both doing our jobs. Just a domestic gone wrong, I pulled the wife away and was talking to her and I heard a gunshot from the other room. By the time I ran in, the husband had turned the gun on himself. I have no idea why he would have shot Oscar, but I found out later that he was suffering from a major psychological disorder. His wife said that he had never been violent before, he just snapped."

"She must have been grateful to you," she said. "You saved her."

"At Oscar's expense."

"No," she said. "He signed up, just like you did. You both knew the risks. And you can't possibly know what happened in a room that you were not in."

"I know," he sighed. "I went through the counseling, remember? I just know that I was useless in that situation, and it didn't make me feel good. Yes, I pulled the wife out and who knows, maybe saved the kids too. But it still ended with her losing her husband, their kids losing their dad. And Oscar's family losing him. I honestly thought that I was done with police work after that night. I couldn't imagine going back."

"I don't blame you," she said. "But I'm glad you ended up here."

"Me too," he said, rolling over. "Imagine how different our lives were ten years ago, and somehow we found our way together."

"Lucky me," she said, her voice teasing. But when he pulled her into his arms, she rested her head on his chest and really felt that way for the first time.

***

Kendra was in her office when Zoe arrived the next morning, surprised to see her boss there. As the end of the pregnancy got closer, she was less likely to be spotted in the restaurant.

"How are you feeling?" she asked, leaning against the door jam.

"Like a beached whale," Kendra grinned at her. "But I wanted to sit down with you and discuss all the ideas you brought in before I'm out. Do you have time now?"

"I do," she said, dropping her bag on the floor and sitting across from her boss. "I hope I didn't overwhelm you."

"Not at all," she said. "Honestly, I'm thrilled. I thought you would leave me, and you could do any of these on your own. I'm a little surprised you wanted to partner on them."

"I don't enjoy the business side of things, and you're good at them. And I'm not ready to leave the kitchen," she explained. "Maybe down the road I will be, once these have grown and need me to be more managerial. But for now, I feel like I could do both."

"Catering," Kendra said, pushing some papers across the table. "That's an easy start. I looked at some pricing from other places and did a sample menu and price list based on what we offer here. Obviously, I would never dictate what you offer, but I wanted to do a cost analysis. It looks like it would be very profitable, if we can make it work."

"This is great. Most of these options do travel well, but I'd want to tweak the menu a bit," Zoe said. "Did you also consider staffing?"

Kendra handed her a second sheet, and she studied it in silence for a minute. "You thought of everything. The initial investment is pretty steep, for the truck, trailer, grills and equipment."

"It is," Kendra agreed. "But we can afford it. And I happen to know a few guys who would be willing to invest, if need be. But I thought it might make sense to start with your second idea first and offer the catering on a smaller scale to start."

She passed over more papers, and Zoe studied the plans to purchase the space next door and expand. The new space would offer ready-to-go meals, cooking lessons, as well as the ability to rent space for parties. Zoe had a million ideas of what they could do, from offering weekly wine nights where women could put together their own meal kids for the week to kids baking birthday parties. "This looks amazing," she said. "You already talked to Julie about buying it?"

"I did," she nodded. "That I will have help with, Patrick said he's more than willing to help with the cost and we can pay him back. That saves us a bundle on bank fees and interest, although I told Dan he needs to draw up an agreement and Patrick has to allow us to pay him back. No forgiving the loan three months in."

Zoe laughed, knowing that Patrick's generous spirit would struggle with that arrangement. "How long would it take to get it ready to go?"

"Not long for the counter service and selling meals," Kendra said. "Jake looked and said he could do that quickly based on what's there. If we wanted to gut it and start fresh, it would be months. I thought he could just touch it up, and then once it's open we can add the big tables in the front to use for the cooking classes and whatnot?"

"Quickly, as in by the festival?"

"Not likely," Kendra said. "That's only a few days away. But we could announce it and promote it at the festival. I was thinking you might want to bring some packaged meals to see if they sell?"

"Perfect," she said. "Let's also get a possible start date for cooking lessons. I can do some small demonstrations and get people to sign up, maybe give a small festival discount."

"I love that," Kendra said. She stood to get something from the shelf behind her and winced, holding her back. A small gasp followed by a laugh had Zoe looking at her with concern.

"Are you okay?"

"Would you mind calling Dan? And Stella, so she can get Calle. I think we're about to have a baby," Kendra laughed. "I have been having this back pain since yesterday, and it just occurred to me that it's just like when I had Calle. Of course, I didn't figure that out until my water broke."

"What?" Zoe jumped to her feet. "Sit down. Or should you lie down? Do you want me to call an ambulance?"

"No, just Dan. He's right across the street at his office, he didn't want to be far away. Calle was at Jake and Shea's for the morning, so Stella can grab her easily," Kendra said. She frowned and started breathing in measured breaths, which prompted Zoe to grab the phone and get to work. She knew nothing about delivering babies, and today was not the day to change that.

***

The kitchen was closed for the night when Emma burst in, a big smile on her face. "Did you hear?"

"No," Zoe said. "But I'm guessing the baby came?"

"Yes, we just left the hospital."

"And?"

"Came straight here," Emma said, a big smile on her face.

"You're doing that on purpose," Zoe accused. "Tell me everything. Boy or girl?"

192

"A boy," Emma shared. "Calle was very unhappy and demanding he be returned for a sister, but then Charlie convinced her that boys are good too."

"Does he have a name yet?"

"Declan Benjamin," Emma said. "And he's just perfect."

"How is Kendra feeling?" Zoe asked, putting the lid on the last container that needed to be stored and then wiping her hands on a towel. The kitchen was clean and ready to be closed for the night, so she flipped off some lights.

"She's doing great. Come on out, Patrick and JJ are at a table waiting for us," Emma said.

"I'm exhausted," Zoe groaned. "I've been thinking about my bed for hours."

"Come on, it's one drink with your sister. And then your handsome hubby can get your right back to that bed," Emma winked at her over her shoulder as she opened the door. "I want to hear if anything has happened with your mom. Oh, and Nat arrives tomorrow, so you have to help me plan things to do with her. How do I entertain a super celebrity here?"

"You live with one," Zoe pointed out. "It can't be that hard to figure out."

"But Patrick grew up here," Emma replied. "He has friends and was happy to be here long before we met. Nat only has us."

"Okay, okay," Zoe laughed. "I'll have a drink to celebrate the baby and talk about a few things for Nat, but then I'm going home to bed."

"Anything with Marise?" Emma asked as they walked through the kitchen.

"Nothing," Zoe said. "I kind of hope she gives up and leaves, but she's probably too stubborn for that."

Her eyes caught JJ's as soon as she walked through the door, and as usual, she felt the zip. She had pushed it aside for so long, determined to ignore the pull he had over her, and she was still getting used to the idea that he was all hers. It was more than chemistry and attraction, although they had that in spades. It was as if he could see right into her heart with one glance, and he proved it as she sat down.

"One quick drink and I'll get you out if here if you want," he whispered in her ear. "I know you must be tired, you started so early this morning. It's not just because I want to get you alone."

She laughed, leaning into him slightly. "I am tired, but I don't mind. I feel like we haven't seen you guys much since Vegas," she said to her sister and Patrick.

"We've all been pretty busy," Patrick admitted. "I've been doing some voiceover stuff from home and getting ready to shoot again in a few months."

"Where will you go this time?"

"Atlanta, mostly," he said. "Then back to Los Angeles for a bit. I'll be back and forth as much as I can when we're on the east coast, but when we get to California I'll be busy. I've already convinced Emma to come with me for the whole thing, I apologize for stealing her away."

"You are going?" Zoe looked at Emma in surprise. "I thought you were determined to keep working."

"I talked to Piper, and we worked it out," Emma explained. "Patrick is very persistent and used to getting what he wants."

"Keep it clean, you two," JJ joked.

Zoe rolled her eyes and elbowed him. "Patrick, how are Dan and Kendra doing? We'll have to try and get over to the hospital in the morning."

"Kendra has every intention of going home tomorrow," Patrick said. "She doesn't like being away from Calle. You might be able to catch them at home, if the doctor agrees."

"Wow," Zoe said. "She's a champ."

"She said she didn't even realize she was in labor for twenty-six hours," Emma laughed. "I'd say she's a champ."

"Who has Calle tonight?" JJ asked.

"Stella and my dad," Patrick said. "Dan was thinking of going home, but then Charlie agreed to sleep over as well, so he feels okay about staying at the hospital. Calle was excited about a sleepover with Mimi and Papa."

"Is that what she's calling them now?" Zoe asked. "That's so sweet."

"Yes, and Charlie switched to calling Stella Mimi too," Patrick said. "Although he slips up a lot. He's always called my dad Grandpa, but Calle was stumbling on it, so he suggested Papa instead. I think they are in their glory, now with four grandkids to spoil."

"Until you give them one," JJ teased them.

"Hey, wait until your parents get a taste of it," Patrick laughed. "I can't believe they aren't pushing you two already."

"Oh, my mother makes regular comments," JJ said. "I just pretend I don't hear her."

"She does?" Zoe turned to JJ in surprise. "I didn't know that."

"Well, you don't need that kind of pressure," JJ said. "I told you I'm okay with whatever you decide, and with whatever timeline you're good with if we do decide to have kids. No pressure here."

"Can I pressure you a little?" Emma laughed. "I'd be a fantastic aunt."

"You are now," Patrick argued. "My nieces and nephews are yours too."

Emma held up her left hand and studied it before turning to her boyfriend. "Huh," she smiled at him. "I don't see a ring here proving that."

"Oh, if you want me to," he stood, then started to bend down on one knee before she grabbed his arm.

"Don't you dare," she laughed. "Imagine what would be on the front of every magazine tomorrow if you got down on one knee here, even for a joke."

"She toys with me," Patrick stage whispered to Zoe and JJ.

"You're impossible," Emma laughed. "Enough about us. Let's plan some things for Nat and compare schedules for the festival to see if the four of us can do anything together that weekend."

One drink turned into two, and soon Desmond was pushing them out the door so he could close. Zoe had forgotten how tired she was as the four of them talked and laughed, and they all hugged outside, promising to do it again soon. Walking home, she couldn't help but reflect on the changes her life had undergone over the last year, and feel grateful for all of them. Last year at the Autumn Festival, she was happy to work sixteen hours days, and looked forward to Thanksgiving so she would have a day to watch movies and eat junk food. Now she had a husband, sister, circle of friends, and plans to look forward to. Surreal as it all was, she was really starting to love her new life.

Chapter 22

JJ was woken up at three a.m. by his ringing cell phone, which he hit answer on quickly before ducking out of the bedroom so he wouldn't disrupt Zoe. The officer on duty reported that an alarm was sounding at the pet store, and that he had already notified the state police but thought JJ should know as well. He thanked him and promised to be right in, grabbing clean clothes from the laundry room rather than risking waking his wife.

The drive into town was quick, and he saw the flashing lights of the state police cruiser as he parked and jogged the last few yards to the store. The glass door on the front was completely smashed in, and glass littered the sidewalk and entry way. The officers finished checking the store before meeting him back on the sidewalk, surveying the damage.

"Looks like they were just after cash," the trooper told him. "The register was pried open, and the door to the office where there is a safe. But they didn't damage anything in the store. And at least we've moved away from armed robbery, I'd rather a million of these than one where someone tries to fight back."

"Totally agree," JJ said. "I was hoping it was over."

"We had a few hits down near White River that fit the same description," the cop said. "We were under the same impression, that the individual was on their way to New Hampshire. This makes me wonder why they would come back."

"We have our annual Harvest Festival this weekend," JJ replied. "Lots of vendors on the town square, a lot of cash around. I've been working for weeks on plans to secure it, but I just don't know how I'll control all those people. It's not like I can provide an armed guard to every vehicle at the end of the day or tell people not to accept cash. I encouraged them all to use digital payments when possible, but I'm very concerned now."

"Makes sense why they would come back," the cop agreed, scratching his head. "If you call the precinct tomorrow, we might be able to get some extra units down this way. I heard a rumor from my teenager that you have a big celebrity in town, so that might add things to it."

"What?" JJ studied him, curious if news about Natalie's arrival had already gotten out.

"The superhero guy? Peter something?"

"Oh, Patrick. Yes, he grew up here," JJ said. "He usually volunteers to help raise money."

"Might be a good idea to have him get some private security," the officer suggested. "If he'll be here, his house will be a possible target."

"True," JJ groaned. "I'll talk to him this morning. Thanks for your help here."

"No problem. You'll get this boarded up?"

JJ nodded and the cruiser pulled away, flashers off now. It drove slowly down Main Street before turning toward the road that would take them back to the highway. Somehow the thought of Patrick's house being empty, other than possibly Natalie in it, had escaped his mind until now. He needed to alert the pet store owner, Ralph, and get the door secured. Then find coffee. And then he could figure out what to do about Patrick's visibility over the weekend.

***

A knock on his office door hours later pulled him away from the stack of paperwork he had strewn across his desk. Zoe stood in the doorway, a cup of coffee and a bag from the bakery in her hand.

"You left without breakfast," she said, sounding shy. "I thought might be hungry."

He stood and stretched as he walked toward her, feeling the grin spread across his face. "Thank you, my love." He kissed her before taking the items from her. "What did you bring me?"

"An egg sandwich on a plain bagel, so you won't have to worry about your breath later," she said. "Although from how stressed you look, it might be better if people were scared off by onion breath."

He sighed and gestured for her to sit in the chair across from his desk, choosing to sit next to her rather than in his normal spot. "It's been a long day already, and it's barely nine."

"What happened?"

"Our thief hit the pet store," he said. "Fortunately, no one was hurt, but it shows that they are sticking around. The state police are worried that they may be hoping to make some big scores over the festival weekend."

"All that cash," she said. "It's way too late to switch to a cashless requirement for the vendors, but that's a good idea for next year."

"Agree," he nodded. "I'm going to go door to door today and ask everyone to try and accept as much through Venmo or anything other than cash. But a lot of charitable booths will have trouble with that, they bank on people just parting with a couple dollars. The hockey team is doing their dunk tank again, and I know they only collected cash last year."

"I doubt anyone will jump a bunch of teenage athletes," she said.

"You'd be surprised. One of those kids is going to be in charge of the money, and has to go home at some point," he said grimly. "I think the safest bet there is to ask Jake to do it. No one in their right mind would look at him and think he's an easy target."

"Good idea," she said. "Maybe I can have him be in charge of mine as well."

"Can you do digital? Although I'll make sure you get home safely," he said. "If you don't have a lockbox of some kind, please make sure to get one."

She nodded. "We have one, I'll make sure it goes in the boxes we have set aside for the festival."

He sipped his coffee and took a bite of the sandwich, before noticing she had nothing for herself. "Do you want to split this?"

"No, I ate over there while chatting with Emma," she said. "You enjoy."

"This has made my day significantly better," he said.

"If I knew it was as simple as a breakfast sandwich and coffee, I'd have done it before."

"No, it's not the food, although that is a bonus," he said. "It's you coming here like this. Shows me how much you care about me."

She blushed slightly and looked at the floor. "Why are you such a cornball?"

"Hey, I love my wife. It makes me happy when she shows she loves me back," he laughed. "This was really nice of you. Did you know you've never come in to see me at work? I'm in the kitchen daily, so having you here just hits different."

"I haven't been here? I thought I was after everything that happened with Calle," she frowned as she thought. "Or at some point over the last couple years."

"I'm sure you've been in the station, but not specifically to see me," he said. "With the way you drive, I'm sure you had a speeding ticket to pay."

"Hey," she laughed. "Take that back."

He laughed and threw his trash in the bin by the doorway, before leaning over to kiss her again. "How's my breath?"

"Not terrible," she said. She stood and grabbed her bag off the floor. "I should get to work; I have a lot to do."

"Thanks again for this," he said. "I'll walk you out."

"You don't need to do that," she protested.

"I want to show off," he said, taking her hand. "And I need to start talking to the store owners before they get busy."

They walked through town together, pausing to talk to neighbors on the street as they did. When they reached the empty shop next to the restaurant, Zoe paused and looked through the window.

"This is where we'll open the catering and lesson space," she told him. "Jake is starting to work on it today."

"That's great," he said. "You didn't tell me that you and Kendra decided to move ahead with it."

"Well, she went into labor just after we decided," she laughed. "It kind of put a pin in it. But she texted me late last night that Jake would be here today getting things started."

"I can't wait to see what you do with it," he said. "But whatever it is, I know you'll make it a success."

"Try not to work too hard today, okay?" she studied his face as she talked. "You look exhausted."

"Is that a nice way of telling me I look hideous?"

"You couldn't look hideous if you tried," she rolled her eyes. "Just remember, you have a whole team of people who work for you. The safety of the entire town is not on your shoulders." She kissed him lightly and disappeared into the alley between the buildings to go into the restaurant through the kitchen door. He watched her go, then went back to his task. Despite her words, he still knew it was his responsibility to make sure the festival was safe and fun for everyone.

He had just finished his rounds at the local businesses when he got a text from Patrick letting him know that Natalie had arrived. Natalie Cloud was one of the most famous actresses in the world, and one of Patrick's costars in the superhero blockbusters that they filmed regularly. Having both of them in town together was an interesting problem to have, but one he was sure he could manage with Patrick's cooperation.

After sticking his head into the station to let them know where he would be, he hopped into his truck to drive up the mountain to Patrick's house. Nestled halfway up the mountain, it was a private area with only Patrick's family as neighbors within walking distance. Patrick's SUV was parked in front of his garage bay, the back open revealing more suitcases than JJ had ever seen together in one spot. Other than a baggage carousel at the airport, that is.

Patrick came out the front door, hair sticking up in the front and wearing sweats. "Hey," he called. "Want to help me?"

"Sure," JJ agreed. "How many people did she bring with her?"

"This is all hers," Patrick groaned. "I told her to pack light, that she didn't need a ton up here. But she said she never knows what might come up and she wanted to be prepared. Honestly, two pairs of jeans, some tees and a few sweaters would have been plenty."

"Has she ever dressed like that?"

Patrick paused, setting down the suitcase he was carrying next to the front door as he thought. "No, I don't suppose she has. At least as long as I've known her."

When they went in the front door, Natalie was lounging on Patrick's couch. As if to prove Patrick's point, she was wearing a long, billowing skirt, a tight tank top and a sweater that was more scarf than sweater. She jumped off the couch and crossed to JJ, smiling as she did.

"So good to see you again, JJ," she gushed. "I'm so excited to be here."

"It's nice to see you as well," JJ said. He gently extricated himself from her and pointed at the suitcases. "Where should these go?"

"I'm going to stay out back in the cottage," she said. "It's adorable."

"About that," JJ said. "Would you both mind if Nat stayed in the main house for the next few days? Just until the festival is over?"

"Of course not, but what's up?" Patrick frowned as he asked. "The cottage has a security system as well."

"It would be a pain to move all this stuff twice," Natalie added. "I don't think anyone will bother me up here. After all, no one knows I'm here."

"We do need to keep it that way, at least until this weekend is over," JJ said. "I know that makes it harder on you, to be trapped up here, but it's just too much if you're both here. The town is used to Patrick at least, and the visitors already know to expect him. If you suddenly appear, I'm afraid of what crazies would come out to find you."

She shuddered and stepped closer to Patrick. "That is exactly what I'm trying to avoid."

Before JJ could say anything, a sharp knock rapped on the door and it started to swing open. "Not sure if you know this, but a luggage delivery just came," Mike's voice called out. "I grabbed a few, who's stuff is this?"

They watched as the trainer walked in, holding four of the large suitcases, and came to a dead stop at the sight of Natalie. His face lost all color and JJ started to worry that he would pass out, but before they could do anything, Natalie moved toward him.

"Oh, my," she purred. "You are even bigger in person than on Facetime. Look at all those muscles holding my little bags." She ran her hand up his arm, and Patrick and JJ erupted into laughter. It seemed to snap Mike out of it as he glared at them.

"Thank you," Mike said to Natalie. "Are these yours? Where should I put them?"

"I'll show you," she said, crooking a finger at him. "Follow me."

JJ and Patrick watched as the two crossed through the kitchen and disappeared through the back door, which led to the cottage. "I guess that means she won't be staying in the main house," JJ said. "Make sure she knows how to set the security system, please."

"Did you see his face? I can't believe I didn't take a video of that. Dan and Jake are going to kill me," Patrick laughed. "I have to text them."

Chapter 23

"I don't know what to do," Zoe moaned to her sister. "I know I'm being whiny and difficult but tell me what to do about my mother."

Emma slowly wiped the counter in the bakery, looking deep in thought. "You aren't being whiny or difficult," she said. "Give yourself some grace. But I do think you need to make a decision, and I'm a little surprised that you haven't yet."

"Why do you say that?"

"You're always so decisive and confident," her sister replied. "I've never seen you unsure about anything. Other than your feelings about JJ, maybe. But even that, I think you know deep down how you feel about him, you're just scared to admit it."

Zoe felt herself bristle and took a few slow breaths before responding. "I don't think that's fair," she finally said.

"Which part?"

"About JJ," she said. "You make it sound like I was stringing him along. I was trying to avoid being in a relationship, I wanted to focus on my career."

"You left France, the culinary capital of the world, to come to Windsor Peak to focus on your career?"

"Well, I didn't come for JJ," she sniped. Seeing the hurt look on Emma's face, she softened. "I'm sorry. You know what I mean, I wanted to just focus on cooking and helping Kendra grow the restaurant, not waste time falling in love."

"Was it a waste of time? You seem happy with him," Emma asked.

"I don't even know how it happened, but yes, I am happy," she admitted. "He's my best friend. He just kept showing up and being nice and making it impossible not to like him."

"Are you saying that you married him just because he's your friend?" Emma's face showed the doubt behind her question. "Sparks were flying between you two to the point that I thought we would have to call the fire department."

"You know we got involved way before Vegas," Zoe said. "I can't believe I'm admitting this, but the first night we spent together I had to talk him into it."

"What?" Emma laughed, putting a hand on her hip as she stared at her. "No way that's true, he was chasing you for all that time and then said no?"

"Yes," Zoe nodded. "We had all gone to karaoke that night, and something just clicked for me that night. We were sitting closely together, he kept leaning over to say things right into my ear, because it was so loud. And all night, I just kept staring at his hands and wishing they were on me. By the time he walked me home, I practically dragged him inside. He was worried that I had too much to drink and wanted to wait, but I had barely had anything. I was so worked up over him, and freaking out a little about what it meant, but mainly just knowing what I wanted."

"Good for you," Emma said. "I can't believe you never told me that before. But it goes to show, when you make a decision, you can't be talked out of it."

"Which brings us back to my original question," Zoe sighed. "What should I do about my mother?"

"She's been here for days, and you haven't talked to her at all?"

"No," Zoe said. "She showed up at our house that day with JJ's family, and that was the last time I saw her. I don't know why she's here or what to do. Remember, I told you I hoped she would just leave? That didn't happen."

"I think you need to talk to her," Emma said gently. "You would have told her to leave already if that was what you wanted. It's okay to admit that you are hurt by her, and that you still want some kind of relationship because she's your mom."

"She was horrible, though. Does she deserve yet another chance? She's the reason my whole life in Paris fell apart," Zoe said.

"And that might be the best thing that ever happened to you. Not the immediate aftermath," Emma said quickly. "That was horrible, and you didn't deserve that. But coming here, to Windsor Peak? You and I found each other again, and you met JJ. What would your life be like if that hadn't happened?"

"I'd probably still be slaving away in that kitchen, putting up with his abuse," Zoe admitted. "Hanging on to the hope that I'd eventually get my own kitchen."

"I know this isn't a fair card to play, but I'm going to anyway," Emma said. "You deserve better from your mom, there is no question about that. But you still have a chance to fix things and maybe have her for the rest of your life. I'd give anything to have more time with my mom, to have her see me as an adult. To have her here when I have babies one day. I think that's what you really want, to have her in your life and to have her be proud of you. If you didn't, you would have sent her away."

"Why do you have to be so rational and smart," Zoe grumbled. She knew her sister was right, but giving her mother yet another chance was a huge risk. "Will you go with me to talk to her?"

"Of course," Emma agreed. "Just let me know when. I can get Piper to cover out front if you want to do it now."

"Probably a good idea to get it over with, then I can go to work and forget about it." Zoe checked her watch and nodded. "I still have at least an hour before I need to get to work. Jake is working on the new space now, so I can't do anything over there yet. And most of my prep for the festival is done."

"Piper," Emma called through the kitchen door. "I have to run out with Zoe. Can you watch the front until I get back?"

"No problem," Piper yelled back. "I'll be out in just a minute."

Emma pulled on a sweatshirt and gestured to the door. "Let's get this over with. I'm sure your mom will be delighted to see me," she laughed.

Zoe's mom had never extended any kindness towards Emma as they grew up, refusing to have her to their house when they were children. Instead, Zoe had spent summers at Emma's house with her loving mother, up until she died suddenly. When she did, Zoe's mother hadn't even told her where her sister had gone, instead hinted that they had moved and didn't want to see her anymore. It had caused Zoe to spiral and get wild in her teenage years, losing the only stability and love that she had felt in her childhood.

The sisters walked silently across the town square toward the Inn, where Marise was staying. As they walked into the lobby, Emma reached over and took Zoe's hand, squeezing quickly before letting go. They went to the room Marise had sent in many text messages and Zoe took a deep breath before knocking. The door opened almost instantly, as if she had been standing on the other side waiting for someone.

Marise looked shocked to see Zoe, but her face fell slightly when she saw that Emma was with her. "Come in," she said, stepping aside. "I thought you would be the housekeeper; she usually comes early to exchange the towels. You know how I hate having wet towels laying around."

"Yes, I remember well your aversion to them," Zoe rolled her eyes. She and Emma sat side-by-side on the small couch, facing where Marise perched on the end of the bed. "You wanted to see me, I'm here. What do you want?"

Marise didn't look surprised at her daughter's abrupt tone, so Zoe knew she must have been expecting some hostility from her. She cleared her throat and then stood to get a bottle of water out of the small refrigerator, holding it up to see if either of the other women wanted one. They both shook their heads, so she came back and sat across from them.

"First, since you're here, I want to apologize to Emma," she said. "I know that it is long overdue, and that it should not be accepted. How I treated you as a small child is unacceptable. And although I didn't find out about your mother until almost a year after it happened, I should have tried to find you, to keep you two together. I was selfish and wrong, and I'm deeply sorry. I don't believe you should accept that or forgive me, because I was so wrong, but I had to say it."

Emma's mouth was slightly open, matching the shock that Zoe was sure she had on her face. Marise had rarely acknowledged Emma's existence though their lives, never mind admitting any fault.

"Are you dying," Zoe blurted out. It was the only possible explanation for her mother's complete change in attitude.

"Not anymore, I hope," Marise replied. Zoe and Emma again looked at each other, both with shocked looks, and then back at her. She shrugged and scraped at the label on the water bottle, staring at it before she looked back at Zoe again. "I had cancer. I finished treatment six months ago, and just got the all clear from the doctor."

"You had cancer, and you didn't tell me?"

"It wasn't fair of me to tell you," Marise said. "I had been going to counseling and was finally ready to reach out to you when I was diagnosed."

"You were going to counseling? What is happening," Zoe murmured.

"I was. I started when I got home from France," Marise nodded. "I met a man—"

"What a surprise," Zoe said, her voice dripping in sarcasm.

"I knew you would think that," Marise said. "But he's not like anyone else I ever met. He saw through me, and he encouraged me to get help. He said we couldn't be together if I was going to remain who I had been my whole life. Selfish and toxic to relationships, among other things. He said he would be my friend, but that I had to make changes before he could be in a relationship with me. I started seeing a counselor, and she was helpful in many ways. She still is."

"I'm sorry if this all seems to be shocking to me, but it really is," Zoe said. "You actually admitting you've been selfish alone is a lot to take in, never mind the rest of it."

"I understand," Marise said, nodding slightly. "I wish I was a different person. I wish I was the mother that you deserved. All I can do now is try to make changes to be worthy of your time for all I have left."

"Are you dying? I have to ask again, because that sounds ominous," Zoe said.

"No," Marise said. "I promise, I got a clean bill of health. I still have to go for scans every six months, but they are confident they got it all."

"Where was it?" Emma asked quietly.

"Breast cancer," Marise replied. "They caught it early, fortunately, and it hadn't spread. I had a mastectomy and chemotherapy to be safe."

"And you didn't tell me?" Zoe was shocked that her mother had kept this all from her, even with their strained relationship. The person she knew would have demanded that her daughter return home and care for her while she underwent the medical treatments.

"I couldn't do that to you," Marise said, hanging her head. "I knew how badly I had treated you, especially in Paris. I honestly did come there thinking we could have a fresh start, as two adults. Your wild years were over, and I felt more settled. I thought we could reconnect as adults and enjoy Paris together, maybe. But I ruined that as soon as I met Antoine."

Zoe nodded, unable to speak. The thought of her former boss caused her stomach to roll, and it was all she could do to stay in her seat. Emma's solid presence beside her gave her the strength she needed to continue to listen.

"When I got home, I met Henri. And then I started going to the counseling, and the reality of what I had done to you really hit me. I was scheduled for my mammogram, and I almost skipped it," Marise went on. "But something made me go. I wanted to stay in bed, wallow in the misery that I had once again let you down. Once I got the diagnosis and started treatment, the doctor recommended I get some counseling to deal with all of it. I was the only person who was going through all of it without anyone to be by my side."

Zoe took a sharp breath and felt her spine stiffen, the unexpected dagger cutting right through her. Marise looked started at her response and held up a hand. "I don't mean that to be negative toward you. I didn't deserve your help. And those days alone gave me time to really think about my life. The changes that I should be making."

"What role did this man have in your attitude? And why wasn't he with you when you were doing the treatments?"

"I didn't tell him until after I was done," Marise said. "I was already on the right path, believe it or not. I don't know that I would have paid any attention to him if I hadn't already realized how flawed I was and how badly I treated you. We met in a coffee shop, and he said I was the saddest person he had ever seen. After a little time together, he said he couldn't feel like he was saving me, I needed to want to change for myself. I didn't want to tell him about the cancer and have him feel like he had to spend time with me, it was my fault I didn't have a support system. Going through the treatments alone made me realize that I was still only thinking of myself, when I should be thinking of others. If I had died, how would that impact you? And in my good health, how can I be someone worthy of your time? When I told him he was shocked, but he said he felt like the old Marise would have forced everyone to take care of me, but instead at my sickest, I was thinking of others. It showed him I had changed."

"He sounds like he has a good head on his shoulders," Emma said encouragingly.

"He's a teacher," Marise said with a smile. "He teaches math, and he always has a little bit of chalk dust on him. He wears this hideous sweater vests that I can't convince him are out of fashion, and half the time he leaves the house with two different shoes on. But he is the kindest person I've ever met, and he's patient enough to help me be better."

"For yourself, or for him?"

"Can't it be both?" Marise said. "I want to be worthy of him. And he's not asking me to change for him, not like other men. He simply told me that he thought we should be friends, because our outlooks were too different to be compatible. But fool that I am, I was already fallen for him and fought for a man for the first time in my life. I told him all about my therapy, and what I went through with the cancer, and told him that I could use someone like him. But that I understood if I was too selfish for him, because in my earlier days, I certainly was."

"Not just your earlier days," Zoe muttered.

"Be nice," Emma whispered. She looked at Marise appraisingly, and then smiled. "I hope you are able to succeed. As I told Zoe earlier, I would give anything to have more time with my mom. I hope you two are able to repair what was broken."

"That is very gracious of you," Marise said. "Zoe, I plan to leave today, now that we've spoken. I want to give you some time and space to process what I've said. And I want to be able to prove to you that I'm changing. I don't need or want you to instantly forgive me or grant me time with you, I want to be able to show you that I'm changing. If you're agreeable, I'll come back down in a few weeks, maybe bring Henri with me, and we could spend some time together. But we can talk about that later, I'll call you in a few days and see what you think."

Zoe stood, feeling suddenly unsteady and off balance. This was not the mother she knew, and it was almost too good to be true. She said a stilted goodbye and wished her a safe trip back to Canada, then followed Emma out of the room. All she could think about was getting to the kitchen, where she could lose herself in the magic of cooking and where things made sense.

Chapter 24

JJ dug through his desk to find his ringing cell phone, smiling when he saw his sister's name on the screen. "Hey, Fin," he said. "What's up?"

"Does something need to be up for me to call my big brother?"

"Of course not," he laughed. "But you never call me in the middle of the workday."

"Colin has been acting weird," she said. "I don't know why, but I figured you could get to the bottom of it if any of us could."

"What's he been doing?" JJ switched the phone to speaker and started sorting through the papers in front of him.

"Pouting," Finley replied. "He comes and sits at the bar at the Palace most nights but doesn't really talk to anyone. He found a rental in town, thankfully, so it's not mom and dad driving him crazy."

"He moved out already?" JJ was surprised, he hadn't heard anything from Colin since the last night at the Palace.

"Yes, but focus. It's not like him to be sulking," Finley said. "You need to talk to him."

"Fin, I'm up to my eyebrows with plans for the festival. Can this wait until after that?"

"If you're not concerned about your brother," she sniffed.

"Can't Des talk to him? Or you? He'd probably rather talk to you about whatever it is," he suggested.

"I already tried. He shot me down, told me to mind my business," she said. "And Des sees him every night at the bar, and he barely talks."

"Fine," he sighed. "I'll text him, see if he can come to dinner tonight."

"We'd love to," she replied. "Des is off too, so this is perfect. Family dinner, we can hit him from all sides."

"I said Colin," he said. "Not the whole family, I can't spring that on Zoe."

"She won't mind," Finley said confidently. "Want me to call mom?"

He sighed, glancing at his watch. "Yes, please. I need to make sure Zoe isn't going to divorce me over this. I probably should have just said I would meet Colin at the Palace."

"But then we wouldn't have a delicious Zoe meal to look forward to," Finley said. "I'll see you tonight. And I'll bring wine."

He dialed Zoe's number and left a voicemail explaining when she didn't pick up. Hopefully she wouldn't mind, and it would give her a chance to talk to Colin. Sending his brother a quick text before he got back to work, he instructed him to arrive before the rest of the family. Easier to let them have their time to talk about the events in Paris before everyone else arrived. JJ suspected that was what was behind Colin's foul mood, so the sooner they addressed it, the faster they could all get back to normal.

***

Zoe was busy in the kitchen when he arrived home, carrying the dessert she had asked him to pick up at the bakery and fresh flowers he had wanted to get her. She smiled and smelled them quickly, then frowned, looking around the kitchen.

"I don't think we have a vase," she said. "I never unpacked one."

"Well, I certainly didn't have one before living with you," he laughed. "I'll just use a mason jar." He pulled one out of the cabinet, filling it with water before placing the flowers inside.

"Just leave them on the island and I'll fix them when I have a second," Zoe said.

"Fix them? What's wrong?"

"It's like when you load the dishwasher," she answered. "And I let you do it, because I really do appreciate the effort. But then I have to redo it the right way."

"Is there actually a wrong way to put dishes in?"

"There is," she laughed. "And you somehow find even more inventive ways to do it every time."

"You must really love me if you're putting up with that," he said. He wrapped his arms around her from behind, kissing her on the back of her neck.

"You can't imagine the chaos you bring to my life," she laughed. "The dishwasher is the least of my trouble. You also move all my spices around, so they are out of order, put hand towels in the laundry after drying your hands, and I swear you're using my expensive shampoo."

"Guilty of it all," he grinned. "And I can't think of anyone else I'd rather be sharing all this with."

She gently elbowed him in the stomach. "Let me finish this before your family gets here."

"Can I do anything to help?"

"Just make sure the bathroom is clean," she said. As he started to walk down the hall, he heard her call out again. "And make sure there's a towel in there!"

He wiped down the counter quickly, replaced the hand towel, and placed an extra roll of toilet paper in the holder. Satisfied that it would meet his mother's white glove standard, he went back to the kitchen. Spotting a bottle of wine open on the counter, he pulled out two glasses and poured before placing one next to Zoe.

"You going to be okay talking to Colin," he asked.

"Yes," she sighed. "I'm a little nervous, but I feel like it will help me put the whole thing behind me. I do need to tell you about what happened with my mother this morning, it feels like a lifetime ago."

He listened as she recounted her meeting with Marise, and he saw the hope in her eyes. As much as she protested the need to have her mother in her life, she clearly wanted to believe that Marise had changed.

"How are you feeling about all of it," he asked when she finished.

She sipped her wine and wiped at an invisible spot on the island before answering. "I'm not sure, if I'm being honest. She let me down so much as a kid, and even as an adult, so trusting her is going to be hard. At the same time, if I don't give her another chance, what does that say about me?"

"You're allowed to be hurt," he said quietly. "And you're allowed to protect yourself. Seeing your walls come down over the last few months with me has been beautiful, and I know how pure your heart is. Whatever you decide, I'm with you."

"You really have changed my whole outlook," she said. "I moved here and thought I could just work and live a solitary life. And the first night that I'm at work, you come sauntering in the kitchen, and just never left. I can't believe you never gave up on me."

"Never," he said. He was cut off from saying more when the doorbell rang, and he cursed Colin for his punctuality before he went to open the door.

"Hey," Colin grunted at him. "Here for the command performance."

"Dude," JJ said. "Relax. We're going to eat some good food and drink a little. It's not prison."

Colin frowned at him and held out the planter he had been holding. "I brought this for Zoe. It's a spice garden for the kitchen."

"She'll love it, bring it in and give it to her yourself," JJ said.

"About that," Colin hesitated after coming through the door. "Are she and I okay? She was really off when I was here last. And I don't know what she told you."

"She told me everything," JJ said. "And she wanted to talk to you herself."

Colin still looked hesitant, so JJ bumped his shoulder. "She's tiny. She can't possibly hurt you."

"You're the worst," Colin groaned.

JJ led the way into the kitchen and went to stand behind where Zoe sat at the island. She smiled slightly at Colin, and looked uncertain, so he started rubbing her shoulders lightly.

"I brought you this window spice garden," Colin said, sliding the planter in front of her. "I thought it would like nice in your window and give you fresh spices year round."

"That's so thoughtful, thank you," she said. "Especially after I was so rude to you when we first saw each other again. And really, when we were in Paris."

"You were never rude to me," Colin objected. "You were focused on work in France, and I know I was caught off guard seeing you again, so I can only imagine how you felt."

"Like my worlds were colliding," Zoe said. "And once I told JJ about everything that had happened, I realized I never thanked you. Or even found out what happened after I ran off."

"I wanted to beat him senseless," Colin said. "But instead, I called the police and he was arrested. Once he was charged, other women in the restaurant came forward and talked about how he had been handsy with them. One of them said he had forced himself on her after drinking in the kitchen all night, very similar to what it seemed like he planned to do with you."

Zoe shuddered slightly under JJ's hands, and he rubbed her arms. He wished he could take the memories away for her, or go back in time to protect her, but was so glad his brother had been in the right place to do it for him.

"Did he go to jail?" Zoe asked Colin, who shook his head.

"No, he took a plea deal and went to rehab for three months," Colin said. "I thought it was getting off too easy, but without you all they had were some older claims that hadn't been reported. If you and I could have both corroborated the story, it may have been different."

"That means he's free to do it again," Zoe said softly.

"I went back to Paris to see him when he got out of rehab," Colin said. "Told him I'd be watching. I reached out to the owner, who had hired you to begin with. She was horrified when I told her what had happened, and wants you to reach out to her, by the way. She said she owed you an apology but couldn't get in touch with you. I advised her that to make up for it, she should hire a female general manager, one who was tough but that the other women would trust. She keeps a very close eye on things, and he's been on his best behavior. His reputation took a huge hit with all the bad publicity, he can't afford any more."

"That's good, I guess," she said. "I honestly can't thank you enough. Even after how I acted towards you all those weeks, you were there for me. I was borderline rude to you, when you were nothing but nice to me."

"Again, you did nothing to me," he said. "Just because I thought you were attractive doesn't mean you owe me anything. And honestly, I really enjoyed watching you cook, and being around you made it feel a little more like home."

"You're too nice," she said.

"Let's not inflate his ego any more than it already is," JJ joked. The doorbell rang again, and he kissed Zoe on the head before leaving the room. "I'll get that." As he walked out, he saw

Colin stand and hug Zoe, and both looked far more relaxed than they had when the night started.

"Hi, honey," his mom said when he opened the door. "Take this, please." She shoved a large tote bag into his stomach and followed it with a tray that his dad had been holding.

"What did you bring? We told you we didn't need anything," he said, gesturing for his parents to go in front of him.

"Your mother doesn't go anywhere empty handed, you should know that by now," Frank said.

"I made some cookies, and I brought a few things Colin forgot at our house," his mom said. "Since he moved out on us so quickly, he barely remembered to pack."

"That's not true," Colin objected as they walked into the kitchen. "You were probably holding clothes hostage. I told you I could do my own laundry."

Maggie sniffed, then accepted the kiss Colin was placing on her cheek, before turning to give Zoe a hug. "Still hurts when your children abandon you."

"I didn't—"

"Although we do enjoy the empty nest," Frank said, patting his wife on the bottom and making his sons groan. "If you know what I mean."

"We all know what you mean, Dad," JJ said. "Please stop. Or at least wait until the twins get here so we don't have to suffer alone."

"Suffer? How do you think you got onto this earth?" Maggie put her hands on her hips and glared at her sons.

Colin and JJ exchanged a look before Colin replied. "We'd just rather not think about it, if you don't mind."

The doorbell rang, and JJ ran to let the twins in, filling the space with their noise and providing a nice distraction from the subject at hand. Soon everyone was standing or sitting in the kitchen, drinks in hand, enjoying the snacks that Zoe had placed out.

"You should sell these," Finley said, pointing at the charcuterie board in front of her. "This is beautiful, and way too much work to put together. But my friends love them for girls' nights or parties. You could definitely sell them with your takeout options."

"That's a great idea," Zoe agreed. "We're still working on the options, so I'll add that to the list."

"You're going to be so busy when that opens," Maggie said. "How is your search for more kitchen staff going?"

"Great, actually," Zoe said. "I reached out to my college, and they had a few graduates who were interested. I also talked to Wyatt, who owns a small spot near Stowe. He has a friend who cooked in the Marine's who's looking for a quiet spot. He is coming to town next week to meet us and see the restaurant."

"Hopefully it will work out, so you'll have some free time," Maggie said with a smile.

"What are you getting at, Mom?" JJ demanded.

"Oh, you know," she said, a twinkle in her eye. "I wouldn't mind being a grandmother one of these days. Stella is constantly sending me pictures of the babies and talking about Charlie and Calle. And I have nothing to share."

"We aren't having a baby so you can brag to your friends," JJ said.

"It would be a celebration of your love," she argued. "Speaking of, your father and I were talking about your wedding."

"What about it?" JJ put cheese on a cracker and tried to make out the look his parents exchanged, and the guilty expression on his siblings faces. Suddenly, he felt as though he had been set up for something.

"We want to throw you a reception," his father said. "None of us had a chance to be at the wedding, and we want to share in the occasion."

Zoe stared at him with shock on her face, and he knew he had to tread carefully. The last thing Zoe ever wanted was to be the center of attention, she liked to be in small groups and behind the scenes, not the middle of it. Whatever his family had planned would probably be her worst nightmare, especially when she hadn't fully embraced her feelings for him.

"Let's talk about this later, okay? Zoe has dinner just about ready," JJ said. "And I have a lot going on this weekend with the festival, so I'd appreciate it if we could shelve this at least until after that. Give Zoe and I a chance to talk about it."

His family all nodded, but he could tell by the look on his mother's face that this subject was far from closed. And as much as he would love to celebrate his marriage with his family and friends here in town, the idea of it might be just the thing to scare Zoe off.

Chapter 25

"Knock, knock." Zoe heard her sister's voice call from the back door to the space next to the restaurant, where she was putting together trays to sell at the festival. Jake was still working on the new design, so it wasn't ready for the public yet, but it was functional enough to give her the room she needed to create.

"I'm in here," she called back to Emma. She placed a cover on the tray she had just completed and looked up when her sister came in, followed by Natalie. "Nat! Welcome to town." She went over and hugged the other woman, who she now thought of as a friend rather than the star she was.

"I was going stir crazy," Natalie said. "Emma had the idea that we might be able to sneak me down here to see you. Maybe I can help?"

"You both can, if you want. I have all the ingredients set out, it will be much faster if three of us are doing it, rather than just me. I'm doing some trays that can be taken home and cooked, like the baked ziti and stuffed chicken dishes," she gestured to one side. "I'm doing those first so they can go into the refrigerator. Then some sandwich and salad selections that can be eaten at the festival. And finally, Finley had the idea to do charcuterie trays, so I'm doing large and small."

"And you thought you could do this all on your own?" Emma turned in amazement, taking in all the tables set up with ingredients. "It's okay to ask for help once in a while."

"I know, I was going to get it all prepped and then see if I could grab a few people from next door," she answered. "But now that you're both here, I don't need to."

"I'm not so great in the kitchen," Natalie warned.

"You don't have to do any cooking," Zoe said. "You can do the sandwiches and salads if you want, that is easy. You just place the sandwich on this side, then a scoop of whatever salad you choose in the smaller section. You have four salads to choose from, and six different sandwiches, so you can do lots of different combinations."

"You're amazing," Nat marveled. "I can't imagine being able to do all of this."

"I'll get you into the first cooking class that I host here," Zoe promised.

"If I'm still here," Nat said glumly. "My publicist is going nuts that I've dropped off the radar. I told them I needed some time off, and they know the trouble that I've been having. I'm really excited about being able to be normal for a change."

"Once you're set free, you mean," Emma laughed. "Patrick is so nervous, thanks to JJ. We had the security company out to review everything, and he's debating hiring private guards for the weekend. Not for the stuff, that can all be replaced, but he's nervous about Nat and I being alone there."

"I don't want that," Natalie objected. "I came here to escape all the craziness, having a bodyguard will just make me feel like I'm back in Los Angeles."

"It might be a good idea," Zoe said. "I know JJ is really stressed about all of this. But once it's over, we'll be back to normal, I hope."

"Although ski season will be here soon enough," Emma laughed. "It's hard to find a quiet time around here, although Patrick keeps telling me how it usually is."

"Maybe before he put Windsor Peak on the map," Zoe guessed. "Now our tourist traffic is almost year-round, all people just hoping to get a look at him. Or pass him a script. What have you been doing since you arrived, Nat?"

"Reading, riding horses with the trainer," she said. "I got to know the Burrow's family over the years, so it's been great to spend time with them. And the babies are so cute, it's nice to go sit with one and give Kendra and Shea a chance to sleep or shower. Stella is trying to teach me to bake, and I've managed to avoid burning down their house. Oh, and that delicious looking trainer comes by to work out with Patrick, which makes for good entertainment."

"You should see Mike," Emma told Zoe. "He's completely tongue tied around her. She went down in workout clothes the other day and he practically ran out of the house. Patrick said he's going to have to send her next door so he can get his workouts in without the distraction."

Zoe carefully filled a tray with baked ziti and closed the lid as Emma and Natlie told stories about life at Patrick's house. They provided the perfect distraction from her thoughts and gave her the energy she needed to prep for the festival opening the next day. The restaurant would be packed this evening with tourists anxious for the fun to start, and her staff would be on edge with so much pressure. Adding the new options to sell at the booth would have added more stress for them all, so she was grateful for the free help.

"What are you lost in thought over?" Emma demanded, hand on her hip. "I just asked you the same question three times."

"Sorry," she laughed. "What was it?"

"How was the family dinner the other night?"

"Oh, it was good. JJ's family is amazing," she said.

"Why do I feel like there is a but in there? You're frowning," Emma said. "Isn't she, Nat?"

"Definitely," the star nodded.

"JJ's parents want to throw us a wedding reception," she said in a rush. "I guess I didn't realize that it was still festering, because that's not even what I thought I would say."

"That's nice of them," Natalie said. "What's the problem?"

"I don't know," she admitted. "Our wedding was a rush, I never really had time to stop and think about it. I mean, obviously I knew what I was doing, and you both asked me if I wanted to do it or run away. But it still doesn't feel real all the time, although I am getting more comfortable."

"You bought a house together," Emma said. "I thought you were all in?"

"I am," she said slowly. "But my mind and my heart are two different things. My mind is telling me to be careful, not to get too invested or do things that mean this is forever."

"And the reception would mean that?" Emma asked, looking concerned.

"I think so, yes," she said. "I don't know why. I really like his family, I always have. I adore his parents and getting to share them now and have his mom text me and Finley together. Did I tell you she named the group chat 'my girls'?"

"That's sweet," Emma said.

"What if I break all of their hearts? This isn't natural for me, being open and letting people in. If I do that, and then it all becomes too much and I have to leave—"

"That's not happening," Emma said. "You are already in way deeper than you even realize. I'm here, and I know you won't leave me. And look at all of this, you thought this up and are seeing it through. Kendra can't do this alone, and I know you wouldn't let her down. Plus, this is a dream come true, having this space here and being creative. And I think you know how you feel about JJ. You're in deep, Zo."

"I have to agree," Natalie said. "This gives all the signs of someone who has dug in roots. I think you belong here."

The two other women looked so certain, but Zoe couldn't quiet the voice inside her head. The one that pointed out yet again that she was most likely unlovable and stood to lose all of this if JJ left her.

***

The next morning Zoe supervised the sous chefs who had signed up to help her stock and man the table for the first day of the festival. They had been able to secure a spot near the road, so

233

loading and unloading for stock would be easy. The rolling refrigerated carts were pulled off the trailer and placed behind the tables, where menus and some samples would be kept. Kendra also had a small hot workstation where she could demonstrate some of the dishes she had prepped for cooking lessons.

JJ pulled up after they finished unloading and surveyed the offerings. "I know where I'm stopping for lunch."

"Nice of you to come when everything is done," she quipped.

"I know how to time things out," he answered. "You were late last night and out early this morning, want me to get you a coffee?"

"I'd love that," she said. "Emma said they would be setting up with coffee early, if you want to pop over there. I'm sure she'll have some pastries too."

"I can take a hint," he said, winking at her over his shoulder as he walked away.

She helped to finalize the details and then watched as people began filing into the area. Even as early as it was, locals and tourists alike came in looking at the vendors items and beginning to play the games that would raise money for charity. Of course, the biggest line was for Patrick at the animal shelter space, and she laughed as he picked up a puppy from the pen to hold in a picture. Soon the person he had taken the picture with was holding the dog, and she was confident that puppy would be finding a home today.

The cooking demonstrations were well attended, and they sold out of the prepared meals faster than anyone had planned.

Before lunch she had to send the sous chef back to the kitchen to prepare more, and they had to call in two more staff members to make them fast enough. Kendra would be thrilled to hear that their trial was working, and that busy locals were clamoring for more options in both the crockpot meals and ready to cook trays.

"How's it going?" Emma popped up next to her in the booth, having snuck in the back to avoid the crowd. She carried a cup of coffee and a pastry bag, which Zoe accepted with a smile.

"It's been so busy," she said. "I feel like the crowds are even bigger than last year."

"I wasn't here last year," Emma replied. "But I'm sure the advertisements that Patrick was going to be here helped. I heard the Inn has been sold out for months, and most of the other hotels and rental properties as well."

"I guess it's good that he met someone and wanted to stick around," Zoe smiled at her sister. "Here, I put some sandwiches aside for you both." She pulled the trays out of the cooler and passed them to Emma.

"Patrick will be thrilled, he was starting to look hangry," Emma said. "And no one likes when that happens."

"How is Nat holding up?"

"She's spending the morning with Kendra," Emma said. "Helping with Calle and the baby. Shea was going to stop over as well, I think. And Stella was going to be around, she said they would come to the festival tomorrow when Charlie is working at the dunk tank. Everyone wants to have a chance to sink him."

"I'm glad she has company, I'm sure for someone who's used to being busy this must be boring."

"I think it's what she needs," Emma said. "Of course, if you want more attention here, we can always get her to come down."

"I barely have enough food as it is," Zoe laughed. "And the demonstrations are going well. I think we'll have a full class for the first round of lessons."

"Whenever they are, sign me and Nat up," Emma said. "We both need to improve our cooking."

"I'll end up with a class full of men, trying to get her attention," Zoe laughed.

"Might be a good advertising technique," Emma said as she started to slip out the back of the tent. "Have Nat do one night and Patrick the other, you can have the best of both worlds."

Zoe surveyed the crowd, frowning as she realized that JJ still wasn't in the area. She had saved him lunch, figuring he would come by to say hi when he got hungry, but it was getting late. JJ had been convinced that the festival meant the criminal activity would amp up, but she had been hopeful that the increased police presence and more people would chase them away. His absence here made her think that maybe he was right with his concerns after all.

****

It was late afternoon by the time JJ made his way into the festival area, and he was stopped every few feet by locals and vendors. Zoe was finishing a demonstration when he finally made his way to her booth, and she smiled at him standing in the back of the crowd.

"Need a taste tester?" he called out when she finished, and the locals in the crowd laughed.

"JJ is my biggest fan," she told the tourists who looked back to see who had asked the question.

"Also, her husband," Piper called out, causing the crowd to smile.

The crowd dispersed, and she handed him the plate of stir fry that she had just completed. All day she had been dividing the portion up among the crowd watching, but she knew he must be hungry and had made the decision to save it for him.

"Thank you for this," he said before kissing her. "And for that. You have no idea how much I needed both."

"I had saved you a sandwich, and you never came by," she said. "Busy day?"

"Very," he said. "I feel like I can't walk two feet without someone stopping me. Rumors are flying that everyone is in danger, and people are nervous about everything from their dog being home alone to having their purse stolen. But no major issues, outside of the usual parking situations."

"That's good," she said. "Must be a relief for you."

"It is," he agreed. "Patrick texted and asked if we wanted to go up to his house after this closes for a late dinner and drinks. You up for that?"

"Sounds perfect, if you can get away."

"Yes, by then I should be free," he said. "My parents went and picked up Tedy for us, they thought it would be easier if they kept her for the weekend. I think they're going through the empty nest syndrome all over again, since Colin and the twins are both out of the house."

"That's good, I was worried about Tedy being alone all day," she said. "I was actually going to see if I could leave her with Nat tomorrow, I figured she would have more fun running around with the horses than being home alone."

"Problem solved for us," he said, putting his empty plate in with her dirty dishes. "I feel so much better, that was delicious. Why don't I pick you up at the restaurant, we can leave your car for the night? We both have to be down here early tomorrow anyway, makes sense to just come together."

"That's fine. I'll be there when you finish, don't rush. I'll find something to throw together to bring up to Patrick's."

"He said he would order pizza," JJ called as he started to walk away.

She laughed, yelling back to him before he was out of sight. "It's as if you don't know me at all!"

Chapter 26

After seeing the last vendor safely to their car, JJ shook hands with the state troopers who had been working the detail and said he would see them in the morning. Despite all his nerves about the weekend, the first day had gone off without a hitch. The typical situations with locals finding strange cars in their driveways, or people taking spots in private lots for the entire day, but nothing that indicated his criminal was still in town. All he had to do was get through one more day, and then he could relax.

He made sure everything was secure, then pulled his truck around to the back door of the restaurant to get Zoe. It looked packed, with people waiting on the front porch and the sidewalk, and a peek through the window showed the bar was three people deep. Good news for Kendra, and for Des, who was hard at work and probably raking in tips.

Zoe looked up as he walked in, and her smile helped him relax further. She looked happy to see him, and had thought to feed him earlier, showing she had been worried about him. The little things that she did to show her feelings meant so much to him, since she was still reluctant to tell him directly.

"Ready to go?"

She glanced around the busy kitchen and shrugged. "Everything is running smoothly here, so yes. Let me just grab the trays I made."

He took them from her, laughing at the amount of food she had prepared. "I told you he was going to order food."

"You know I can't show up empty handed," she argued. "I just thew a couple salads together, and some snacks. Oh, and a few desserts."

He placed everything carefully in the back seat of the truck before opening the door for her. "Are you okay with going straight there, or do you want to stop at home first?"

"I already changed," she said. "I keep an extra set of clothes here just in case. But if you need to stop, we can."

He gestured to the jeans and long-sleeve raglan he wore, smiling at her. "Clearly, I'm already changed."

They chatted about the rest of the day, and the people they had seen, as they drove up to Patrick's house. Former neighbors tended to return for the weekend, and it turned into an impromptu reunion for many of their friends. Since they were both transplants to the area, they missed out on a lot of the festivities but enjoyed meeting the former residents.

When they pulled into Patrick's driveway, Dan and Jake's cars were already parked, and Mike pulled in just behind them. "I can't believe he's going to have dinner with Natalie," JJ said. "Patrick said he completely freaked out when he saw she was here."

"Poor guy," she said. "You guys need to leave him alone. He just needs to get used to her being around."

"Kind of like when you met me," she laughed. "Knocked you right off your feet."

"Sure did," he said, smiling as he helped her from the truck. "Still do every day."

"Hey guys," Mike called out. "Want some help?"

The two men grabbed the trays, and they walked up to ring the bell, hearing Patrick call from the other side to come in. JJ shook his head, opening the door to the party and meeting Patrick's eyes when he did. "I told you to make sure the house is locked up tight this weekend," he said.

"I did," Patrick objected. "We're all here now."

"Two major celebrities under the same roof, with an unlocked door," JJ grumbled, making a point of locking the door behind him.

"I wouldn't have let anything happen to them," Jake called out from the couch, where he sat holding a sleeping baby.

"You look ready to attack," JJ rolled his eyes. "Tell your brother to keep the door locked and it won't be a problem."

"Wow, someone is grumpy," Dan laughed. He was also holding a baby, walking from the kitchen to the living room with the baby on his chest and a glass of wine in his hand.

"It's been a long week," JJ sighed.

"Have a beer," Patrick said. "Relax."

"I have to drive us home," he said automatically.

"I'll drive," Zoe offered. "I'm tired anyway, so a cup of coffee sounds better than wine."

"Do you have news for us?" Shea appeared from the door that led to Patrick's lower level, which contained a gym and a media room.

"News?" Zoe looked at JJ with a confused look on her face, and he laughed.

"They think you're pregnant," he told her.

"Oh! No, nothing like that," Zoe said. "I was just on my feet all day and I'm wiped. Plus, I know how much JJ needs to be able to unwind right now. Nothing more than that, I promise."

"I guess we have enough babies for now," Shea said, hugging her quickly. "I'm happy to see you guys."

Before either of them could respond, a noise from above had them all looking up. Natalie, striking in a cream-colored ankle-length cardigan, worn over a tank top and a skintight pair of jeans, descended the stairs. "Did everyone make it?" she paused to hug Zoe on her way to the sitting area. "Oh, hello, Michael."

They all laughed as Mike's face turned a bright shade of red and he stuttered out a greeting to her. Zoe linked her arm through Natalie's and pulled her toward the kitchen, discussing whether the sweater was cashmere as they walked away.

Patrick handed JJ a beer and gestured to the couch. "Take a load off." They moved to sit with Dan, Jake and Mike, while the women clustered around the island in the attached kitchen.

"You might want to figure out how to talk to her," JJ said to Mike, nodding in Natalies direction. "Maybe you could practice in the mirror or something."

"It's not that easy," Mike argued. "You guys just don't get it."

Dan handed his sleeping baby to JJ, then leaned back on the couch. "Want some advice from an old married guy?"

"First of all, you're not that much older than me," Mike said. "And b, it took you almost twenty years to figure out your mistakes and win Kendra over."

"It wasn't that long," Dan argued. "I feel like you're underestimating my wisdom."

Jake laughed. "Don't ask me. I'm fully aware that I'm lucky Shea saw something in me and was able to wait until I came back. If she hadn't been persistent in writing to me all those years, who knows where I would be."

"We're all glad for that," Patrick said. "But in all honesty, Nat isn't that scary. You can talk to her just like anyone else."

"I think it would be easier if you all would butt out a little," Mike said. "Too many eyes on me, know what I mean?"

"Maybe you can help us out tomorrow," Patrick suggested. "The girls kept her busy today, but they want to go to the festival tomorrow and show off the babies. I'm worried about leaving Nat alone here, because if she gets antsy, she might just come to town. Want to come up and go for a ride with her, or you could do a workout with her?"

"You want me to work out with Natalie Cloud?"

"That is what you do for a living," Patrick said drolly. "Why not work out, then go for a ride. That will take up a lot of the day and keep her out of trouble."

"And probably get *me* into a world of trouble," Mike said softly.

"It would be a huge help," JJ threw in. "I'll feel better knowing that she's not alone."

"Fine," Mike sighed, as if they had asked him to walk barefoot up the mountain in the snow.

The other men all looked at each other and laughed, getting the attention of the women in the next room who demanded to be let in on the joke. Dan quickly covered for them all, talking about a noise one of the babies had made, and Mike looked less terrified when they seemed to believe it. The two babies were collected by their mothers to be put down in portable cribs when the pizza was delivered, and the adults all crowded around the table to eat.

JJ relaxed, content with a full stomach, a beer in his hand, and his wife at his side. The festival was half over, and all was good in his world. He just needed to get through the next twenty-four hours so he could settle back into his normal, quiet life.

***

Early the next morning, JJ walked Zoe over to the festival tent, where sleepy vendors were starting to set up. The state troopers were visible around the perimeter as people set up their cash boxes and carried in inventory, and JJ felt safe leaving her there. JJ kept scanning the town, feeling as though something was off, but he couldn't see anything out of place.

"I'll definitely be by for lunch," he promised. He leaned in, kissing her softly before placing her tote bag under the table for her. The two restaurant staff members who would be helping her for the day were busy setting up, and Zoe was already distracted as she checked their work.

"Okay, I'll see you later," she said.

"Zoe?" He waited until she looked up and focused on him. "Have a good morning. Remember that I love you."

He went to the station to get a briefing on the night before, happy to hear that other than a few people sleeping off a day of drinking in their holding cells, not much had happened. One local had reported their car stolen, only to find out their teenage son had taken it out to go for a late-night ride with his girlfriend. And one fight had been quickly broken up, the two men making up before either could be handcuffed.

Nick Sharp walked joined him in his office to go through the plan for the day, helping to plug in officers where they would be most needed. "The parking lot at the library and the school might need attention," he said. "People were parking on the grass and blocking other cars in. Not to mention, that's a lot of unsecured vehicles that could be targets."

"Good idea," JJ said. "But where can we pull them from?"

They huddled over the town map, deciding where two officers could be reduced to one, and radioed the new assignments out. A groan came back over the radio as one was moved from downtown to the library parking lot. "Is this because I ate too many free samples yesterday?" he asked, causing both men to laugh.

"Yes, Jeff," Nick replied. "The pizza shop especially has had it with you."

"Thanks for helping with all of this," JJ said. "Where are you headed first? I know you're on rove patrol, keeping an eye on everything like me."

"I thought I would do a quick sweep through the rentals near the base of the mountain," Nick replied. "All those Airbnb rentals that will be checked out of this morning, and the cleaning crews going in. I want to make sure we don't have another unexpected guest there. Then I'll stick with the back roads, since most of the downtown is covered."

"Perfect, I'll call if I need you," JJ said. They both took a final sip of their mugs of coffee before pulling on jackets. "One last day of this."

"You're forgetting that the new Christmas Festival will be coming up in just a few weeks," Nick laughed.

"One thing at a time," JJ groaned. "That's all I can handle."

***

The crowds were slower to grow on the second day of the festival, with a lot of the tourists sleeping in after late nights in town. After the checkout times at the Inn and other rentals passed, the town square would fill with everyone wanting to get their last bit of fun in before their drive home. JJ was able to stop in the tent just before that crush of people would arrive, grabbing his lunch and a kiss from Zoe, before any calls came in.

He ate the sandwich in his car as he drove over to the school parking lot to help settle a debate over the last parking spot, then visited the animal shelter which reported a faulty alarm sounding. Realizing it was a smoke alarm, he called for the fire department to handle it before setting back out.

He quickly dialed his parents' house on his cell phone, amused as always that they were still determined to maintain a landline. His father answered on the second ring, the sound of Tedy barking present in the background.

"Is everything okay, Dad?"

"Of course," he replied, crunching on something. "Why do you ask?"

"Why is Tedy going crazy?"

"Oh, your mother decided to make a big Sunday breakfast," he answered. "Bacon and sausage and waffles. Tedy seems keen on the bacon."

"She's a dog, she'll eat almost anything," he said. "Don't spoil her, Zoe doesn't want her to beg for food."

"What's the point of a grandparent if we don't spoil? Hang on, your mother wants to talk to you."

"Jeremiah," his mom said, and he closed his eyes briefly. The only time his mother used his actual name was when she wanted something, and it was never good. "I was thinking about something."

"That's not good for anyone."

"Don't be fresh," she chastened him. "I really think you and Zoe should have a wedding here. I know you didn't want to talk about it and push her, but everyone wants to celebrate. And this whole Vegas thing is really bothering your father."

"Is it? Or is it bothering you?"

"Both of us," she replied. "Will you please talk to Zoe? Tell her how much it means to us."

"I'll see what I can do," he sighed. "After this weekend. And a few days to recover, we are both exhausted. She's also got a new business starting up, and it might not be a good time."

"There is always time to celebrate love," his mother said. "Make it happen."

"I have to run, Mom."

"Be safe. I love you."

"Love you too," he said, clicking end on the phone screen. As much as he would love to have a huge wedding in Windsor Peak, until Zoe broached the subject herself, he was going to keep quiet. He might be able to drop a few ideas here and there, but that was it. He wasn't risking losing her over a party, no matter how much he might agree with his mother.

His phone rang, and he frowned when he saw Patrick's name on the screen. His friend should be busy at the festival, not making social calls. "Hey, Patrick."

"Hey bud," Patrick said, the sound of the crowd around him almost drowning him out. "My alarm keeps sending me faulty messages. The service guy was out last week and must have reset something wrong. Everyone is down here, and I hate to disrupt their day, do you have anyone in the area that can swing by and make sure all is okay?"

"I'll go up myself," JJ said. "I'm not far."

"Thanks, I appreciate it. Mike was there with Natalie, they might still be out on the horses now," he said. "Neither of them is answering their phones, but they might have left them behind when they went out for a ride."

The hairs on the back of JJ's neck stood up, sensing something was wrong. There was no way Natalie would have left without her phone, he knew that for certain, even after only knowing her a short time. She was never without it, even in outfits where it seemed physically impossible for her to hide it. Forcing his voice to stay calm, he told Patrick he would update him shortly and ran to his car.

Chapter 27

Zoe felt herself hit the wall in the late afternoon. Shoppers from out of town were pulling crying children out of the tent to start the drive home, denying them the last bit of candy or a try at the carnival games. They looked even more exhausted than she felt, and they had to drive home, so she felt bad for them. Other vendors were yawning and checking their watches, looking forward to the closing time just before dinner.

Emma came through with a tray of coffees and cookies to hand out to her neighbors, all of which were taken with gratitude. "How are you doing," she asked Zoe when she stopped by.

"Good," Zoe said, choosing a coffee and cookie. "Thank you for this, I had no idea this would be as exhausting as it's been."

"But hugely successful, from the looks of it. You've been slammed all weekend with people watching your cooking class and buying food," Emma said.

"Yes, that's true. We are almost full already for the first run of cooking lessons, and we don't even have a start date yet," she laughed. "And the premade meals are selling like hotcakes, as are the crockpot dump meals. I have a list of recipe ideas from talking with people, so that will keep me busy all week."

"When does Jake think you'll be able to open?"

"I saw him this morning, and he said he would really put a rush on it," Zoe said. "He said Shea was excited about it, so that means he needs to get moving."

"Good plan, always appeal to the wife," Emma laughed. "And the man's stomach."

"True. How are things over your way?"

"Good," Emma said. "Piper is over there now, so I was able to make the rounds quickly. The Burrows are all over watching Charlie get dunked, with Dan and Jake being the two primary dunkers. Patrick took a quick turn too, and once people found out that was his nephew, the line grew."

"What do they hope to accomplish with that?"

"Who knows," Emma shrugged. "Any connection to him is a good one, I guess. Piper said our sales are at least triple what they were last year, and she thinks it's just people who want to get a look at me. Apparently, being Patrick's girlfriend makes me worthy of gawking."

"That's both flattering and totally creepy," Zoe said. "I'm surprised you didn't run for cover."

"I thought about it, but Piper's my friend. And if me drawing attention gets her more business, I'm okay with it." Emma glanced over to where Patrick was still surrounded by fans, the last of the dogs and cats who needed new homes sitting next to him. "I am going to check on Patrick before I get back to the booth. I'll see you when we close up."

Zoe checked her schedule and saw she only had two more cooking demonstrations to do, which meant there was a light at the end of the tunnel. She double checked ingredients while the other two staff members handled sales and started heating a pan just before the next session.

A small crowd started gathering right when the hour changed, and she was due to start. She greeted everyone with a smile and indicated the hot pan. "Hi everyone, thank you for joining us. I want to warn you all that this pan is very hot and ask that you please keep any little hands from reaching over to touch. I love having kids here to learn about cooking, I just want to make sure everyone stays safe," she said.

A woman in the crowd, holding a little girl, asked about mommy and me cooking lessons. "I think we could absolutely do that," she nodded. "Let me touch base with Kendra and we can make plans. I know Calle would love it too, so I'm sure she will say yes. Keep an eye on the website or ask next time you come in for dinner."

She poured some olive oil in the pan and took a tray of scallops from one of the staff members. "I'm going to show you how to do seared scallops with a garlic butter sauce," she told the crowd. "I know this seems like a fancy dish, but it's very easy to make at home. The first thing you want to do is dry the scallops and then season them with salt and pepper, so we'll do that while the oil heats." She quickly prepped the food to be cooked, and when the oil looked hot, placed them carefully in the pan. "They will cook quickly, so I'll keep an eye on them. We'll flip after just two minutes, and as you can see, I already have the other ingredients ready. This is not a dish you can walk away from to search for things while it cooks."

The crowds laughed softly, and she flipped the scallops, happy to see they were perfectly caramelized and browned on the bottom. She looked up to explain to the crowd what the coloring indicated and frowned when she saw them part for Nick Sharp to come through. He looked intense and his gaze was focused on her, and his uniform let everyone know who he was, so the crowd parted easily.

"Hi, Nick," she said uneasily. "I'm just in the middle of something."

"I need someone to take over," he looked at the others in the booth. "You need to come with me right now."

"What's wrong?" She glanced around, seeing Emma hurry toward Patrick with a worried look on her face. Patrick was talking intensely with another local officer, Jeff, and glanced over at her.

Eduardo, one of her sous chefs, gently took the spatula from her hand and removed the pan from the heat. She watched as he slid the scallops onto a plate and then gave her a head nod indicating she should slip out and he would take over. As she stepped back and removed her apron, she heard him start talking to the crowd about melting butter, taking the attention away from her.

"Nick, please tell me what's going on," she said.

"Let's get out of here for some privacy," he said. He led her through the back of the tent, where she found Patrick and Emma, along with the other officer. "I'll just get right to it. There was apparently a break-in up at Patrick's house. You have a houseguest, correct?"

"I do," Patrick said, his face going pale. "Is Nat okay?"

"She's fine," Nick nodded. "But she and Mike were there when the guy broke in. They were able to send a distress code through the alarm company, which came through to you as a fault, from what I understand."

"Yes," Patrick said. "I called JJ and asked if he could go take a look. It just kept alerting my phone that something was wrong with the system."

Zoe felt lightheaded, seeing the look the two cops exchanged. She reached for Nick's arm and knew when he looked at her what he was going to say. "JJ went there?"

Nick nodded, then cleared his throat. "Yes," he said. "He was injured. We need to get you to the hospital right now."

"Injured how?" Emma cried.

The two cops exchanged a look again, and this time Jeff stepped forward. "He was shot. We need to go, now."

"Is he alive?" Zoe whispered, feeling the tears falling down her cheeks. She felt Emma's arms go around her and heard her sisters soft sobs.

"Last we heard, yes. But we have to go. Now." Jeff put an arm around her and pulled her toward the state police cruiser sitting at the curb. "The state police are going to take you guys to the hospital. One of us will meet you there as soon as we can."

They climbed into the back of the waiting SUV, and it took off, siren blaring into the streets. Zoe watched numbly as friends and tourists stopped to look at the noise as it flew by but wasn't able to comprehend anything. She felt Emma's tight grip on her hand and saw Patrick frantically texting from the other side of her sister.

"Is Natalie okay? And Mike?" she asked Patrick, her voice breaking as she did.

"Yes," he said. "Mike just texted me that they are on the way to the hospital, but both are fine. Nat is really shaken up, but nothing that we can't deal with. I'm trying to get Stella to go get JJ's parents, and his siblings."

"Oh, I should have thought of that," she said, fumbling for her phone before realizing it was still at the festival, in her tote bag. She hadn't thought to grab it when Nick had approached her, and she wasn't going back for it now.

The drive seemed to take forever, although the cop was going as fast as he could. The traffic leaving town for the highway was backed up, and getting through even with the siren was difficult. Zoe nervously chewed on a fingernail and stared out the window, trying to wrap her head around the possibility of a world without JJ.

He was so full of life, and just radiated joy. He always had a smile on his face, even when he was having a bad day, and he had told her once that it helped others to see someone happy. He chose happiness always, because he knew it would help those around him, and that was who he was at his essence. From the first day she had met him until this afternoon when she last saw him, he had never faltered in trying to make her smile. And he succeeded more often than not, helping her to relax and settle into a new town, and accept people as friends.

It simply wasn't possible to have him gone. She refused to allow herself to think of it, to even allow the universe the option to take him away. He was to good to be taken out of the world, too bright of a light for so many people. Not to mention, he was the air she breathed, and the reason she was a part of this town. His leaving her not of his own accord had never entered her mind, and now was she not only against that, she didn't want him leaving her for any reason.

They finally pulled up to the door to the emergency department of the hospital, and the state trooper got out to free them from the car. "I can't come in with you," he said. "But I am thinking of him and hoping he will pull through. If we can do anything for you, Mrs. Monahan, please just let us know."

"Thank you," she murmured. *Mrs. Monahan. Mrs. Monahan.* The words reverberated around her head, and she found herself twisting the ring on her left hand, desperate for any connection to JJ. Patrick hesitated as he started to lead the way into the hospital, which spurred Emma into action. She led them both into the waiting room, holding out a hand when a fan tried to approach Patrick.

"This isn't the time," she said quickly. "Please." The fan backed down instantly and apologized, and the trio made their way to the information desk. "We need to find out where my sisters' husband is," she said to the nurse behind the desk.

"Who is your husband," the nurse asked Zoe, who found herself unable to respond.

"Monahan," Emma replied.

"First name?"

Emma hesitated and looked at Zoe. "Sorry, Zo, I only know him as JJ."

"Jeremiah," she said dully. "Officer Jeremiah Monahan, of the Windsor Peak police."

The nurse's eyes locked on Patrick, as if seeing him for the first time, and her attitude changed instantly. "Of course, Mrs. Monahan," she said quickly. "Follow me."

They followed her at a fast pace through a busy emergency room, and Zoe blocked out the sounds of people crying and all the beeping. All she wanted was to hear JJ's voice calling out to her, telling her that he loved her, and he was safe. But they walked all the way through and came out a back door into a hallway, where they racewalked behind the nurse to a different waiting room. "Wait here," she said, then disappeared.

Patrick guided each of them into chairs, positioning Zoe between himself and Emma. He stood again and crossed the room for a box of tissues, passing them to Emma before sitting down again. The three of them sat in tense silence, the only sounds that of the staff talking in murmurs as they walked down the hall.

"What is taking so long? I'll go find someone to talk to," Emma said, starting to stand.

"Please, don't leave me." Zoe started to feel like she couldn't breathe, as though someone were sitting on her chest.

"Are you okay?" Emma looked at her with concern.

"No," Zoe heard herself say. "I can't breathe. And I feel cold." She realized her whole body was shaking, and Patrick quickly pulled off his sweatshirt and wrapped it around her.

"You could be going into shock," Patrick said. "We should get a doctor for you."

"No," she said. "I just need to know what's happening with him. There's nothing wrong with me."

"Let me see what I can find out," he stood to leave, but the nurse from the lobby reappeared.

"The doctor is on his way out now," she said.

As she finished speaking, an older man appeared, wearing scrubs, his head covered in a surgical cap. "Which one of you is the officer's wife?"

"I am," Zoe said, standing. Patrick moved to stand next to her, Emma on the other side.

"We are taking him in for surgery. He's lost a lot of blood, but he was conscious when he came in. He was asking for you, the nurse will come out and share more about that," the doctor said. "The bullet didn't come out the other side, so we need to get it out and see what damage was done."

"Is he going to be okay?" Patrick asked, since Zoe wasn't able to form the words.

"A few inches away, and he'd be gone already," the doctor replied. "I'm going to do my best to make sure he pulls through. If you believe in a higher power, this would be a good time to call on them. I'll have a nurse update you as we go."

The doctor turned to leave, and Zoe found her voice. "Can I see him first?"

"I'm sorry," he shook his head. "He's already being prepped. I need to get in there."

"Please save him," she whispered, and it appeared that he heard her as he walked away. Patrick took her elbow and guided her back to the chair, then pulled out his phone, texting quickly. The silence of the room was only interrupted by his fingers flying over the screen, but she didn't have the energy to ask him what was going on.

Maggie and Frank came flying around a corner and almost ran right past them, but Emma called out to them before they went too far. "Oh, honey," Maggie cried, stretching her arms to Zoe. "Come here. We're here, we'll get through this."

Zoe hadn't realized she was crying again until she found herself on her feet, wrapped in the arms of JJ's mother. And his father, she realized, feeling his arm join Maggie's around her shoulders. The unexpected comfort brought new tears, and it took her a minute to compose herself and step back.

"The doctor was just here, he's taking JJ in for surgery," she said. "We don't know much."

"He's alive," Maggie said. "That's all we need to know right now. He is going to be okay."

"How do you know that?"

"I'm his mom, and I refuse to believe anything else," she said, her eyes shining with tears.

Chapter 28

Colin, Desmond and Finley all arrived minutes after their parents, and soon Dan and Jake Burrows appeared, taking the last two empty seats. Patrick stood when his brothers came in, hugging both of them quickly.

"How is Nat?"

"She's okay," Jake said. "Stella and Dad are with her, and Kendra and Shea. Plus, Mike is still up there."

"Is he doing alright?"

"Best as he could be, considering," Dan answered.

Zoe realized that both Natalie and Mike must have been present when JJ was shot, and she looked up at the Burrows brothers. "What did they say happened?"

Jake looked at Patrick, who indicated that he should tell Zoe. "Mike and Natalie went to ride the horses," he said. "They left the back door unlocked, not thinking anything would happen. When they got back, there was a guy there, waving a gun. Saying he was going to take Nat; he would be able to finally get his big payday."

"Oh, she must have been terrified," Emma murmured.

"She was," Jake said. "Mike stayed between them, wouldn't let the guy touch her. He said Nat noticed the alarm pad beside the door and knew it was similar to the one she has in her house, so she just kept putting in random codes. That triggered the alarm company that something was wrong, although they didn't get a distress signal, so they only called Patrick."

"And I called JJ," Patrick admitted. "I feel terrible about that. I thought he would just be able to check it out, I never thought something like this would happen. I'm sorry, Zoe."

"Don't be sorry," she said automatically. "He wouldn't have wanted it any other way."

"He must have seen what was happening through the window, because he came in with his gun already drawn," Jake continued. "Mike threw Natalie on the ground and covered her, and said he just heard JJ yell at the guy to drop it, and then shots were fired. When he didn't hear anything else, he got up and found both of them on the ground."

"He called for help right away," Dan said. "The other guy was already gone, but Mike was able to put pressure on JJ's wound and said he was talking to him when they came to get him."

Jake and Dan exchanged a look, and Zoe's heart felt like it was in a vice. "What did he say?"

"That he wanted you to know how much he loves you," Jake finally said quietly. "And made him promise that we would all look out for you if he didn't make it."

"He has to make it," she said. More tears came, and Emma helped her back to her chair.

Patrick's phone rang, and he stepped out of the waiting room to answer it. He came back a moment later and took his spot next to Zoe. "That was my agent," he said. "I texted her and asked her to make sure JJ was in the best hands possible. She said this doctor has a stellar reputation, and she has a jet ready and waiting in case he needs to go to Boston or New York."

Before she could answer, Kendra's longtime best friend Tina came around the corner. Zoe knew that Tina was a nurse in this hospital and was relieved to see a familiar face.

"I came to give you an update," she said, after greeting everyone. "Dr. Ortiz is still operating, he said it was a little worse than what he was expecting."

Gasps filled the room, and Zoe covered her mouth to keep from screaming. He couldn't die. She met Maggie's eyes and saw the same thing in them, before they both turned back to Tina.

"He's the best we have," she said. "He wasn't even on today, but we called because it's JJ, and he always comes in when it's a first responder. He's a good man and an even better surgeon. There is no one I would trust more."

Zoe nodded numbly, glad to have Tina back up the report that Patrick had gotten. "Is there anything you can tell us?"

"The bullet went into his left upper abdomen," she said. "It missed his heart, which is the good news. A few inches higher and we would be having a much different conversation. It looks like his spleen will need to be removed. His left lung collapsed, so they are putting in a chest tube to help. He did lose a lot of blood, which we are trying to fix now with infusions."

"Is he going to make it?" Zoe whispered, scared to look at Tina.

"He's young, he's strong, and he has a reason to live," Tina replied. "I can't make any promises, but I'd bet on him."

"How much longer do you think it will be?" Maggie asked from behind Zoe.

"Hours, I would think," Tina said. "Dr. Ortiz is meticulous and takes his time. He won't keep him open longer than necessary, but he will make sure he has done everything he can before he closes. I would suggest going home and waiting for us to call, but I don't think any of you would listen."

"Nope," Dan said, crossing his arms. "We're here for the long haul."

"Okay," Tina said. "We're doing everything we can to keep it quiet where Patrick is, but rumors have been spreading since he walked through the emergency department. I was able to get permission to move you all to a room right near the nurses' station, which will be more comfortable and private."

"That's not necessary," Patrick objected.

"It's easier for everyone," Tina explained. "Security is freaking out, so having you out of sight will help."

"Just listen to her," Dan said, clapping Patrick on the back. "Show us the way, Tina."

They all followed her to a room just past the nurses' station, which held a large table, comfortable chairs, and a TV on one wall. "Is this your break room?" Patrick asked Tina after surveying the space.

"It's the doctors lounge," she said. "Our room is not nearly as nice. But they are all in agreement that you should use it, no one is upset."

"Are you sure?"

"Positive," she nodded. "It's a Sunday anyway, so any surgeons who are here are here for a reason, and then they'll be with their patients until it's safe for them to go home. No one has downtime to relax like they do during the week."

"This is so nice of you," Maggie said, hugging Tina quickly. "We appreciate this."

"It's no problem," she said. "I'll be back as soon as I have an update. Zoe, if you need me, I'm right out here, okay?"

Zoe nodded, and then let Emma lead her to a soft chair in the corner. Finley surprised her by coming over with a cup of tea that she handed off before sitting in the chair next to her. Emma slipped away to stand with Patrick, leaving Zoe alone with JJ's sister.

"This is so crazy," Finley said. "We all thought something like this would happen when he worked in the city, but never up here."

"I know," Zoe said. "Even with all the things he was worried about over the last few weeks, this wasn't one of them."

"I feel bad," Finley whispered. "He kept trying to get me to have lunch with him, but I was mad, so I kept putting him off. And now he's like this, and I realize how stupid it was that I was mad at him."

"Why were you mad?"

Finley stared at her cup, as if the answer would appear. Taking a slow sip, she finally turned to Zoe. "I was upset that I wasn't at your wedding, and I acted like a jerk. He accused me of not being happy for him and told me I was being selfish. I told him he was selfish to get married without all of us, and then I stormed off on him."

"Oh, Finley," Zoe said. "I'm so sorry."

"I realize now that it shouldn't matter," she said. "What matters is that you guys are in my life, and I get to be a part of it every day. But my big brother getting married, and me finally getting a sister, and I didn't find out until later? It hurt."

"I feel terrible. I should have thought of it and put him off," Zoe said.

"Would you have still married him if you had time to think about it?"

It was Zoe's turn to sit in silence, trying to wrap her head around the question. What would she have done if JJ had proposed, but she had time to think about it? To let her inner voice panic and try to push him away? He had structured the entire thing for her and sacrificed his own wants in the process. Of course he would have wanted his family there, and he gave that up to make sure she was happy.

"I shouldn't have asked," Finley said. "I'm sorry."

"No," Zoe shook her head. "I was just trying to think of how I would have behaved if we were to come back here. And you're right, I would have found a reason to make it difficult for him. I did that the entire time, really. For two years, he came to see me every day and was nothing but good to me. He asked me out on dates every day, and I said no. When he started asking me to marry him, I thought it was a joke."

"Well, he did tend to ask you after having a good meal," Finley said with a smile.

"And even when things started happening between us, which I'll spare you the details on," Zoe said, making Finley laugh. "I wouldn't let him tell anyone. I wouldn't commit to being in a relationship with him. I made it so hard for him, and he never gave up."

"He loves you," Finley said softly. "He told me that the day after he met you, and I didn't believe him. I didn't think it was possible to fall in love at first sight, but he said it was. That he had met the girl he was going to marry. And then we all met you, and saw him with you, and we knew he was right. He was always so happy when he was with you."

Zoe choked back a sob, feeling as though her heart were breaking. "What if he doesn't make it?"

Finley moved, kneeling in front of Zoe and holding her hands. "And what if he does?"

Zoe was saved from answering by Maggie, who interrupted to tell them that she and Frank were going to spend some time in the chapel. "Have one of the boys run down and get us if they come back with an update," she asked, pulling Finley to her feet for a hug.

The simple moment between mother and daughter had Zoe wishing she had a similar relationship with her own mom. She was so lucky that Maggie had welcomed her to the family and would be a dream of a mother-in-law, but it stung to not have her own mother to turn to in times of crisis. She pushed the thought away, because even if she wanted to call her mom, she didn't have her phone. Better to let the idea fade away and focus on thinking about what she could do differently when JJ was better.

Colin dropped into the chair that Finley had left empty, shooing her away when she glared at him. "How are you holding up," he asked Zoe.

"Not great," she answered. "I just wish we knew what was happening in there."

"Same." He leaned back in the chair, crossing his arms.

"You don't have to babysit me," Zoe said. "If that's what's happening here."

He glanced at her, one eyebrow raised. "You've never had brothers. This is what we do."

"What's that?"

"We'll have your back, always. I'll always be here if you need me," he told her. "Des too."

"And Finley."

"Yes, but she's here for different things," he said. "Girl stuff."

"Girl stuff?"

"You know," he waved his hand. "The tears and whatnot. Plus, when JJ is better, you can get your nails done or go shopping with her."

"Wow," Zoe laughed. "Women do more than that, Colin. I'm surprised at you."

"I don't mean it that way," he said. "I just mean that you'll be able to hang out with Finley all the time. But Des and I will always show up when you need us. That's all I meant."

"I can't hang out with you guys?"

He rolled his eyes. "Not at this rate. You're making me regret coming over here."

She laughed lightly. "Well, at least you made me think about something other than what's happening with JJ right now."

"He's going to be okay," Colin said.

"How do you know?"

"He's my big brother," Colin said. "He's never let me down. He won't start now. Plus, he has something to live for now."

They sat in silence for a minute before Zoe responded. "I hope you're right."

"I always am," he said with a wink. "I'm going to see if the Burrows boys can get this TV on, at least we can have a football game on to distract us."

The Burrows brothers and Colin pulled chairs over to the TV, putting the football game on mute. Finley and Emma came and settled on either side of Zoe, chatting quietly about light topics in a clear attempt to distract Zoe. Someone brought in a tray of sandwiches and refilled the coffee carafes, and time seemed to crawl.

The minute the door opened, revealing Dr. Ortiz, everyone jumped to their feet. Zoe went from feeling as though time had stopped to suddenly feeling like it was moving too fast. Desmond jumped to his feet and ran out of the room in the direction of the chapel, and she was glad someone had the foresight to get Maggie and Frank.

"Should I wait for him?" the doctor asked, looking in the direction Des had disappeared.

"He went to get our parents," Colin explained.

Desmond came crashing back into the room, his parents just behind him. "Sorry, we're here."

Maggie started crying, rushing to link arms with Zoe. "Please, tell us doctor. Is Jeremiah going to be okay?"

Chapter 29

The doctor took a deep breath, and took his time pulling the surgical cap off his head and throwing it into the trash can in the room. "It was a long day," he said. "He was in rough shape when he came in. The bullet went in a few inches below his heart and was lodged inside, so I had to get it out. He lost a lot of blood, and we had to take out his spleen."

"But he's alive?" Zoe whispered, hope filling her heart.

"He is," Dr. Ortiz said. "The next few hours will be crucial. He went through a lot of trauma and his body needs to recover. Once he wakes up, he will be in a lot of pain. But first, we need to monitor him closely to make sure that he will wake up. He will be in the ICU, at least for tonight, so that he will have a nurse with him at all times."

"Can we see him?"

The doctor hesitated, looking at the large crowd in front of him. "One person at a time, and I'd prefer it just be his wife and his parents for tonight. I know you all care about him, but we need to focus on his health."

Tina appeared behind the doctor, catching Zoe's eye and smiling. The doctor turned and noticed her, then looked back at Zoe. "If you want to go with Tina now, she can take you to him. Unless you want his mother to go first?"

"No," Maggie said, giving Zoe a push. "You go."

"Maggie, I feel like it should be you," she said. "You're his mom."

"And you're the love of his life," she said. "I know my boy, and I know who he wants next to him right now."

Finley stepped forward and hugged Zoe fiercely. "Remember what I said. This is your second chance, don't be afraid to make the right choices. Love him the way your heart wants to."

Zoe blinked back tears and hugged Emma quickly before turning to follow Tina. She turned back just before leaving the room and met the doctor's eyes. "Thank you. I can't tell you how grateful I am for you. I don't know what I would have done if he hadn't made it."

"You're very welcome," Dr. Ortiz said. "It's my great honor to work on a hero like your husband."

Tina led the way out of the room, walking quickly so Zoe rushed to catch up with her. "I want to prepare you for what you'll see," she said. "He is still intubated, so he has a tube down his throat. That's to help him breathe, and to help his lung heal. He also has a lot of leads on him, monitoring his blood pressure, pulse, and oxygen. There is a tube coming out of his chest on the side of his injury, which is helping with the collapsed lung. He's heavily sedated right now, to allow his body time to heal, so he will not wake up while you're in there."

"Can he hear me if I talk to him?"

"We think so," Tina nodded. "A lot of people wake up and know who had been with them, others are so out cold they don't remember anything. But it certainly can't hurt, so go ahead and talk."

"How long will he be sedated?"

"I don't know," Tina answered. "It could just be a few more hours, or it could be longer. They want to get his lung to reinflate first, so that he can breathe comfortably on his own. In order to keep him intubated, they have to keep him sedated. He would fight and pull it out if he were to start waking up, so they closely monitor."

They stopped outside a glass door, and Zoe could see activity on the other side around a bed. All she could see from her angle were legs that were covered with a blanket, and more still than she had ever seen JJ. "Tina," she said, just as the other woman was about to open the door. "Do you think he will wake up and be okay?"

"Yes," Tina said confidently. "I know this is scary, and we never really know what will happen. But I think that he will be fine. And I don't say that often, or lightly."

"Thank you," Zoe said softly.

"You ready?"

Zoe nodded, making a point to stand up straighter and force herself to act as though she was strong enough for this. If the roles were reversed, she knew JJ would be strong and hold it together, and she wanted to do that for him. She wanted to be someone he would be proud of when he woke up, and that was worthy of his and his families love.

Tina pushed the glass door open, and Zoe was surprised at the amount of noise on the other side. Through the glass it looked like a silent ballet, with three nurses working quickly and efficiently around JJ's still body. Once she was inside, she could hear them talking, along with the beeps and other sounds from machines on either side of him. Tina indicated a chair that was close to JJ on the side away from his injury, and she sank into it gratefully. She reached for his hand and then hesitated, seeing all the wires attached to him that were across the bed.

The nurse opposite her smiled and gestured for her to touch him. "It's okay," he said. "You won't disrupt anything."

She smiled at him and then laced her fingers through JJ's, aware of the cooler temperature of his skin and the heaviness of his arm. Forcing herself to stay sitting up and not collapse in a heap of tears on his bed, she focused on what she could handle. The nurses finished their work, and only the young male nurse stayed in the room next to the machines as the others left. She tentatively lifted his arm to rest his hand against her cheek.

"Hey," she said softly. "This was not on our weekend agenda. But of course, this is just like you, why take a leisurely vacation when you can get shot and be forced to take time off? I'm sure you'll be pacing the streets soon, ready to get back but not cleared yet.

Everyone is here. Your parents, the twins and Colin. Dan, Jake and Patrick, who feels terrible, by the way. He looks like he has the weight of the world on his shoulders, so you need to wake up soon and let him know that you're fine so he can relax. He's so grateful to you, but still worried."

She kissed his hand before putting it back against her cheek, using her other hand to smooth his hair. "Emma is here too, of course. I had the oddest moment a while ago, when I was watching your mom with Finley. I almost wished that my mom was here, but that's ridiculous, right? I really need to talk to you about that, because it's confusing. I'm realizing how heavily I've leaned on you for years, without even realizing it. You're my constant, the one thing that I know I can always depend on. I always knew I could talk to you about anything at all, and you would help me without judging. I wish I hadn't wasted two years pretending that what we had wasn't real."

A new noise started, and she jumped, looking across the room to the nurse in confusion. "It's just the blood pressure cuff," he said, pointing to JJ's right arm. "It's right next to you, and it's going to inflate every fifteen minutes."

"Oh, okay. Sorry."

"No worries. I'm here if you have any questions, but otherwise ignore me completely," he said, turning back to the laptop in front of him.

"Will you be in here the whole time?" she asked the nurse, curious about his presence.

"Yes," he nodded. "If not me, another nurse. But someone will be in here around the clock until he's awake, and then we'll probably be moving him to a regular room once he's stable."

She nodded and focused her attention back on JJ. "I know this is pushy of me, but could you hurry up and get back to me? I have a lot that I need to say to you, and I'd prefer to be looking in your eyes when I do. It's been a long time coming and might be worth waking up for."

She sat with him for another half hour, before realizing she should tear herself away so that Maggie could come in. Leaning over to kiss him on his forehead, she told him she would be back, before going to change places with his mother. She let herself out, shocked to see nursing staff running into another room, where a blue light flashed. They were pushing a cart and calling instructions to each other, and it looked like at least ten people surrounding the bed. After looking quickly to make sure that JJ was still okay, she rushed down the hall to get Maggie. She didn't want to waste a single moment that they were allowed to be in the room with him.

***

A short time later, she was back in the room with JJ. During the time his parents had been with him, she had been force-fed a sandwich by Emma and Finley, who were insistent that she needed nourishment. Dan produced her small tote bag that had been left behind at the festival and explained that the staff manning the booth had found it and delivered it on their way home. Fortunately, the bag also contained her charger and a book, as well as a pair of leggings and a sweater that she had planned to slip on after dismantling the booth. Grateful to be able to take off the less comfortable chef coat and pants, she had changed quickly in the bathroom. Emma had taken the dirty clothes and tucked them into her bag, promising to get them back to her.

Somehow Patrick had conjured up a water bottle, which he had filled for her, and a few granola bars that he tucked into her tote. "I have a feeling you'll be with him all night," he said. "I wanted to make sure you would have something to keep you going."

"You guys should head home," she said to the room. "Maggie and Frank can't sit here all night, and they will if you all do. Everyone should go home and sleep, and I'll call if anything changes."

"We don't want you to be alone," Colin objected.

274

Patrick nodded. "We should stay. At least some of us. Dan, Jake, you guys should go home to your families."

"We're staying too," Desmond said stubbornly.

"Someone has to bring mom and dad home," Colin said. "Zoe is right, they can't sit here all night."

"You do it," Des shot back.

"I'll take them," Finley offered. "I'll make sure they eat and sleep for a few hours at least, and I'll bring them back in the morning if not sooner."

"Thanks, Fin," Colin said, smiling at her. "I always liked you better than Des."

"Nice," Desmond said. "I'm staying with you; you might want to reconsider."

Colin shrugged. "Not sure what to say. She's prettier and smells better, and she's nice."

"If our brother wasn't already fighting for his life, I would make you take that back," Des said.

"Enough," Finley commanded. "We need to focus. Mom is going to fight us on this, and dad will do whatever she wants. We all need to be in agreement over this."

"We'll back you up," Colin said. "You say whatever you need to, just get them to go home and relax. We don't need one of them to collapse from exhaustion or stress."

Zoe turned to Emma as the siblings planned their strategy. "You and Patrick should go home too," she said. "Poor Natalie must be traumatized, and she only really knows you two. I'm sure she will sleep better tonight with you both home. I'll be okay here, I promise."

"Are you sure?" Emma studied her face, looking concerned. "I worry about you. I could send Patrick home, and I'll stay."

"I'll be in with JJ anyway," Zoe said, shaking her head. "You go home and just come back in the morning. You can bring me clean clothes, that would be helpful. Colin and Des will be here if there's anything that I need, and I'll send out an alert if anything changes overnight."

Emma sighed, looking at Patrick. They both looked torn, and she was sure the weight of worry about her, JJ and Natalie was heavily on them. "I promise, I'll be okay. If I need you, I'll call."

"Promise?" Emma asked, holding up her little finger to make her pinky swear like they had as kids.

"I promise," she said, twisting her finger with her sisters. "Let me know how Nat is doing when you get home, please."

Maggie and Frank came back into the room, smiling through tears at the room. "Zoe, honey, you can head back in," Maggie said.

"Mom, Dad," Finley said, pulling their jackets out of the pile on a chair. "Let's go home. Zoe is going to update us if anything changes, and we all agreed that it's causing her more stress to have all of us here."

"We can't leave her alone," Maggie said.

"We're staying," Colin nodded at Desmond. "Everyone else can come back in the morning. If anything changes, we will make sure everyone knows."

"Are you sure?" Frank asked, looking back and forth between his sons, who both nodded. "Okay, honey, let's listen to the kids. We'll both feel better with a little rest."

Zoe ducked out as everyone was saying their goodbyes, happy to be able to return to JJ's side and stay there the remainder of the night. If she got tired or needed a break, she knew one of his brothers would happily take her place, but she wanted to be there when he woke up. This nightmare needed to be over, with a happy ending for once in her life.

Chapter 30

Shortly before dawn, Zoe woke up suddenly, realizing there were more voices around her than there should be. She realized with a start that she was sitting in a hard chair, her head resting on a bed next to JJ's arm. He was still and quiet, and proof that she hadn't just dreamt the events of the last twelve hours. Turning, she noticed two doctors who were studying the monitors along with the nurse who had been with her all night.

"Is everything okay?" she asked, rubbing her eyes.

"Yes," the nurse replied quickly. "We may try to extubate him shortly, since his lung appears to be recovering well. If they decide to go ahead with that, I'll have you step out for a few minutes."

"Okay," she agreed. "Nothing changed while I dozed off?"

"No," she said. "He's holding strong."

One of the doctors met her eyes finally and nodded. "Everything looks good. We're going to see how he does breathing on his own, so it would be a good time for you to go get a cup of coffee. Give us about twenty minutes, and we'll have someone get you."

She stood, feeling her whole body cry in protest, and leaned over to kiss JJ again before leaving. "You got this," she whispered. "One step closer to waking up. Just breathe."

Exiting the room, she was flagged down by a nurse behind the busy desk. "Would you like some coffee?" she asked, pointing to a huge display of carafes behind the desk. "Or a pastry? Your family sent all of this over, so you should take advantage too."

Patrick, she thought. Only he could coordinate such a thing in the middle of the night in Vermont. "You guys should enjoy," she said, shaking her head. "We're so grateful for all that you do."

"And we appreciate that, honestly," the nurse said with a smile. "We also know how horrible the cafeteria coffee is, so when you change your mind, just let us know."

She smiled at them and made her way to the rest room, where she tried to clean up as best she could. Then she backtracked to the room where Colin and Desmond were sound asleep, feet up on chairs and looking more comfortable than she had been. There was a similar setup of coffee and food in the corner of the room, so she quietly made a cup of coffee and grabbed a pastry to nibble on. Before she could sneak back out, Colin stirred and jumped to his feet when he saw her.

"How's he doing?" he asked softly, since Desmond was still sound asleep.

"They are trying to take the breathing tube out now," she told him. "If he does okay, that's one step closer to him waking up."

"That's great news," Colin said. "Want me to text everyone?"

She checked her watch and saw it wasn't even five in the morning and shook her head. "Let's wait and see how he does and let them sleep a little longer. I don't want to wake them and then have everyone be disappointed if it doesn't go well."

"Text me and let me know," he said. "I'll hold off on any updates until you give me the go ahead."

"Thanks," she smiled at him gratefully. "What time do you think your parents will be back?"

"My dad is usually up early, but last night was late for him," he said. "Finley will try and keep them at home until the sun comes up at least."

"Word has started to spread," she told him, holding up her phone. She had at least one hundred text messages from the people in town, all wanting to know how JJ was. "I can't possibly respond to all of these."

"Leave it to me," he offered. "When we have any news to share, we can get word out to the town."

"Thanks. I should get back there, see how it's going."

"Text me when you can."

"Will do," she said, opening the door to leave.

She walked slowly down the halls, wanting to give the doctors time to finish with JJ before she made her way back. Waiting was torture, but it would only be worse if she was right outside the door and envisioning everything bad that could happen. *Positive thoughts,* she told herself as she approached the ICU wing.

Just as she entered the area, a nurse raced by her with a cart, and she heard the alarms she had heard the night before. The nurse was headed right for JJ's room, and she could see people at his bedside through the glass. His door was open, but thankfully, the nurse went right past it to the room next door. She leaned heavily against the wall, catching her breath and letting her heart slow down at the realization that it wasn't JJ in crisis mode.

"Mrs. Monahan?" The nurses voice came from behind her, and she turned to see the same one who had offered her coffee. "It's okay if you want to go back in, the doctor told us to keep an eye out for you."

"Thank you," she whispered, her eyes trying to avoid the activity in the next room. She walked in through the open door, seeing that there was a doctor on either side of JJ, and the tube that had been in his mouth was gone.

"He did fine," one doctor told her quickly. "His oxygen saturation is staying above ninety, and his respirations are good. He's breathing a little shallow right now, but that could be due to pain, or the lung. We'll keep an eye on it either way."

"Do you think he'll wake up now?"

The second doctor frowned slightly. "He's still mildly sedated, and the drugs are in his system still. It will take a few hours for them to clear his system, since he was on them for a while. We'll just be giving him pain medicine from now on, so within the next few hours, you should see him start to rouse."

"Is there anything I should be doing?" she asked, desperate for a purpose other than watching him sleep.

"The nurse will be monitoring his oxygen and vital signs," the first doctor said. "You can talk to him; he might hear your voice and fight through the medications."

She settled back into her chair, watching as the two doctors left to continue their rounds. Texting Colin quickly to let him know that all had gone well, she then sat quietly as the nurses did their report for change of shift. Although she could hear them discuss JJ, half of what they said went right over her head, it was so complicated. Once it had settled down to just her and the new nurse, she felt more comfortable talking to JJ again.

"Good morning," she said. "The doctor said that you're doing well, which is good news. I already told Colin, and he'll spread the word to everyone. It's still so early that we're the only ones awake, but since you're a morning person, I'm sure you love that. The doctor said you're doing good breathing on your own, so you don't need to stay asleep any longer. I know it's going to be painful, but anytime you want to wake up, I'd really appreciate it."

When JJ didn't respond, she rubbed his cheek, hoping it would cause his eyes to open. Noticing his lips were chapped and dry, she pulled a tube of Chapstick from her bag. She hesitated before putting it on his lips, holding it up for the nurse first.

"Is it okay if I put this on him? His lips look painful."

"Sure," the nurse said. "I can get you some ointment too if you need it."

"I think this will be okay for now," she said. "When he wakes up, he might want something different. Luckily this isn't a tinted one, if he thought I was putting that on, he might wake up just to stop me."

The nurse laughed softly, reaching over to check on a bag on an IV stand. After she finished entering something on the computer, she turned back to Zoe. "It looks like we'll be moving him to a regular room in a few hours," she said. "He doesn't need to be in ICU anymore, since he's stable."

"But he's not awake," Zoe said. "Shouldn't he be monitored until he wakes up?"

"He still will be," the nurse assured her. "But not quite as intense as this. He doesn't need us in the room with him around the clock, and it will make it more comfortable for you. The other rooms have a daybed in them, so you could get some sleep. Plus, other family can be in the room as well."

"Oh, that's good."

"It's a positive step, I promise," the nurse said. "And I bet he will wake up in a few hours anyway, probably before he moves."

***

The few hours passed quickly, and before she knew it, Zoe was following the bed as it moved to a different part of the hospital. JJ remained asleep, now connected to only about half of the machines that he had been in ICU. The nurse had explained to Zoe that he would remain on the IV fluids and medication until he woke up, and they would still monitor his vital signs, but from the nurses station rather than the room.

When they arrived at the new room, she was shocked at the size of it. There was a wall of windows overlooking the mountains, and a small garden outside the hospital. There were several comfortable chairs around the perimeter of the room, as well as the promised daybed under the window. A door led to a private bathroom, which the nurse assured Zoe she could use.

"This is bigger than some of my apartments," she marveled, looking around.

The nurse laughed as they positioned JJ's bed in the room and started hooking the wires up to the new monitors. "It helps to have friends in high places."

"What do you mean?"

"Tina was already pushing for him to have a good room," she explained. "And then Patrick Burrows pledged a huge donation, and Natalie Cloud matched it. They're going to put a whole wing on the hospital, they are so grateful to Dr. Ortiz and everyone who saved your husband. That gets him the VIP treatment for sure."

"I didn't realize," Zoe stuttered. "He wouldn't want to be treated differently than anyone else."

"Don't worry," the nurse said. "We'd probably be doing this anyway, since he's one of us. First responders stick together, you know? But if Patrick Burrows and Natalie Cloud want to help the hospital grow, we'll be happy to let them."

The nurse left the room after showing Zoe how to call for help. She had the button that was laying on JJ's bed to call for regular help, as well as a button on the wall that she could press if JJ stopped breathing or anything alarming happened. When Zoe had paled at the thought, the nurse assured her that they could see his vital signs from the nurses station and would be in way before he was in crisis. And that they weren't expecting a crisis, so she shouldn't worry.

Trying to distract herself from the thought of JJ dying, she turned to face the window and admire the view. The windowsill was already full of flowers, and Zoe started reading through the cards, realizing half the town had already sent something. Well wishes from the mayor, the state police, his staff at the sheriff's department, Zoe's staff at the restaurant. There were so many that she felt tears brimming again, especially when seeing that people she had gotten to know had reached out. Apparently, she had settled into this little town even more than she had thought.

"Listen, JJ," she said, her tone firmer than it had been earlier. "It's time to wake up. You need to see how many people have already sent flowers, and it's not even been a full day. I can't imagine what will arrive today."

He didn't respond, and she sat down with a sigh. Having him be so quiet was throwing her, he was always so full of life and led most conversations. Without him, she would be an introvert who just worked and went home. He was the reason all these people were her friends, why she suddenly had a family. And his still body reminded her that it could all disappear, and the greatest loss she would feel would be if she were to lose him.

The door opened, and Maggie's face appeared. Frank followed her in, with Colin, Desmond and Finley all trailing behind. "He's not awake yet?" Maggie whispered, looking crushed.

"Not yet," Zoe said at full volume. "But I'm determined to wake him, he's slept long enough. JJ, your family is here, time to get up."

Everyone stood still and watched him, sighing in disappointment when he didn't move even an eyelid. Maggie pulled a chair next to Zoe and patted her hand. "I was in labor with this one for three days," she said. "He'll come around when he's good and ready. Stubborn as can be, and never did turn away an audience."

"I really need him to come back to me," Zoe said softly to Maggie.

The older woman nodded, and then reached over to pull Zoe close to her. "He will, honey. I know he will. And you have all of us to help you through this, and for always."

JJ's siblings filled the space with their usual banter, teasing each other and JJ, and telling stories from their childhood. Zoe laughed for the first time in a day as they recalled the time JJ had gotten his leg stuck between the slats on his bunk bed. "He was screaming and crying, as if it was broken," Maggie chuckled. "All he needed to do was straighten it out so that it would fit through. But he wouldn't listen, would he?"

Frank shook his head, laughing. "I had to go get the saw, and when he asked what I was doing, I said I was going to have to cut the leg off. He straightened it right out then to get away from me."

Mid-morning, a cart filled with breakfast offerings and drinks was rolled in, courtesy of Patrick. "He has meals set up for you guys for as long as you'll be here," the aide told them. "The staff as well, please tell him that we said thank you."

Before he could leave, the door opened again, revealing Emma and Patrick. The aide tripped over her own feet, nearly crashing into the wall, before Patrick offered her a hand. He accepted her thanks before she disappeared through the door, looking as though her day had just been made.

"Any changes?" Emma asked, looking hopeful.

"No," Zoe replied. "He's breathing on his own and only on pain medications, but he should be waking up soon. Or should have by now. I'm not sure what to think."

"Think positive," her sister said, squeezing her hand. "He fought for you for two years, he's not going to stop now."

There was a searing pain in his chest, which got worse with every breath he took. It was the first thing he became aware of, and it seemed to take over his entire being. All he could focus on was the pain, and trying to breathe through it. He became aware of voices around him, people he didn't know. As much as he wanted to open his eyes and see who was causing him this pain, he couldn't. His eyes wouldn't listen to his brain, or his brain was so busy just trying to deal with the pain that it couldn't do two things at once.

Relief came suddenly, one second he was in agony, and the next he felt like he was floating on a cloud. He became aware of other noises in the room, and the feel of a small hand in his, holding tight. Feeling Zoe's heat, and hearing her voice asking him to wake up, helped him relax. She was here, and she didn't seem to be panicked. He squeezed her hand lightly and went back to sleep.

***

The hum of voices woke him from what felt like the deepest sleep of his life. Trying to open his eyes was a struggle, but he managed to get his eyes to open a slit. Zoe was next to him, still holding his hand. His mother was next to her, their two heads close together as they talked. He could make out other figures in the room, but the light was too bright so he closed his eyes before seeing who they were.

"JJ," Zoe's voice came close to his ear. "Can you hear me? Squeeze my hand if you can."

He squeezed her hand and tried to tell her he was just tired, but his mouth was so dry, it barely made a sound.

"Here, take a small sip of water. It's a straw, just a small sip, okay?" He took a sip and would have drank more if she hadn't snatched it away. He groaned, and she laughed softly. "Can't have you overdoing it when you aren't fully awake yet."

He managed to open one eye and saw her face just inches from his. "What happened?"

"You were shot," she said. "You had surgery and you've been unconscious for twenty-four hours. You've given us all quite the scare."

"Where?" The words made sense, but he had no memory of anything. When he pushed his brain past the exhaustion that fogged the corners, he could remember driving to Patrick's house with Zoe. "Are you – okay?" Getting the words out was a struggle, but he had to know.

"I'm fine," she said. "I'm just so glad that you're alright."

He could hear her crying, and wanted to wake up and take her into his arms, but the heaviness won, and he was back to sleep before he could say more.

When he woke up again, he felt clearer than earlier. The windows were dark, and only Zoe and his parents were in the room. His parents were huddled together by the window, looking tired. Zoe was at his side, looking at something on her phone, and if he had to guess, she hadn't moved from the spot all day.

"Hi," he whispered.

Her head snapped around, and she smiled when her eyes met his. "Hi," she said back. "How are you feeling?"

"Terrible."

"Do you want me to get the nurse?" she looked worried, and held up the call button that he knew would summon help.

"No, I want to talk to you for a minute before I fall back to sleep," he said. "What day is it?"

"Monday night. It's just after eight." She turned as his parents approached and smiled at them before looking back at him. "Everyone is still here, we just thought you needed more quiet than your siblings and the Burrows can provide."

"You guys should go home," he said to his parents. "You too. I'll be okay."

"I'm not going anywhere," she responded, a stubborn look in her eye.

"How are you feeling, son?" Frank stood at the foot of the bed, and JJ could see how worn out he was.

"I'm in pain, but I'm alive. You guys look like you need rest," he said. "Go home. I'll still be here tomorrow."

His parents looked at Zoe, as if waiting for her approval. She smiled at them and then stood to hug them both. "He's right, go home. I'll call you if anything changes."

"Do you want us to send your brothers and sister home? Or have them come in?"

"Give me a few minutes alone with Zoe, please. Then I'll have her grab them."

They both leaned over to kiss his forehead, the way they used to when he was little and had a fever. The stress this had put on them was evident, and he hoped it didn't take a toll on their health. But before he could worry about them, he needed to figure out what was wrong with him, and it would be easier to talk about if his mom wasn't in the room crying.

Once they left, he tugged on Zoe's hand to move her closer. She leaned on the mattress lightly, but jumped up when he winced. "No, it's okay. I want you near me."

"Not if it causes you pain," she said. "How are you feeling?"

"Like I got hit by a truck."

"Looks like it too," she smiled softly at him. "I'm sure you have a million questions, but let's try to keep it simple so you can rest again."

"Were you there?" The fear that had been nagging at his brain came out first, even before wanting to know what was wrong with him physically. He could recover from anything, as long as he knew she was okay.

"No," she shook her head. "I was at the festival. You don't remember anything?"

"Nothing."

"I'll give you the brief version that I know, and you'll get more details later, I'm sure," she said. "You got a call at the festival that Patrick's alarm was malfunctioning. Apparently, when you got there, it was Natalie using the system to call for help. There was an intruder there, determined to take her with him so he could get a big ransom. You came in, and you shot at each other. Luckily, you're a better shot."

"I got him?"

She nodded. "You did."

"Must have made a mess out of Patrick's house," he said with a frown.

"He's just happy that you, Nat and Mike are alright," she said. "His manager had someone at the house within hours to clean up, once the police left. And he said he'll have Jake replace the flooring."

"That's good." He studied her face, seeing the fatigue around her eyes. Even in the most extreme situations in the kitchen, or when he had put her on the spot in Vegas, she hadn't looked this stressed. "I'm sorry."

"You're sorry?" She looked at him in shock, and shook her head. "You have nothing to be sorry for."

"This must have been horrible for you. I hate that I put you through it," he said. "I don't remember what happened, but I probably could have been more careful."

"Don't say that," she said. "You were protecting your friends. I know you would only do what you felt necessary at the time."

"Still, I wish I didn't cause you stress," he said. "And overall, I probably have put you under a lot of that over the last few months. I shouldn't have pushed you to get married so fast, without any time to think about it. Being a cops wife is not like a regular marriage, and I shouldn't have rushed you the way I did. I completely understand if you want to go."

"What?" She looked either confused and fully pissed off, and he wasn't sure which was safer for him. "I've been sitting here for twenty-four hours, begging you to come back to me, and now you want me to leave?"

"I don't want you to leave," he said, stopping to cough. Only once he started coughing, pain seared across his chest and made it hard to breathe.

Zoe pushed the button to call the nurse, panic on her face as he coughed and gasped, seeing his vision narrow and darkness try to take over. His body desperately wanted the release that being unconscious would allow, but he was afraid if he allowed it, he might not wake up.

The nurse came in, and quickly called over the walkie-talkie in her hand asking for a doctor. She pressed a pillow to his chest softly, and encouraged him to hold it against his wound when he coughed. The doctor rushed in, quickly giving the nurse orders, who left the room again.

The doctor slipped an oxygen mask over his face and checked the monitors next to his bed. "I know it feels like you can't breathe, but you are. We're going to get you something for the pain, and to help you relax."

He shook his head, but the doctor frowned at him. "I can't have you overdoing it. You have stitches and healing wounds. Trust me, you don't want to be back in the OR repairing something that we can avoid. Tomorrow we'll scale back what you're taking so you can start getting up. This is a slow process, you need to give yourself time and grace to heal."

JJ watched as the doctor injected a needle into the IV tubing, and although he wanted to fight against it, the relief was immediate. He reached for Zoe's hand as he drifted off, wanting to apologize but unable to say the words. One he felt her fingers link with his, he allowed the darkness to take over.

***

When he woke again, he could see dawn peeking in through the window. The light was soft, the rest of the room darkened other than a nightlight shining in the bathroom. With the door closed to the hallway, the noise was muffled. He had felt someone in regularly all night, checking the machines and giving him medications, but no one had woken him fully, and he was grateful. Although he still had an aching pain in his chest, it was dulled by whatever medication he was on.

He rested his head back on the pillow, trying to go back to the night he was shot in his head. As hard as he pushed his memory, nothing would come. The last time he could remember was being at Patrick's house with Zoe, having a fun night with their friends. He had a vague recollection of getting ready for the day and dropping Zoe off, but even that could be his imagination. They had done it so many times, maybe his brain was just creating the memory for him. There was nothing about what he had done all morning, or what had prompted him to go to Patrick's, never mind what happened when he got there.

Anyone who could answer questions for him was notably absent, and he had to assume it was at the doctor's request. He knew getting riled up would be bad for him, but the need for answers was strong. His phone was out of reach, so he made a mental note to text Patrick later and ask him to come by. And maybe he could get Nick and Jeff to come as well, surely they would be able to fill in the blanks.

The light outside the window had started to brighten, and he glanced that way again, grateful that he had lived to see a new day. He wasn't normally a guy who appreciated the sunrise, but he would from now on, he vowed. Suddenly, he realized the couch by the window wasn't empty. Zoe was curled up, sound asleep, covered by a blanket. He had assumed she had gone home after he had fallen back to sleep, but instead, she was still here at his bedside. He couldn't make out her features in the weak light, but it made him happy to know she was there.

For two years, he had fought to get her to love him back. He knew it was there, just under the surface, and she needed encouragement to bring it out. When she had agreed to marry him, as crazy as the situation was, he had felt like he won the lottery. He had long suspected that she shared his feelings, but just couldn't express it. Granted, he was an open book and sometimes needed to close his mouth, but she needed him to be that way to feel safe enough to expose her soft side.

Her sleeping on an uncomfortable couch, just a few steps from where he lay, was all the proof he needed about her feelings for him. If he had any doubts about their marriage, or about her loving him, this put them to rest. Just as he had been saying to everyone for years, she showed it when she couldn't say it. And that could be enough for him, as long as she needed it to be.

Chapter 32

The doctor was shaking his head, saying something she couldn't hear. His face looked sad, as if he was giving her bad news, but nothing was coming out of his mouth. Behind him, she could see them pulling a sheet up over the bed, and she wanted to scream, to tell them that JJ was there. Why were they covering him up? She lunged forward, trying to get to him, and woke up when she hit the cold floor.

"Are you okay?" JJ's voice came through clearly, and she looked up to meet his gaze where he was laying on the bed. Perfectly fine, no doctor in sight.

It was a dream, she realized, shaking her head. She hadn't fallen out of bed since she was a toddler, and here she was falling face first in front of JJ. "I'm fine," she said, standing slowly. "A little embarrassed. Are you okay?"

"You were talking in your sleep, kept saying no over and over again. Are you sure you're alright?"

"I was having a dream," she admitted.

"About?"

"Good thing you're already a cop," she said. "You have a gift of interrogation."

He laughed, but looked at her, waiting for her to respond.

"I dreamt the doctor was here, and he was trying to tell me something, but I couldn't hear him. And they were covering you up, like you had died."

"I definitely did not," he said. "Come here."

She walked toward him, her feet slipping slightly since she still had on her fuzzy slipper socks that had no traction. JJ laughed slightly as he watched her. "Don't laugh," she said, settling back into her chair next to him. "Although I'm sure I looked like those giraffe on ice videos you love."

"I do love those videos, but fortunately, you are much shorter and have two less legs," he said. "But you do look like you might need some skating lessons."

"I can ice skate fine," she objected. "This floor is slippery."

"Sure it is."

"Why are you so infuriating? I'm supposed to be glad you're alive," she said with a sigh.

"Thank you for staying with me," he said.

"Of course," she said, feeling surprised. "You thought I would leave you?"

"I wasn't being my best self when I last fell asleep," he admitted. "I never meant that I wanted you to go away, it just came out wrong. I wanted you to get some rest, and it sounded as though I wanted you to leave. I always want you next to me if it's my choice, you know that."

"I do," she said. She took a deep breath, ready to finally tell him the truth about her feelings.

Before she could start, the door swung open, and a nurse appeared. "Oh, you're both awake," she said. "Great. My shift just started, so I wanted to come check on you. And you,

Jeremiah, are going to have a chance to actually try to eat some breakfast this morning. It's a big day."

"Coffee too?" he asked, looking eager.

"Let's not push it too much," she responded. "Maybe a small decaf, but we'll see how you do with some bland foods first. Your wife is welcome to get some coffee from the very elaborate offerings at the nurses station while I check you over."

"I'll do that," Zoe said, standing to leave. She heard JJ laugh softly as she slipped again, so she reversed directions to put her socks and sneakers on before leaving the room.

The nurses at the station were clustered around the coffee, tea and pastry station, but quickly made space for her. They all thanked her and asked her to pass along the message to Patrick and Nat, which she promised to do.

"Do you think either of them will come by to visit?" The youngest looking nurse asked shyly.

"I don't know for sure," Zoe said, unsure of how Patrick would want her to respond. "But I know they are very grateful for the care he's receiving, and Patrick was here the night JJ was shot. There's a good chance he might come by, and I know he'll be happy to say hello."

The nurses all looked at each other, wide eyed, and giggled. "We promise not to make total fools of ourselves," one of the older nurses told her. "Especially since we all know he's dating your sister."

"He is," she said with a smile.

"She's so lucky," the young one gushed. "Do you think they'll get married?"

"That I can't say," Zoe laughed. "They would both have my head if I was speculating about it."

She poured her coffee and grabbed a muffin, heading back into JJ's room as the nurse was leaving. "He's all yours, honey," she said in passing. "I'll be back in soon to get him up."

"He's getting out of bed already?" Zoe was horrified, thinking of the pain he had been in the night before.

"Yes," she nodded. "He needs to get moving so we can avoid the risk of a clot. His medications have been adjusted so he will be able to tolerate small walks, and we want him to be up using the bathroom and moving around a bit. If the pain gets to be too much, we'll adjust."

"But he's still hooked up to everything."

"I just unhooked it all," she said. "And the chest tube came out before he came up here, so he's ready to go. He had a catheter until now, so he's going to be asking to get up in a few hours one way or the other."

"Oh," she said, not sure what to say. Obviously the medical team knew best, and she shouldn't push. "Thanks for the info."

"No problem," the nurse smiled at her kindly. "We know this is all overwhelming, feel free to ask as many questions as you have. We don't mind."

"That's very nice of you."

"I'm going to have them bring him his breakfast," she said, starting to walk away. "Prepare yourself for him to complain and try to steal yours. He has to start with oatmeal and some plain toast and work his way up to better food. His stomach has been empty for almost two days now, with only the IV fluids and medications. Food can be upsetting for some people's stomachs, so we always start slow."

"JJ has a stomach of steel," Zoe laughed. "But I'll get him to prove it."

JJ smiled at her when she came back in the room, pointing at the coffee. "That for me?"

"No, you heard the nurse. No coffee just yet."

"That seems like cruel and unusual punishment," he said. "Especially since I can smell yours."

"Want me to dump it?" She stood back up, gesturing to the bathroom.

"No, don't be silly. Drink it, I know you need it." He watched as she took a sip and a bit of her muffin. "Have you left here at all?"

"No," she shook her head. "Emma brought me some clothes, and I've just been here. Tedy was with your parents, so I didn't have to worry about her. Apparently they have a neighbor who was thinking of getting their kids a dog for Christmas, so they were happy to take Tedy when your parents were here."

"She's going to have them thinking all dogs are that well behaved," he said. "Watch, they'll get a puppy and be shocked that it's not housetrained."

"Maybe your parents can encourage them to visit the shelter and adopt," Zoe suggested.

JJ nodded and looked as though he was going to say something, but stopped as the door opened. An aide walked in with a tray, containing the promised oatmeal and toast, and a small bottle of water. "Gourmet right here," JJ said. "Good thing I married a chef so I know this is a once in a lifetime meal."

The aide laughed and backed out of the room, leaving them alone again. "The nurse said they plan to get you up today," Zoe said.

"She told me that," he nodded as he took a bite of toast. "Unhooked me from everything, even things I didn't know I had."

Zoe laughed, and let him eat. He obviously had regained his appetite quickly, because he finished everything quickly and then was eyeing the other half of her muffin. "You're going to get me in trouble if you eat that," she said.

"One bite would probably be okay," he tried.

She shook her head stubbornly and moved it further away. "Let's wait and see how your stomach does. As soon as they clear you for regular food, I'll get you whatever you want."

"Well, I'd want something cooked by you, but I don't want you to leave," he said. "I'll think of the second best option."

"JJ, I have some things to say to you," she blurted out. "This might not be the right time or place, but I have to get them off my chest."

"This could either be very good or very bad," he said slowly. "Go ahead."

"I've been stubborn, and hard on you," she said. "From the very first time we met, you have been amazing to me. So kind, and patient, and loving. You do that with everyone you meet, and you make them feel safe. It's a gift you have, that you make people happy when you're around. I know I'm always happy when you're around, you have made me smile more in the last two years than I think I ever had in my life."

"I'm glad to hear that," he said. "I feel the same way about you."

"I don't think you do," she said, then held up her hand when he was going to object. "What I mean is, I was in a dark place when I moved to Vermont. There wasn't a lot of light in my heart or my life. Then you walked through the kitchen door, and it was like you radiated it, like you were the sun. Or maybe like Tedy, just all infectious joy."

"Not sure how I feel about being compared to a dog," he laughed. "But go on."

"Everything about you was wrong for me," she said. "You're loud and you like to be the center of attention. You are social, you love being around people, and I'm happy in the kitchen alone. Behind the scenes, where people aren't looking at me. But you dragged me out from there, away from my solitary life, and I made friends. I started to find my place in the world, and to find people who liked having me around. For the first time ever, I felt like I belonged."

"You do."

"That's because of you. I would never have extended myself if you weren't there, pulling me along," she said. "Everything I have right now, it's because of your determination. You saw something in me that I didn't see in myself, and you made me want to be that person. You gave me the confidence outside the kitchen to push for more responsibility, to share new ideas. When I left Paris, I felt small and meaningless as a chef, and now I'm helping Kendra expand the business and try new things.

And on top of that, you helped me be able to breathe again. I was finally able to relax, to feel good. And that was before anything happened between us."

"Hopefully you were better than good after that," he winked at her.

She rolled her eyes, then continued. "You never pressured me to do anything that I didn't want to do. I obviously always knew you were interested, but you helped me to settle in and get my confidence back, without asking anything of me in return."

"Other than asking you on a million dates, and asking you to marry me, you mean?"

"You consistently showed me your interest, but without strings," she explained. "I didn't feel like I had to do any of that to have you still be nice to me, and that's not usual for me. Any other man I met always wanted something from me, expected to be physical because he bought me dinner. You didn't do that. You let me set the pace, as slow as it may have been, and you even made me make the first move."

"I can't help it that I'm irresistible," he said with a smile. "But in all honesty, I knew from the first time that I saw you that I wanted to be with you forever, and I was okay with that taking a bit. I wanted you to be on the same page as me, and it was easier to let you lead the way."

"Which meant I never felt pressure from you. Just kindness, and love, and patience. All things I really hadn't had in my life before you," she said. "And when I got the news that you had been shot, and I sat out there waiting for the news—" She took a shuddering breath, choking on tears once again.

"I'm sorry, Zo," he said, squeezing her hand. "I'm sorry you had to go through that."

"It was like I couldn't breathe," she said. "All the light was gone. I felt the darkness closing in, and even though I could see your family, and Emma, and everyone, I felt alone. I don't know that I could have gone on without you."

"Yes, you would have," he said. "You're strong and capable, and it's okay that you fall down sometimes. But you let people help you up, and you keep going. I'm happy that I'm your main person, but all those other people love you and would have gotten you through it."

"I don't even like to think about it," she said. "Because the truth that I've finally come around to, and that I need to tell you, is that I—"

The door to the room swung open, while the nurse knocked at the same time. "Ready to get up, Officer?" she asked, hands on her hips.

Zoe sank back in her chair, seeing the emotions on JJ's face. He was clearly upset at being interrupted, and she sensed that he was about to ask for more time. Not wanting to make it harder on him, she jumped up and grabbed the tray off his table. "I'll just run this outside," she said.

Once she got in the hall, she leaned against the door. That had been the most honest conversation of her life, and maybe the interruption had come at the right time.

Two days in the hospital was two days too long, JJ decided. In total he had been in for three days, but the first spent unconscious had been easier than the last two. He had been through a battery of tests, been encouraged to walk as much as possible, and had finally been granted a shower. Between the gradual increase in his diet finally allowing him to eat whatever he wanted, and the shower, he finally felt human again. Now he wanted to go home, be alone with his wife, and see his dog again.

The room seemed to have been filled with friends and family, in addition to the medical staff, since he and Zoe were interrupted to get him out of bed. He desperately wanted to continue the conversation and see what it was that she was trying to tell him, but by the time everyone left, they were both exhausted.

His parents and siblings were currently in the room, along with Emma, while Patrick took pictures and accepted hugs from the staff in the hallway. "I'm ready to go home," he announced, stopping the conversations.

"Oh, honey," his mom said. "Not yet. They want you to heal a bit more, and maybe do some physical therapy. A bullet went into you, that's more than a two day recovery."

"And the spleen removal," his father added. "Don't forget that."

"I don't think the spleen is causing him pain," Colin said.

"It probably does," Frank insisted. "There's tissue in there that has to heal after it was removed. It's not like the game Operation, where things are really attached."

"Thanks for all the help," he tried again. "But what I really want is my own bed, and my couch, and to not be here anymore. Let's try and make that happen."

"Let me get Patrick," Emma said. "Maybe he can talk to someone."

"No, that's okay," he sighed. "I'll wait until the doctor comes in. The nurse said they would be doing rounds in about an hour."

Like clockwork, the doctor came in an hour later, reviewing the chart as he came through the door. "Good afternoon," he said to the room. "How are you feeling?"

"Good," JJ responded. "And ready to go home."

The doctor chuckled, then moved to his side to check the wound. "This is healing well," he said. "What's your pain like?"

"Four out of ten most of the time," he admitted.

"When is it higher?"

"When I try and do too much."

"And do you get lower than four?"

"Yes, when I'm icing. Or sleeping."

"You think you can manage your pain at home," the doctor asked, looking worried. "And be able to get around?"

"Yes," he nodded confidently. "I have way too many people available to help me if I need it. But I need my own bed, and the comfort of home."

The doctor frowned, crossing his arms. Before he could answer, Patrick jumped into the conversation. "I can get him a visiting nurse, whatever it takes," he offered.

"That's no necessary," JJ said.

"Well, it might be," the doctor said. "You'll need the dressing changed, and you definitely need to do some physical therapy to regain strength. Plus I need you to make sure you're working that lung, so pulmonary therapy would be a big plus."

"I'll get that all set up," Patrick said.

"Where is your bedroom in the house?" the doctor asked, looking between him and Zoe.

"First floor," he said quickly. "It's a Craftsman, everything we need is on the main floor."

"You can't be home alone at all," the doctor warned him. "Not even for a few minutes. I don't want you to overdo it and open the wound, or cause anything to get worse. You need constant supervision."

"I'm not a —"

"We'll make sure of it," Zoe cut him off before he could say something stupid, which he appreciated.

"As long as your labs come back normal, you can go home. But I need you to be seen in the office on Friday, and I'll readmit you in a heartbeat if you are pushing yourself too hard."

"Done."

"Absolutely no working," the doctor warned him. "I know you want to get to the bottom of what happened, but you are not to be investigating, got it?"

"Got it." Asking questions and investigating were two different things, after all.

The doctor studied him, and then laughed. "I feel like I'm losing this conversation, and I don't know why."

"I'll be good, I promise. I just want my own bed, and some quiet."

"Hey," Desmond said, sounding offended.

"But you won't be alone," the doctor said. "You have to accept help from your loved ones. And from the staff that I'm sure Patrick will have at your beck and call."

"Already on it," Patrick responded, holding up his phone.

"Please don't steal any of my nurses, no matter how much they beg," the doctor laughed. "Give me an hour, and I'll get you out of here if all is good."

The doctor left to the chorus of thank you's from everyone in the room, and then everyone looked at him happily. "I'm so glad you're going home," Maggie gushed. "It will be much more comfortable for everyone."

"Mom, I really just want to sleep in my bed and have some quiet."

"But you heard him, you can't be alone," she argued.

"Zoe will be there," he tried.

"Yes, but she'll also need to rest. And have some time to herself, so we will fill in."

There was no point in arguing with his mother, he realized. A few days would be fine, and it would go much faster than the time in the hospital was. "Colin, why don't you take the twins and head to the house? Can you grab Tedy and bring her home too?"

"She might be too excited," his father warned. "Maybe she should stay with us a few more days."

"Are you trying to steal our dog?" JJ looked between his parents' faces. "She can stay on her leash until she settles down, but I miss her."

"We'll get her," Des promised. "Anything else you need at the house? Zoe, need us to run to the store?"

"No," she shook her head. "Kendra had people from the restaurant run up a bunch of the freezer meals I had prepared for the festival, so we have plenty of food."

"Wine?" Finley asked, slipping on her jacket.

"I'll take care of that," Patrick promised.

"JJ can't be drinking," Zoe said.

"No one said it was for him," Colin laughed.

The three of them left, followed by Patrick and Emma, who promised to be at the house when they arrived. Zoe had never left the hospital and didn't have a car there, so they were going to be leaving with his parents when they did head home. Zoe started moving around the room, picking up items and either throwing them in the trash or stacking them on the bedside table.

"What are we going to do with all the flowers?" she wondered as she surveyed the room, where almost every surface was covered by arrangements.

"Let's just bring the cards home so I can thank people," he said. "And then have the nurses either take them home or spread them to other patients."

"You sure you don't want to take them? I can get some boxes," Frank offered.

"No, we don't need them," he said. "And honestly, it's been smelling like a funeral home for days in here. I'll be happy to be free from the flower smell."

His mom started helping Zoe gather items, and he was amazed at all they had accumulated in a few days. Emma had regularly brought Zoe clothes, and everyone had supplied phone chargers, books and magazines, a deck of cards, and several of the kids from town had sent hand drawn get well cards for him. Plus, he had all the medical items, including a tool he had to breathe into every hour to help his lungs stay healthy, and a ridiculously tight pair of socks they made him wear to avoid a clot.

Zoe disappeared and came back with a few large plastic bags, which she filled with all their items. By the time she was done, the nurse came in pushing a wheelchair with paperwork in hand. "I heard you called for an uber," she joked, pointing to the chair.

"I really can walk," he objected.

"Nope, not allowed," she said. "It's wheels to get out, or you can stay. Your call."

Which is how he found himself being pushed through the halls as the staff applauded for him, his wife and parents trailing behind carrying all the bags. It was both touching and humiliating, and he knew he would never forget.

The nurse leaned down and spoke into his ear. "You're a hero, enjoy it."

That alone almost brought him to tears, but instead he made a point of looking at as many people as possible and thanking them. Soaking it in seemed a better choice than hanging his head in embarrassment, and he had never been one to shy away from attention.

The drive home felt like it took forever. Despite feeling thrilled when he first got into the SUV, five minutes and three bumps in the road later, he realized how painful it could be with a hole in your chest. His father slowed down every time JJ hissed in pain, to the point that he was practically crawling. Zoe sat behind him, lightly rubbing his shoulders and coaching him through breathing exercises. When they finally pulled into the driveway, he decided he wasn't going back in a car for a long, long time.

His siblings' cars were parked in the driveway, Patrick's behind them. The front door opened, and everyone piled out, surrounding the car. Patrick opened the passenger door to help him out, while his brothers started unloading the bags from the back. Tedy was bouncing around on a leash that Finley held, straining to get to him and Zoe.

His family got him settled on the couch and then bustled around the house. Zoe disappeared into the kitchen with Emma and his mother, Finley following them when she realized she was outnumbered. He heard car doors in the driveway, and Jake stood to look out the window.

"Mike and Nat," he said.

"Oh, good," JJ said. "I haven't seen them, I wanted to see how they were."

"Mike is doing better than Nat," Patrick said. "She's still a mess, but we're trying to get her through it."

JJ frowned, but didn't have time to respond before Jake ushered them into the room. "Hey," he said. "How are you guys?"

"How are you," Mike asked. "You're the one who was hurt."

"Physically, yes," he answered. "But I have no memory of what happened, and you probably do. I'm glad you're both okay though."

Natalie looked pale, and had black circles under her eyes. Her hands were shaking slightly as she pulled her coat off, and she overall had the look of someone who was riddled with anxiety. She smiled at him, a tight one that didn't reach her eyes. "I'm glad you're okay. Thank you for saving me."

"I wish I knew what happened," he said. "But I'm very glad you are safe."

Her eyes darted around the room, and Patrick put his arm around her, hugging her to his chest. "Want to go in the kitchen with Emma?"

"Sure," she said, walking out of the room with him.

Mike perched on a chair near JJ, his big frame dwarfing the seat. He also looked exhausted, though less so than Natalie. "Tell me what happened, please," JJ said to him.

"You sure you're up for this? We were told not to excite you."

"Just fill in some blanks, and maybe my memory will pick up the rest."

"I spent the morning with Nat, we worked out and then had some coffee in the kitchen," Mike said. "We both wanted to get outside for a while, so we decided to go for a ride. The trainer helped us saddle the horses and we headed out. I think we were gone for about two hours total. When we got back, I was starving. I offered to order some food, and we handed the horses off to be cooled down and went back into the house. I had left the back door unlocked, thinking that since the staff was in the stable, no one would go in there."

"Understandable," JJ said. He didn't want his friend to feel badly, or feel responsible, for making the decision that led to him getting injured.

"We went in, and I was distracted. She is so beautiful, you know? And we were having fun together, it was all surreal," Mike continued. "I opened the door for Nat, and I was looking at her when I walked in. She just stopped right inside the door and was in the way. I joked that she was going to need to move inside a little if she wanted me to come in. When I finally realized she looked scared, I looked past her and saw him."

"Did you give a description to the other officers?"

"JJ," Mike said slowly. "They saw him. You shot him."

"Oh," he said, then thought. "I guess someone did tell me that."

"Anyway, when I looked into the house, he was standing there with a gun pointed at Natalie. I pushed her behind me, hoping she would go through the door and run. It was still open, and I kind of shoved her, thinking I could close the door once she was on the other side. But she was just frozen, and she didn't move. He must have realized what I was doing," he said. "Told her to come in and close the door or he would shoot me. I was still nudging her back, but she came in. I kept her behind me the whole time, even when he was getting mad. When he didn't shoot me right away, I figured he wasn't going to."

"That was a big gamble," JJ said. "You were brave to protect her like that."

"It was the right thing to do," Mike said humbly. "I kept trying to talk to him, ask him why he was doing this. I said we could just give him money, and he could leave. He said he kept trying to get enough money to be able to live, and told me that he had robbed those stores. I told him we wouldn't tell anyone, no one would ever know he was there. But he said if Nat went with him, he would be richer than he could ever dream. He said all his problems would be over if he had her. She started crying when he said that, and I told her it wasn't happening. I was just trying to find the opportunity to jump him, but he stayed far enough away that it was a risk. Then you came in."

Zoe was in her glory puttering around in her kitchen again, putting together trays of snacks while the meals heated up. Emma, Maggie and Finley were sitting at the island sipping on wine, and a fragile-looking Natalie had joined them a short while ago. Everyone was talking to her gently, easing her into feeling comfortable and less anxious. As she worked, ideas were floating around in her head, and she finally decided to share with the room to see if the other woman could help her.

"I was thinking," she said. The others quieted quickly and faced her, making her more nervous, but she pushed through. "I want to do something for JJ, once he's up for it. But I might need help."

"Anything at all," Maggie said. "What can we do?"

"Good, because it involves both of you," she said, looking at Maggie and Finley. "Actually, all of you."

"What is it?" Emma prodded her.

"I want to have a wedding reception," she blurted out. "It means a lot to him, and it's a way to show him how I feel."

"Oh, honey," Maggie cried. She stood and came around, hugging Zoe as she cried. "This means so much to me, and I just know he's going to love it."

"I'd like to surprise him, if we can," she continued once Maggie had returned to her seat. "I know he wants this, and I hope he won't be upset to not be involved in the planning. But he planned everything for Vegas, and it was so beautiful. I want to do the same for him."

"Where do you want to have it? The Palace?" Finley asked.

"I was thinking Palace Plates, if Jake can make it work," she responded.

"Is that the name for the new space? I love it," Maggie gushed.

"Yes," she smiled as she answered. "Kendra and I decided but were waiting for the sign to go up to announce it, so keep that quiet."

They all nodded and indicated they would keep the secret, so she continued. "We designed it so it's mainly an open space. The tables are adjustable, so they can be raised to be used as prep surfaces for classes or lowered to have seats for functions. There is a wall that can be closed to hide the ovens and the retail area, making the front just a function space. It's plenty of space for what we'll need."

"We need flowers, music, decorations, and a photographer," Emma ticked off. "Should we each take one? Or how do you want to do it? Patrick could take care of most of it with one phone call."

"I know, and I appreciate that," she said. "But I want to make sure that it's me doing this for JJ. The one thing that I could definitely use his help with is a great photographer. I know he has more resources than I could ever dream of, and I want to make sure we can look back on this day forever."

"Let's also talk to him about the music," Emma suggested. "Look what he organized for Jake and Dan."

"He's not a party planner," Zoe laughed. "We can get a local DJ."

"No, don't do that," Natalie said, looking better than she had since she came in. "Let me help with the music. I dated a producer for a few months and we're still friendly. What if I could get the country artist who we saw in Vegas?"

Zoe stared at her, open mouthed. "You really think that's an option?"

"Absolutely," Natalie nodded. "I'll work on it and let you know tomorrow."

"That would be amazing," Zoe said. "I never even dreamed that was a possibility, I figured we could just play the song."

"Do you want to redo the ceremony too?" Maggie asked.

"I hadn't really thought about it," Zoe said, considering the words. Although the reception would be enough to show him that she was committed to him, maybe standing in front of their loved ones repeating their vows would be an added bonus. "But now that I do, that might be a nice idea. How could we do that? The space isn't big enough for both the ceremony and a reception."

They all sat in silence, thinking of solutions. "What if we did a small ceremony in the back garden of the restaurant?" Finley suggested. "There's enough space there to set up some chairs if needed, and then people could just walk right inside."

"That's a great idea," Emma agreed.

"I can help organize that," Finley said. "I live right there, so I can go down early and do the setup and decorating."

"Thank you," Zoe said. "We can keep it pretty simple."

"What about decorating it the way the chapel was in Vegas?" Natlie said. "It was a garden theme, and it was gorgeous. We could recreate that."

"You might be overestimating my abilities," Finley laughed.

"I can get help," Natalie offered. "If you don't mind, Zoe."

"No, that would be amazing. I feel bad that I didn't think of it," she admitted.

Emma reached over and clinked her wine glass to Zoe's and smiled. "But you thought to employ the best party planners around, and we can make this perfect for you guys. Let's get some paper out and sketch out some plans, and once you have a date, we can get to work."

***

The night passed quickly, with everyone enjoying the food and time together. After a few hours, JJ started to look wiped out, so Zoe helped him into their room and got him settled in bed. She gave him two pain pills, which he swallowed with the bottle of water she provided. He smiled gratefully at her as he lay back against the pillow. "You make a great nurse," he said. "I'm a lucky guy."

"That you are," she teased.

He grabbed her hand as she turned to leave and pulled her closer. She leaned down and kissed him, careful not to lean on the bed and put any pressure on his wound. "Do you want me to sleep in the other room, so I don't risk hurting you?"

"You'd hurt me if you did that," he said. "I've been looking forward to being back next to you."

"Okay," she said. "Relax, I'll get everyone on their way home and then settle Tedy down, then I'll be in."

By the time she said goodnight to everyone, walked the dog and got her settled in, and cleaned the kitchen, JJ was sound asleep. She got into bed carefully, savoring the comfort of their bed, and the sound of him snoring softly beside her. All was right in her world again, finally.

***

Two days later, Kendra left JJ in the care of his mother as she went to work for the first time in almost a week. It felt good to be back in her domain, making decisions and checking on supplies. Kendra was still out on maternity leave, and the manager Linda had been in charge, along with her senior sous chef. She praised both for keeping things running smoothly and answered a million questions about how JJ was doing. Midway through lunch, a server asked if she had time to step into the dining room to talk to a table. Assuming it was about JJ, she agreed and washed her hands before heading out.

She stopped short when she looked at the table, recognizing the back of her mother's head from across the room. The man next to her was older, with grey hair and a pair of reading glasses perched on his face as he surveyed the menu. Marise glanced over her shoulder and saw Kendra and gave what could only be interpreted as a shy wave.

Kendra wove her way to the table, greeting familiar faces as she went and assuring them that JJ was doing well. When she arrived at her mother's table, Marise stood and started to hug

321

her before settling on a kiss on the cheek. "Thank you for coming out," she said. "We just arrived, and I wanted to introduce you to Henri."

"It's nice to meet you," she said, finding herself smiling. Despite her misgivings, his friendly, open face had her wanting to like him. "I didn't know you were coming to town."

"Emma called me," Marise said. "We were out of town, and when we got back, I got the message about your husband. We got right back in the car and drove down, but we arrived so late last night we didn't want to disturb you. Henri thought if we came here and you were still out, we could call Emma and see what we should do. I really didn't want to add to your stress."

Touched that her mother had actually considered her feelings for the first time in her life, she felt herself soften. "That was very nice of you," she said. "JJ is home now and doing well. He is on forced rest while his wound heals, but knowing him, he will do it quickly."

"That's wonderful news," Henri beamed at her. "We were so worried."

"We won't keep you," Marise said. "We're staying at the Inn, and we plan to stay for a few days in case you need me. But we're happy to entertain ourselves if you're busy."

"Why don't you come for dinner tonight?" Zoe heard herself saying. "JJ's parents will be there as well; we can have a quiet dinner."

"That would be lovely, thank you," Marise said. "If you're sure it's not too much of an imposition."

"Not at all," she said. "I have to get back in the kitchen now. Would you mind if I sent you some options rather than ordering from the menu?"

"We'd love that," Henri said. "I've heard such wonderful things about your cooking, I can't wait to try it."

She walked back into the kitchen, amazed. Her mother appeared to be thinking about her for once, and to think that she had been bragging about her to Henri was even more amazing. Maybe there was a chance for her and Marise to mend their broken relationship after all.

The rest of the afternoon flew by, and before she knew it, she was in her kitchen with both sets of parents. Frank and Henri had hit it off immediately, bonding over a shared love of baseball. Marise and Maggie were talking quietly, leaving Zoe the chance to check in with JJ.

"How are you feeling?"

"Great," he said. "Well, a little sore. But I slept so great last night, and it's just so good to be home."

"Don't overdo it, okay?"

"Never," he promised, kissing her hand. "I'll be the best patient in the world. How are things going with your mom?"

"Shockingly well," she said. She quickly told him about the conversation at the restaurant that had led to the dinner invitation. "I think Henri might be magic."

"Sometimes it's just that one thing that a person needs to let their guard down," he said. "Henri is that for her, he makes her feel safe. That means she can let her guard down with you."

"I hope it lasts," she said softly.

"All you can do is keep an open mind and give her a chance," he said. "Stay positive. If you start doubting it, then it will fall apart. If you believe in it, then maybe you can have a relationship. You can't fix the past, but you can have a future together."

"When did you get to be so wise?"

"Almost dying will do that to you," he said. "But I promise to go back to my normal self soon."

She laughed, putting her head on his shoulder. "Don't ever change."

A short time later, she walked both sets of parents out to their cars. They had already made plans to get together the following day, so Maggie and Frank could be their tour guides. Marise stopped Zoe as they walked, so the other three went ahead.

"Are you okay with me being here?" she asked, looking worried. "We can head back tomorrow if that would be better."

"No, I really am okay with it. Tonight was fun. And I really like Henri," she responded. "He seems like a really good guy."

"He is," Marise said, smiling in his direction. "Not at all what I would have thought I'd find, but I'm so glad I did."

"I'm happy for you," Zoe said with a smile. "That's how I feel about JJ."

"I'm glad he will be okay, I was worried."

"Me too," Zoe admitted. "It was a scary few days."

"I wish I could have been here with you," Marise said, looking at the ground.

"You're here now," Zoe said, then hesitated. Making a quick decision, she carried on. "I'd like it if you could stay. I'm planning a surprise wedding reception for JJ, so we can do our vows in front of everyone we love. It would mean a lot if you could be there."

Marise sniffled, and wiped her eyes quickly. "Nothing would make me happier."

"It might be a few days or weeks, I need to wait until he's up for it," she warned. "If you need to go home, you could come back for it."

"No, I think we'll enjoy Windsor Peak for a while," Marise said. "We're retired, and this is a lovely place to spend some time. Maybe I can help with your plans."

"Maybe," Zoe said with a smile. "I'll let you know."

She watched both cars disappear and couldn't believe how quickly her life had changed. Having a nice dinner with her mother, and accepting help from her, was not something she had imagined happening even three months ago. Suddenly, she was looking forward to seeing her the next day, and of what the future held.

***

Over the next two weeks, Zoe took JJ to countless doctor's appointments as well as the therapy required by the sheriff's department. He was getting stronger each day, and more like himself, and she finally decided that he was ready for their surprise wedding. He would still be sore, but she couldn't wait any longer, she was anxious to tell him how she felt.

Kendra sat in the office with her, going over the final plans, the baby strapped to her chest in a carrier. "I think you're ready to go," she said. "Jake said that he's all set next door. You can have your decorations go in at any point. Finley will direct everyone in the morning to get the garden set up. What else can I do for you?"

"Nothing," Zoe said. "I'm so grateful to you for all your help. Now I just want you there to enjoy the day with us."

"You've got it," she said with a smile. "We wouldn't miss it for the world. Thank you for letting us bring the baby, since everyone we know will be there."

"Of course, I wouldn't want you or Shea to miss it," she said.

"You realize that having babies there will get both sets of parents start thinking about grandkids, right?"

Zoe laughed and stood up, ready to head home. "I think that idea is already planted, but thanks anyway."

"Alright, I'll see you tomorrow for your big day. Let me know if you need anything."

She walked home, feeling as though she was walking on air. Although they were already married, and JJ had no idea about what was happening, she felt as though she were a bride on her wedding night. At the first one, she had felt unsure and hadn't taken it seriously. This one, she was all in.

Chapter 35

The boredom was the worst part, he decided. He could handle the pain, being out of work even, but sitting around at home doing nothing was a major problem. No one at work would discuss anything other than how he was, and some social gossip, but refused to discuss any issues with him. He still didn't even know the name of the criminal that he had exchanged fire with, and the guilt over killing someone had kept him busy in therapy.

The therapist had been employed by the Sheriff's department, tasked with making sure he was of sound mind when he was physically cleared to return to work. He saw her three days a week, wanting to get back as soon as possible. Despite their sessions, he had still been unable to recall anything about the day of the shooting. She told him it was his mind's way of protecting him, but that it could come back to him at any moment. She guessed that he would start dreaming about it, and then it would come back slowly. Or it could hit him all at once. There was no rhyme or reason to it, and it was another layer of frustration for him. He liked things neat and orderly, and this was anything but that.

Fortunately, this morning his doctor had cleared him to begin some light exercise and stated he could start leaving the house. He wasn't to drive, and absolutely couldn't walk Tedy on a leash or lift anything heavy, but he could take short walks or sit on an exercise bike at a low resistance rate. He had thought he could sneak a Peloton class, but Zoe had caught on and put the rules in place about leisurely rides rather than exertion.

"Can we go for a walk?" he asked Zoe when they pulled in the driveway from the doctor. "Take Tedy into town and get some fresh air?"

She glanced at her watch, and then nodded. "Yes, but we can't be out all day," she warned him. "I have stuff I need to do."

"I thought you were off all day today?"

"Yes, but I have things to do," she said vaguely. "I have a whole new business that I'm opening, don't forget."

"Are things on track for the opening this weekend?"

She nodded and busied herself with her cell phone. "Yes, seems to be."

They got Tedy from the house and walked through town slowly, stopping to talk to everyone they came across. When Dan asked him to have lunch, Zoe opted to drop Tedy with Desmond and get work done rather than join them. She disappeared with the dog, and he made his way to Slice Girls with Dan.

"Wouldn't it be easier to eat at the Palace? Isn't Jake working next door?" He questioned Dan as they walked.

"He said he was in the mood for pizza," Dan said. "He probably eats more than he's paid at the Palace, so he's looking for something different."

They settled into a booth, and Jake slid in a few minutes later. "Patrick can't come," he said. "Nat is having a tough day."

"She's still struggling?"

"Yeah," Jake said. "I know you can't remember, and even if you did, your training would have prepared you. She just pretends to hurt people on a movie screen, so it was a lot to take in."

"She'll be okay," Dan said. "Patrick has her meeting with a therapist over Zoom every day and offered to fly one in if she wanted. She's pretty tight lipped about it but seems to be getting better."

"She's looking forward to this weekend," Jake said. Dan made a face at his brother, and Jake seemed to be caught off guard. "For the opening, I mean."

"What's up? Why are you guys being weird?"

"No reason," Dan said quickly. "Let's order."

***

Zoe was up before him on Saturday morning, which was unusual. "Are you nervous about today?" he asked as he watched her rush around and get dressed.

She stopped and stared at him, mouth open. "What do you mean?"

"The opening?"

"Oh, yes," she said with a sigh. "Very nervous about the opening."

"I'm sure everything will go great," he said. "I was planning to walk down by myself, but Colin had a little fit and said he was picking me up. Something about not wanting to walk in alone, which is the weirdest thing I think he has ever said to me."

She laughed softly, pulling on a sweater. "I have to run, I'll see you there," she said, kissing him quickly.

329

He puttered around the house for a few hours and ate a sandwich that Zoe had left for him. The opening wasn't until four in the afternoon, which was an odd time, but Zoe had insisted it was perfect. He would have thought opening with the other businesses so people could stop in all day would make sense, but she said she wanted to have a cocktail party and a soft opening. Whatever that meant, he was just going as her arm candy.

Colin arrived at three, holding a garment bag. "I brought you clothes," he said.

"I have clothes," he responded, indicating the jeans and sweater he was wearing.

"You can't wear that to your wife's big night," Colin chastised him. "Here, change into this."

He unzipped the bag and turned back to his brother. "I'm not wearing a suit."

"Oh, but you are," Colin said. "I'm doing the same. Go change, I'll use the guest room and put mine on."

"We're going to be way overdressed," he grumbled. "This is crazy."

"Or we'll be the best dressed there," Colin challenged. "Stop complaining and go change."

He pulled off the sweater while swearing under his breath at his annoying brother and started to put the suit on. It was the nicest one he had ever worn, he realized, and a perfect fit, as if it had been made for him. "Where did you get this?" he yelled across the hall to Colin.

"Why? What's wrong with it?"

"Nothing, it's just really nice," JJ said. "I can't imagine they had this in the general store."

"Are you ready? We need to go," Colin said.

"Almost," he said. He turned to the mirror to knot the tie, glad he had gotten a haircut earlier in the week. He wasn't sure why Zoe hadn't mentioned how formal this party was going to be, but he'd have to remember to ask her later.

Colin drove them into town, pulling into a spot on the street just a few minutes before the party was to begin. The two brothers crossed the street, and JJ started for the shop door before Colin gestured the other way. "Let's go around back," he said. "Jake mentioned he put some new pavers in, I want to have a quick look."

"I don't want to be late," JJ said. "I wanted to be the first one here, but you drove so slowly that's probably not going to happen."

"Come on, you're wasting time arguing with me," Colin said, turning and walking away quickly. When he got to the gate that led to the small garden behind the restaurant, he opened it and gestured for JJ to go first. "After you."

"Thanks," he said, frowning at his brother. "You're acting weird."

When he walked through the gate, he came to an abrupt stop, causing Colin to run into him. The space was filled with even more flowers and greenery than usual, reminding him of something he couldn't put his finger on. His entire family was standing there, dressed to the nines. His mother looked about ready to cry, and she rushed over to hug him.

"What's going on?" he asked, looking at them all. "Why do you look like you're upset?"

"Not upset, darling," she said. "This is pure happiness."

He looked past his family, and noticed chairs set up in the garden, all facing the same direction. Friends and neighbors were in the seats, all looking at him. He saw the Burrows family in one row, all smiling at him, Stella and Kendra wiping tears away. His assistant Mary sat with Jeff and Nick and their wives, Danielle and Larissa, across the aisle. But why was there an aisle? "What is going on?"

His mother grabbed his hands and squeezed. "Zoe has a surprise for you," she said. "We can't say much, but just go with the flow. Everyone, go take your places."

"Take their places? Is there a show going on?"

"JJ, stop talking," Maggie said firmly. "I would like for you to walk me to my seat, please."

He offered her his arm, hearing a guitar start to strum as they walked. His mother was beaming, walking slowly as she led him to the front row, where she turned to face him. "Be happy, my love." She kissed him on the cheek, and then pushed him toward the front of the chairs, where his brothers stood.

Colin gestured for him to stand next to him, and he did so, facing the rows of loved ones. The music changed, and suddenly everyone stood, turning to face the back. The doors to the shop opened, and first Emma appeared, and then Zoe. Zoe was dressed in a wedding gown, a simple slip style that perfectly suited her. She took his breath away, and he felt tears on his cheeks as he watched her walk toward him.

"I hope this is okay," she said quietly once she reached him. She wiped his face with a soft handkerchief that she had around the base of her flowers. "I'd really like to marry you again."

"This is more than okay," he said, leaning over to kiss her.

The minister cleared her throat, laughing. "That part hasn't happened yet," she said.

"Sorry," he apologized, not feeling badly at all. His cheeks hurt from smiling, and he took Zoe's hands in his after she passed her bouquet to Emma.

The minister gave a quick speech about love and life, the words flowing around him but not sinking in. He was so mesmerized by the woman in front of him, and so moved by this moment, it was more than he could take in. Suddenly, the minister placed a microphone between them, stating that Zoe wanted to say her own vows.

"I promise, here in front of all our family and friends, to share my life with you, Jeremiah. I promise to be your best friend, and to be by your side, in good times and bad. The last few weeks have taught me a lot of things," she said. "The first and most important is that I love you."

He hadn't thought he could smile bigger but hearing her say the words finally had him doing so. Without thinking, he pulled her closer and kissed her again, causing everyone to laugh. "I'm sorry, I had to."

"It's perfect," she laughed. "I love you. I love how you look out for everyone, and how dedicated you are to the town. I love that you find joy in everything and can always make someone find their smile. I love that you love me so unapologetically."

"I do," he said, smiling at her.

"When you were shot, I felt like the air had left the universe. I couldn't breathe, and I thought that if you had died, I would go right after you. Because you've given me life again, and without you, I don't know how I would have gone on. I want to grow old with you. I want to have babies with you, and grandbabies. I want to laugh together, cry together, and fight with you over the thermostat setting. I want to spend my nights playing cards with you and losing crazy bets," she said. "Because the last one that I lost ended up being the very best thing that has ever happened to me."

"I had no idea I was getting married today, so I don't have anything prepared," JJ said. "But I can promise to love you for the rest of my life. My love for you grows every day, and I know it will only keep growing. I feel like the luckiest man in the world, because the day I met you, I knew you were my forever. Persuading you of that was the most fun I've ever had."

The crowd around them chuckled, and he smiled at Zoe. "I can't wait to see you as a mom, and for us to learn to be parents together. I promise to be patient, and to listen, and to look twice before I ask you where something is. I'll put our relationship first, and always remind you that you're the most beautiful woman I've ever seen, both inside and out. I'll love you forever, with every breath that I take."

The minister finalized the ceremony, finally granting him permission to kiss his wife. After kissing her thoroughly to the hoots and hollers of the small crowd, he led her down the aisle. "This was the best surprise ever," he told her as they stopped to take a picture.

"I'm glad," she said. "I was worried you would be upset it was a surprise. But I wanted you to know how I feel, and this seemed like the best way to show you."

"I also like when you say the words," he said.

"I love you," she said, smiling at him as the camera clicked. "And I have one more surprise." She took his hand and led him into the new shop, which was decorated for a reception.

"You did all this for me?" he asked, looking at all the careful decorations and the waitstaff ready to serve food and drinks.

"I had a lot of help," she laughed as their guests came streaming in from the garden. Soon everyone had champagne, and the small band that had played in the garden had relocated to a stage in front of a makeshift dance floor. "Will you dance with me?"

"Always," he said, leading her to the dance floor. He stopped short when he realized who was on the stage and stared at her. "How is this happening?"

"Natalie," she laughed. "I can't take any credit."

The band started playing the song they had been engaged to, and they danced slowly as they were serenaded. "I know you gave up this moment to get me to marry you spontaneously in Vegas," she said. "You missed out on walking your mom down the aisle and having your family there. I hope this makes up for it."

"It more than makes up for it," he said. Catching sight of Marise at a table with his family, he glanced back at Zoe. "And you get to have your mom here, which you never thought would be possible."

"You make good things happen," she said. "I love this life you have given me."

"The life we have created together," he corrected. "And that we'll enjoy forever."

Acknowledgments

There are so many people who keep me inspired to write, and who help me be brave enough to put the books out for the world to see. Writing is such a solitary activity, but having a support team who are always there when I need them makes it far less scary.

My parents, Jim and Arlene Giddings, who show up at every event and share my books with everyone. If I never sold a copy of a book, just seeing how proud they are to tell people about something I did would be enough satisfaction. I'm so lucky to have you as parents, and for you to be such an active part of our lives. As the years go by, I feel even more blessed to have the relationship that we share, and to be so close to both of you. I love you, and I will always show you the same love and support that you've shown me all these years.

My brother Jeff, sister-in-law Danielle, and Timmy, Tessa and Emmy also show up at every event and even go into book stores when I'm not there just to see if my books are on the shelf. Jeff has always been there for me, from little kids when I would have a nightmare to giving advice as adults, and I hope I return the favor to him. Having a sibling who is also a best friend is a blessing, and the fact that he married someone I love as much as I do my sister-in-law is a double blessing. I think the best thing that ever happened to Jeff was meeting Danielle, and she has been the most amazing addition to our family. Together, they are such great parents, friends and family, and they are raising three of my favorite people. Timmy, Tessa and Emmy, you make me proud with everything you do! I love you all!

My friends, who I can't even list out because I know I would forget someone. You all show up at the book signings, and comment on my social media posts, and show your support in so many ways. It means the world to me, and I'm always so happy to see your faces or hear from you! Thank you for reading, for telling your friends, and for being my friend for all these years!

Brendan and Conor, no matter how old you get, you'll still be the first two nephews who stole my heart. You're becoming men that I'm proud to know, and I can't wait to see what path your lives go down. Taylor, thank you for being the perfect match for Brendan! It's funny to think that the two little kids who played together would be building a life together as adults, but it's so nice to be a witness to. Love you all!

Shae Coon, the genius behind my book covers – thank you for taking one sentence and turning it into the perfect vision. Book Designs by Shae is her handle on social media, and she's both a brilliant graphic design artist and a genuinely good human. Thank you for all you do!

Luke Combs, Ray Fulcher, and Dan Isbell for writing the song "Love You Anyways", performed by Luke Combs, which I knew it was JJ's song to Zoe the first time I heard it. I hadn't planned on doing a book for them when I started out, but that song played and I could feel how JJ felt. Even if she had chosen to walk away from him, he would have loved her – and I needed to write that story. I am a sucker for a good love song anyway, but when I hear one and so instantly feel connected to a character, I use it to pull the story out. I wish I had a count for how many times I streamed that song in the writing of this book!

The little network of fellow authors that I've met along the way, who have provided encouragement, resources, and shared ideas that have helped so much. Again, in this lonely endeavor, being able to message someone who can relate is so valuable. I hope I give as much back as I get from all of you!

My husband, Tommy, and our two boys, Camden and Calum, are the reason I do everything. Tommy gives me a lot of funny stories that I can weave into the books, but he will also do anything for us. My boys are the light of my life, and they make me so proud. Cam only has a few more years before he leaves me for college (I will follow you if you try to go far away), and I'm trying to really treasure this time with them. It's a fine line between getting writing done and also making time to be present for them, and I hope I'm balancing it well. I'll never miss a sporting event or awards ceremony, or a conversation about Roblox, because I know this time with them is so short. And as much as I love my readers, they are first priority always!

My biggest reward from all of this has been in seeing my son Calum and my nephew and nieces decide they wanted to be storytellers. Calum writes stories regularly, sharing them with his teachers at school, and is so creative. Timmy has his whole book mapped out, we just need to get started on writing it! And my girls, Tessa and Emmy, are loving books and writing even more. Something that may have been a struggle before is now fun for them, and that brings me such joy.

To all of you who are reading these books, and are sending me words of encouragement – thank you. I wouldn't be able to do this without you. Each person who has picked up one of my books, or downloaded it onto their Kindle, has played a part in me continuing this series.

Stay Tuned

I have some exciting things planned! I will definitely be staying in Windsor Peak for a while longer, and am already working on the next one! Make sure to follow me on social media (@deniselathamwrites) and sign up for my newsletter on my website (www.deniselatham.com) to be up to date on the latest news!